Max stared as she removed her Stetson

He couldn't move.

Couldn't breathe.

It was an eternity before he felt his partner's viselike grip on his arm, cutting off the circulation.

"Oh, my God, my God," Doug chanted under his breath. "Max...Max. What's going on?"

Max didn't answer. But there wasn't a doubt in his mind that the woman before him was Sandra. He was as sure of that as his own name. He was staring at a dead woman—except she wasn't dead.

His sense of shock faded, replaced by a sense of betrayal. And anger.

ABOUT THE AUTHOR

Evelyn A. Crowe worked for twelve years as a media director in an advertising company before turning her hand to writing in 1983. Her decision to change careers was certainly a stroke of good fortune for Harlequin readers, as Evelyn's bestselling books are favorites around the world.

Books by Evelyn A. Crowe

SO HARD TO FORGET
Evelyn A. Crowe

Harlequin Books

TORONTO • NEW YORK • LONDON
AMSTERDAM • PARIS • SYDNEY • HAMBURG
STOCKHOLM • ATHENS • TOKYO • MILAN
MADRID • WARSAW • BUDAPEST • AUCKLAND

ISBN 0-373-70745-2

SO HARD TO FORGET

Copyright © 1997 by Evelyn A. Crowe.

SO HARD TO
FORGET

CHAPTER ONE

MAXIMILIAN WARNER stood before the wide expanse of his office window on the sixth floor of Warner and Hart Security and stared down at Central Park. He wondered how spring had come and gone and summer arrived without his noticing.

Max sighed long and deeply, then glanced over his shoulder at the files spread out on his desk. It was time to give up. Time to make the call and deliver the bad news. Instead, he turned and stared blindly out the window again. All he could see was the image of the young woman whose pictures were scattered among the papers on his desk. He didn't need to refresh his memory with photographs, though; her beauty and sweet expression were branded into his brain. He doubted he'd ever forget her.

"You look like crap."

"Feel like it, too," Max said on another long soulful sigh, then returned to his desk and faced his partner, Douglas Hart. They had one of the top security and private-investigation companies in the country, with branch offices in Los Angeles and Houston and more than a hundred employees. He and Doug figured that after five years they'd pretty much made it. Warner and Hart was so sought after the company didn't have to advertise. Keeping and maintaining a low profile was its primary goal. With some luck and a lot of damn hard work, the partners were now able to pick and choose the cases and clients they represented.

"You didn't go home, did you?" Doug scowled at his partner's appearance. He didn't expect an answer and didn't get one. Max's dark hair was wildly tousled. There was a bruised look around his eyes that spoke of too many hours reading and rereading. His normally bright blue eyes were dull with fatigue and defeat.

"You going to make the call or am I?" Doug asked. He was more than a little worried about Max. Hell, they'd been through a lot during their twenty years of friendship. As he waited for his partner's answer, he let his mind wander back over the years. He and Max were from small neighboring Texas towns. School rivalries in football and baseball brought them together, and for some reason they'd become best buddies.

They'd attended college together, shared a dorm room, got drunk together, traded and fought over girls. When Max's family told him they could no longer afford a college education, they both joined the military. There they found they had a talent for the twists and turns of intelligence work and a proficiency in the sometimes boring detail-laden process of an investigation. Later they were accepted into the elite Navy Intelligence. When it was time to re-up, they decided together not to and were discharged on the same day.

They were a team, and by then the FBI was eager for their combined talents. After five years with the government, they resigned and set up their own business. They were so close that most of the time one would start to say something and the other could pick up the thought and finish it.

"We've been on this case eighteen months, Max,

used more manpower than on any other. It's time to cut our losses."

Max glanced at the spread of papers on his desk. "You know he killed her," he said, and willed himself not to look at the pictures, but his eyes were drawn to them. Sandra Applewhite Gillman, twenty-seven years old. Daughter of Harry and Helen Hudson Applewhite of the Kentucky Applewhites. Old money on both sides, lots of it. A blue-blood family with an impressive stable of Thoroughbreds and a long list of winners. Sandra was the Applewhites' only child, and except for the death of Harry Applewhite ten years ago, they were a picture-perfect rich family.

That was until Sandra met and married John Gillman. After a shaky year of marriage, they had supposedly been on a second honeymoon, yachting around the Florida Keys, the Bahamas and finally the British Virgin Islands when the so-called accident happened. That was eighteen months ago, and Sandra had died in a yacht explosion off the island of Virgin Gorda.

Sandra's husband, a thirty-seven-year-old playboy, ex-Navy SEAL and con man, was ashore when the yacht exploded. Sandra's body was never recovered, and after an island inquest and hearing, Gillman was cleared of any responsibility for the accident and the death of his wife.

But Helen Applewhite thought differently. After a few discreet telephone calls to those in the know, she was referred to Warner and Hart and hired them to investigate her daughter's death. She knew in her heart that her son-in-law was a murderer. So did everyone at Warner and Hart who'd worked on the case. They just couldn't prove it.

Doug glanced at the thick file. "How many times—" he nodded at the papers on the desk "—did you go through those last night?"

"A couple." Wearily Max rubbed his face.

Doug knew what the problem was, what was eating at Max, but hesitated to voice his opinion. They'd come up against cases they were unable to solve before. Granted, they were few and far between, and the agency always kept those files open just in case a break came somewhere down the line.

Doug braced himself and said, "You've let this get personal." His friend had been staring at the Sandra Applewhite Gillman photograph so intently he didn't think he'd heard him. "Max?"

"Damn right, it's personal." He felt the heat of anger wash over him but held his tongue, knowing he was exhausted. There was no sense taking his ill temper out on Doug. "You know I don't like to lose or give up."

Doug shook his head. "Goes deeper than merely losing."

"What the hell are you talking about?"

Taking a deep breath, Doug plunged on. "You've fallen in love with Sandra."

"Don't be an ass." Max shoved back his chair and stood up. "She's dead."

"Yes, she is."

"Doug, I'm in no mood for your games. If you've got something in your craw, then spit it out."

"Okay. From the first day we took on this case— as we sat in that mansion listening to Mrs. Applewhite tell us her daughter's life story, her fears that she'd been murdered, all the while dealing out those pictures of Sandra like playing cards—I saw you change. You've become obsessed with getting Gillman."

Doug held up his hand to stop Max from interrupting with some snide remark. "Make no mistake," he went on, "I agree one hundred percent that Gillman murdered his wife. After a year I knew we weren't going to nail the bastard's hide to the wall. But you've let it drag on another six months. Deep down I think you know this is one for the dead file, and neither you nor all the manpower we've put into it is going to solve it. But, my friend, you won't admit it because that would mean letting go of Sandra."

"Don't give me any of your armchair psychobabble. Dammit, she's dead. I know that."

"Do you really? Well, love's a funny thing, Max. It seems to have a mind all its own. When you least expect it—wham! It hits you. You're in love with Sandra." Doug was more worried than he let on. Max had changed over the past six months. He'd dropped all his girlfriends, started staying late at the office or shut up in his apartment. Doug had tried repeatedly to pry Max out of his slump but was always rebuffed for his efforts. Hell, he and his wife had, on numerous occasions, invited him to dinner or drinks, but Max always said he had other plans. Which was a lie.

Then there was one particular incident that really plagued him. On a Sunday afternoon a couple of weeks ago, while he and Sara were walking in Central Park, they decided to drop in on Max. Of course as soon as Max saw the way he and Sara were eyeing the scattered stack of photographs on his coffee table, he started making excuses about working on the case at home. Doug knew better. Some of those pictures he'd never seen, and he realized his partner had kept

them for himself. He also remembered that faraway
look in Max's eyes. Like a man lost in his own fantasies. It was damn unhealthy and he didn't intend to
lose his buddy and partner to a breakdown—or a dead
woman.

Doug knew he was treading on thin ice but took the
heavy step forward, anyway. "Well, if you're not in
love with Sandra, then you have some sort of obsession with her, and before it ruins you and this company, I suggest you come to terms with your problem."

"The only problem I have is a conscience. Something that seems to be lacking around here lately. Oh,
hell," Max snapped, then attempted a friendly, if tired,
smile to take the sting out of his words. "Get this
straight, will you? I'm not in love with Sandra." He
stared for a long moment, letting the silence between
them stretch as he watched Doug's nervous habit of
pushing and worrying his glasses, then running his fingers through his thinning hair. Max realized he was
being an ass, had been for months, and was suddenly
sorry about his behavior. "Give me a moment, then
I'll call Helen." Doug sat unmoving and Max favored
him with a tired smile. "Get out."

"I'll make the call if you want."

"Out."

"It might be easier, you know."

"Doug!"

Douglas Hart stood and headed for the door, but
paused before leaving. "When you're free, give me a
buzz. We just got a honey of a case. Exactly what you
need to bring the sparkle back to your eyes, roses to
your cheeks and the spring in your step." His attempt

at humor fell flat, so he quickly left and firmly shut the door behind him.

Max took one last look at the scattered array of photographs on his desk. Her big green eyes, flawless skin, pouty mouth and enchanting smile tore at his heart. Her hair was long and turned under just above the shoulders. He knew it was naturally curly, which she hated, and so worked hard at taming the waves into a smooth swinging style. He could almost feel her bright blond hair slipping softly through his fingers like warm silk.

Sandra was more than beautiful. There was a sweetness in her smile and a gentleness in her eyes that made his heart pound and his throat ache with the pain of loss. He knew she loved children and animals. She was a gentle soul, a woman of great compassion and an equal capacity for love. She was intelligent, cultured and refined. With all her family's money, she did a lot of charity work, mostly with underprivileged children.

Sandra loved chocolate, but it gave her a headache. Her favorite ice cream was plain vanilla. She had a dark crescent-shaped mole behind her left ear. Cats made her sneeze. Her favorite perfume was Joy, and she loved gardenias and the color yellow. She adored horses and was an accomplished rider. She loved the sea and was an expert sailor and a strong swimmer.

Max tried to breathe around the pain in his chest. He'd interviewed so many of her friends that he probably knew more about Sandra and her life than anyone, even her mother. He knew something else: there was no concrete proof she had been murdered by her husband. John Gillman had already received more than a million dollars of life-insurance money, and in five more months he would come into the bulk of his wife's five-million-dollar estate.

Gillman, a man addicted to money, women, and kinky sex, and occasionally indulged in recreational drugs, was going to slip up one day, and Max intended to be there. Resting his head in his hands, he stared one last time at Sandra's photograph and silently vowed that whatever it took, whatever he had to do, he would make sure John Gillman paid for what he'd done. If justice didn't serve them, he would serve up his own brand of justice.

Gathering together the papers and photographs, Max neatly stacked them in the file folder. For a second he hesitated, then closed the file and reached for the telephone.

DOUG WAS PERCHED on a corner of Max's secretary's desk. Neither spoke as they stared at her phone and its one lit line. After half an hour the light blinked out. Doug stood and returned to his partner's office. He decided the best approach was a direct one. "How'd she take it?"

"Like the great lady she is. Sad, disappointed, but resigned. I explained to her about keeping the file open, our policy of reviewing and continuing to work on unsolved cases if new leads come our way." Max leaned back in the big leather executive chair and closed his eyes. "Man, I let this one really get to me, didn't I?" When Doug didn't answer, he opened his eyes and caught his friend reading through a file. Whenever there was an interesting case, Doug liked to play his little games, drag out the facts like a squirrel giving up his hoard of nuts one by one. He wanted to smile, but was just too damn tired.

"How long has it been since you've gone fly-fishing?" Doug asked.

Max sat up at the mention of his favorite sport. "What was it, two, three years ago when you and I took some clients to Colorado?" The idea of getting away, of wading in a river so clear he could count the rocks on the bottom, air so clean and fresh it almost hurt to breathe and nothing but the sounds of nature around him was as alluring at that moment as a naked woman. It peaked more than his interest; it made his pulse race. Then his responsibilities rushed back and he felt as deflated as a pricked balloon. "Tread carefully, Doug. I'm a little wrung out today."

Doug chuckled, then pitched the file onto Max's desk where it lay unopened. This was their game; he always filled Max in on the new cases. "Does the name Carl Bernard Bedford ring any bells?"

"Very clearly. Fortune 500 corporation. CEO of a worldwide publishing empire. What does he need us for, and what does this have to do with fly-fishing?"

"I'm glad you asked." Doug casually raked his fingers through his hair, fiddled with his glasses and grinned, pleased that he'd caught Max's interest. "Bedford's bought up an estimated twenty thousand acres in Montana. Seems he needs a place to get away from all the pressure and a little ranch to play with." Doug's eyebrows arched over the tops of his wire-rimmed glasses. "But he's not satisfied with what he has. There's this plum piece of property with a mountain, spring-fed rivers, a waterfall or two, abundant wildlife and scenery to die for. Bedford wants the property really bad. But the owner..." He picked up the file and flipped through a couple of pages. "Ah, here it is. Fellow's name is Charles Dawson. He won't sell.''

"Good for him," Max grumbled. "Twenty thousand acres ought to be enough for one man.''

"Well, it's not," Doug snapped back. "Let me remind you, before you turn into a bleeding-heart liberal environmentalist on me, that this case is money in our pockets and could open a lot more doors for us.''

Max shook his head. He hadn't realized just how weary, or maybe bored, he was with the company. Warner and Hart pretty much ran itself. Hell, he'd been working, holding various jobs, since he was twelve years old. Maybe he ought to give some serious thought to selling his shares. He did a quick calculation of his investments and realized he had more money than he knew what to do with. Retirement at thirty-two was an appealing idea. But could he do it? "Doug, when did we stop caring about people and let money rule our lives?''

The sarcasm and disgust didn't faze Doug. "When you and I bought apartments on Central Park West and relocated our offices within walking distance of our homes. When we updated our entire computer system, the gadgets and gewgaws, your Lamborghini, my alimony to three ex-wives—no, only two, Babs remarried—and let's not forget Sara.'' He faked a shiver. "She thinks I print my own money just for her to spend. Don't ever get married again, Max.''

Max couldn't help laughing. Doug was a master at the art of placating, constantly juggling his ex-wives' demands and screaming fits with finesse and real style. Secretly he thought Doug loved it—all that female attention. Remembering his own two-year fiasco of a marriage that ended five years ago made Max want to shudder. He couldn't imagine ever marrying again. Then Sandra's face flashed in his mind, and he knew he would have remarried only once, and that would have been for the rest of his life. He had to quit thinking about her.

"Okay, fill me in on all the details of the case. What are we supposed to do? I draw the line at strong-arming this Dawson fellow into selling to Bedford, though."

"Not necessary. Seems Dawson has two weaknesses—drinking and cards. Loves to gamble. The only thing that's keeping the place going is the profitable business—Dawson Outriggers. He takes fly fishermen up to a mountain lodge and treats them to a real sportsmen's holiday. That's the main source of the money. Then there's the other things, some river rafting and hiking trips. Charges a couple arms and legs, but Bedford says nobody's ever come away complaining. Hell, Bedford even spent a week up there. That's one of the reasons he decided to buy in Montana in the first place."

"Has he made an offer to Dawson?"

"Several. All were turned down flat. The last offer, this Dawson fellow kicked Bedford's men off the place. Told them if they came back, he'd load their butts with buckshot."

Max chuckled, then stood up and stretched. He was bone-tired and wanted Doug to finish. "What're we supposed to do?"

"Go out there. Nose around. Do what we do best, get all the information on Dawson. Treat him and his business like any other company we're investigating for our client's takeover. Find his strengths and weaknesses and zero in on his weak points, the ones that will enable Bedford to bring him down. I figure we should go out there, do some serious fly-fishing and our job at the same time. How's that sound?''

Max thought it sounded damn good. He needed the time to clear his head, decide what he wanted to do. Then again, there was the excitement of a new job, the thrill of the investigation. But this time he promised himself he'd carefully weigh the pros and cons of selling up and retiring. Montana, one way or the other, was going to be a turning point in his life.

CHAPTER TWO

MAX GLANCED briefly out the window of the small cramped airplane, then turned his head and glared at his seatmate. "You bastard. You did this on purpose, didn't you?" he said between clenched teeth. He was a white-knuckle flier in the best of conditions. The turbulence they were encountering now had tied his stomach in little knots, then forced it to the back of his throat. His forehead was damp with the sweat of fear, and his fingers were numb from the iron grip he had on the arm of his seat.

He watched with a sense of perverse pleasure the way the laughter quickly died in Doug's gaze and he frantically fumbled with the release of his seat belt when he thought he was about to get Max's lunch in his lap. Max closed his eyes and swallowed hard, trying to think of anything but the way the plane kept rising and falling.

Doug pried Max's fingers off the arm of the seat and shoved a barf bag into his hand. "I didn't tell you about the second leg of the trip because I knew you wouldn't go for it. You'd have rented a car and driven. But this ain't New York or Los Angeles, old pal. You'd be days getting to Dawson's and we'd lose our reservations. Hell, I had to pay extra just to get us included."

The pilot seemed to have found a calm pocket and

Max opened his eyes, but kept his gaze glued to the seat in front of him. "Damn right I'd have rented a car. I'll get you for this, Doug. I swear I will. Where are we heading?"

Doug bit his lip to keep from laughing, then pushed at his glasses and finger-combed his hair. From New York he figured they'd changed planes three times, or was it four? He was as tired as Max. "We'll be landing at an airstrip near a town called Bartlet. Someone from Dawson's will pick us up and drive us to the ranch. We'll stay one night at the ranch house, then hike up the mountain to the lodge. Man, I can't wait. Did you remember to bring those flies I bought you? The guy at the store said they were guaranteed to catch anything we went after."

"I don't understand you, Doug. You're the most suspicious person I know. It takes an act of Congress to convince you of something. Yet put you in a sporting-goods store or a tackle shop and you'd believe a two-year-old if he told you their new shipment of pink-winged flies were found only on the moon and were guaranteed to hook the world's biggest trout."

Doug wouldn't dignify his accusations. "Well, I don't understand *you*. When we were in the service, we flew all the time. Hell, I saw you parachute out of planes without blinking an eye."

"I've got a confession, Dougie. I was scared out of my mind then, too. Just too young, proud and plain stupid to admit it." He would have said more, but the steady roar of the engines changed pitch as they began their descent. Max grabbed the arms of the seat, squeezed his eyes shut and didn't open them again until Doug shook his shoulder.

"We're here, Max. Get up." He leaned over and

looked out the window. "Car's waiting. Move it. I'm dying to get there." Doug rubbed his hands together like a kid, and, picking up some of his gear, rattled and bumped his way toward the open door.

Max peeled himself out of the narrow seat like pulling a suction cup from a pane of glass. He had to hunch his shoulders and stoop to keep from hitting his head on the ceiling as he made his way out on legs that felt weak and rubbery. As soon as his feet touched solid ground, he almost choked on the crispness of the clean air. The beauty of the scenery stole his breath and left him awed, light-headed. He could have stood there for hours soaking up everything like a dry sponge in warm water if Doug hadn't yelled at him to get moving.

As the driver of the old Suburban introduced himself as Reed Bartlet, Max gave him a hard look. Interesting—Bartlet was also the name of the town. He was a good-looking kid with a head of thick, coal black hair and solemn blue eyes. Close to six feet, tanned and fit, he had that gangly loose-limbed build that bespoke that alien mixture of youth and manual labor. His face was losing its adolescent roundness, beginning to show the angularity of manhood.

Max figured the kid probably had girls trailing him around now, and in a few years he'd have to beat them off. The maturity sat awkwardly on his shoulders, and Max, after a second closer look, would have sworn the kid wasn't much older than thirteen. He was about to ask to see his driver's license, but Doug was too busy pushing and prodding him into the back seat. Once comfortable, he promptly fell asleep.

The ride to the ranch took well over an hour, and Doug had to shake him awake as they bounced over the cattle guard. He sat up just in time to catch the blur of a horse and rider racing parallel with the fence as though trying to outrun the car. He fully expected the kid driving to step on the gas and try to outdistance the rider, but even though temptation made the boy's hands tighten on the steering wheel, their slow pace never increased.

Max smiled, wondering if he'd have had that much willpower when he was that age. Then his vision was filled with wide rolling meadows thickly carpeted in green and dotted with yellow and pink flowers, here and there a tree. The scene was like a mirage, the way it wavered and rolled on the heat waves of the July afternoon. He had to rub his eyes to make sure he wasn't hallucinating.

But no, those black-spotted cattle that reminded him of dalmatians were very real. He smiled, feeling the peace of the place as those big docile animals munched away on the rich grasses, leisurely lifting their heads to inspect the car as it passed. For the first time in months he felt the tension in his neck and shoulders begin to ease a little.

Doug said something from the front seat. Max tore his gaze from the fields and leaned forward, trying to catch what was being said. But Doug had fallen silent, and Max followed the direction of his gaze. His heart stopped beating for an instant as he looked at the sprawling, two-story, gray stone house with the varied rooflines. It reminded him of a fine painting, one he could sit and stare at for hours and never get tired of.

The main portion of the house had a severely steeped slate roof, like an arrow with its tip pointing upward as if showing the way to the mountain that rose majestically behind the house. Brushed with hues of green, tinted with shadows of gray and black and topped with snow, it, too, was like a fine painting. This was Dawson Mountain, and it was no wonder Carl Bedford wanted to add it to his collection.

Reed carefully brought the Suburban to a stop, sighed audibly, then smiled. He indicated a man standing on the front porch and said, "That's Charlie Dawson. He busted his ankle and it's made him pretty cranky."

Max recognized the nervous relief in the kid's voice and felt for him. He'd obviously been given the responsibility, however illegal, of picking up the late arrivals and was both glad and excited it was over and he hadn't been stopped by the police. Max remembered the small-town days of his own youth, and how the laws of age and a driver's license were ignored.

As he climbed out of the car, Max slipped the kid ten bucks, nodded and grinned. Then he leaned against the car and watched the old man with the obviously new cast on his leg make a careful but awkward descent down the steep stone steps. The man was hanging on to the railing with one hand and wrestling with the crutch under his other armpit, trying to get the rhythm of the crutch-and-leg movements and keep his balance at the same time. This was the subject of his investigation, Max thought, and took precise note of every detail. It was surprising how much one could learn just from a man's appearance.

Charles Dawson was medium height and looked solid from years of hard work. He was dressed in faded jeans, one new handmade boot and a stylish brown-and-turquoise Western shirt. Max noted that the shirt and boot weren't cheap and tucked away that fact, too. Dawson was a little vain, had expensive tastes and enjoyed being a dandy. It was hard to estimate his age as his face was deeply lined and weathered brown by the sun; his thick hair was more salt than pepper. But Max guessed him to be somewhere in his late sixties or early seventies. Then Dawson lifted his gaze, and Max immediately subtracted five years from his estimate. The old man's eyes were sharp and clear, a startling bright blue in the dark face, and at the moment his gaze was full of frustration at his helplessness.

Charlie cursed and threw the crutch down the remainder of steps, watching it break in two. After a moment of satisfied silence, he smiled at the two city slickers standing by the car as their suitcases were being piled beside them, and he reminded himself they were paying guests. He never understood why all these weekend sportsmen found it necessary to bring half their wardrobes.

"Welcome to Dawson's, gentlemen. Why don't you come on up to the house and join the rest of the guests in the living room for some refreshments? Reed, I see you trying to sneak off. Call Ash to help with the luggage, then come give me a hand." All the while he'd been talking, Charlie was easing himself down the remainder of the steps so that when he finished he was able to shake hands with the two new arrivals. When Reed returned to assist him, he said, "Ring the bell to get Nick's attention, would you?" He shaded his eyes, apparently noticing something or someone in the distance. "Never mind," he said.

Doug glanced down at the cast, then back at Charlie's strained face and grinned. "What happened? Fall off a horse? Get thrown by a bull?"

"Nothing so exciting. I stepped in a damn critter

hole." He tried again to get the city boys moving. "There's ice-cold beer, and lunch is about to be served. You're both a little late, but the rest of the men have voiced a willingness to leave for the mountain lodge after the meal. Are you up to a half-day hike through the most beautiful country in the world, or do you want to wait and ride up with one of the boys early tomorrow morning?"

"We'll leave with the others," Max said as his gaze followed Charlie's. He saw a horse and rider execute a smooth jump over the three-rail fence, then head toward them at a full gallop. Doug automatically moved back, bumping into Max and stepping on his toe as the horse stopped a few feet away.

There was no mistaking the rider's gender, not with the shapely body and long legs encased in tight jeans. As she dismounted, Max admired the firm rounded backside and smiled when he heard her light laughter. Her face was deeply shadowed by the dip of her Stetson. He stared as she removed the cowboy hat and dusted it off with a few thumps against her thigh.

He couldn't move.

Couldn't breathe.

There was a roaring in his ears like the rush of a waterfall.

Everything around her seemed to fade and then disappear. Her hair, a short curly cap, sparkled like gold in the noon sun. Her eyes, when they swung in his direction, were a bright emerald green. The beauty of her face left him numb. It was an eternity before he felt Doug's viselike grip on his arm, cutting off the circulation. His friend's hoarse whisper brought him forcefully back to earth.

"Oh, my God, my God," Doug chanted under his breath. "Max...Max. What's going on?"

But Max's voice had dried up and he couldn't answer, only gawk. There wasn't a doubt in his mind that the woman before him was Sandra Applewhite Gillman. He knew every detail of that face and body. The minor changes—the short hair, the tanned and slimmer figure were all minor details. For this was Sandra. He was as sure of that as his own name. He was staring at a dead woman—except she wasn't dead.

Max's shock quickly faded, replaced by betrayal and anger. It was his turn to grab Doug's arm and squeeze, to stop him from confronting Sandra.

Charles ignored the way the two city boys were making fools of themselves. He'd seen it happen many times before. "Nicky, these are the two gentlemen we've been waiting for." He introduced her and wondered at the rapid change in the big man.

Nicole sighed inwardly as she shook hands with the newcomers. She guessed the clean air and anticipation of a rugged vacation had their testosterone levels running on high. She suddenly had an image in her mind of them beating their chests. Here were two big-shot executives who thought they knew everything there was to know about Montana, fly-fishing and women.

She glanced from one to the other as they stood elbow-punching each other like little boys. Then she locked gazes with the big man, Max. There was something electric in those blue eyes that made her pause. Nicole shivered.

These two were going to be trouble. She just knew it. If she hadn't known better, she'd have thought both men were tongue-tied at just seeing a woman. She nodded politely to the new arrivals, excused herself, then jogged up the porch steps and disappeared inside.

In a fog of confusion Max watched his dream vanish. He drove the seething turmoil of questions aside for the time being and glanced at Doug. His partner looked as bewildered as he was. Then, like a pair of dumbstuck teenagers, they blindly followed as Reed helped Charlie up the steps.

NICOLE DIDN'T SLOW or stop until she reached her bedroom. After the door was firmly shut, she leaned against it as if winded. Her heart was racing a mile a minute. She could still feel the way the big man's eyes followed her every move and was puzzled by the intensity of the attention.

She took a couple of long deep breaths, and when her knees stopped feeling like jelly, she pushed away from the door and headed for the bathroom. After a quick shower, she shampooed and dried her hair. Then she applied a minimal amount of makeup and dressed for work, but her mind wasn't on what she was doing. It was ridiculous, she knew, but all she could think about was the way Max Warner had watched her. Beyond the shock and the anger she'd seen in his face, there was more, something she couldn't put a name to.

"Nicky, Nicky," she said through gritted teeth. "The man is trouble." She pulled a short-sleeved knit shirt over her head, then fluffed out her damp hair. "Trouble in a big good-looking package." Stepping into a pair of khaki walking shorts, she paused before yanking up the zipper and said, "You've done this before." Damn, she was talking to herself again. But the last time she'd been this attracted to a man, she'd married him.

"And look where that got you." She sat on the corner of the bed to put on her hiking boots. "Divorced and back home, living with Charlie." As hard as she concentrated on every task, she couldn't erase the memory of the way his gaze seemed to eat her up. Something hot, dark and sensual shimmered through her.

"Dammit," she said when she caught sight of herself in the mirror. Her eyes looked too big, her cheeks flushed. She bit her full bottom lip. "You're twenty-seven years old, not a silly schoolgirl. Keep your feelings in check this time and your eye on Charlie." The thought of the old man had the sobering effect she needed. She straightened her shoulders and turned toward the door. He'd avoided being alone with her for the past two days. There was no telling what he was up to now.

She glanced around the big airy bedroom, with its tall windows, high ceilings and abundance of glossy white molding and wood. This had always been her sanctuary, her haven. The only room in the house where she could vent her emotions without being seen or heard.

Feeling more relaxed and ready to face the men downstairs and the five-day task ahead, she leaned her forehead against the cold smooth wood of the door. She had to stay focused, professional and above all keep her wandering thoughts from running amok with foolish fantasies. The last thing she needed right now was a man in her life. She quietly closed the door behind her, moved down the stairs—and came face-to-face with Sam Wooten. "Sam!" She didn't try to cover her surprise. "What are you doing here?" She'd been dodging Sam ever since the last day of school and had done pretty well until now. As she tried to move past him, he touched her arm, obliging her to halt.

"I knew you were still interested in a permanent teaching position. I've come to tell you that the school board is meeting in two weeks and I'm going to put your name in for consideration."

She eyed him suspiciously. Sam Wooten was a forty-five-year-old divorcé who seemed to consider himself irresistible to women. It galled him, she knew, that she constantly, but always politely and with diplomacy, turned down all his invitations. The fact that he was much older than she was, that his hair was thinning and graying, or that he had a good start on a potbelly, wasn't the reason she kept turning him away. She just flat out didn't like or trust him. There was something sneaky about him.

But she was always pleasant to him, because he was the principal at the elementary school where she'd taught first grade for the last three months of the school year—a replacement for the regular teacher, who'd been killed in a car accident. Furthermore, he was on the school board and usually got what he wanted.

Montana was a state of great wide-open spaces and mountain ranges, and except for the few cities, most of the territory was ranch land or government land. The ranchers and small-town families had to bus their children to the nearest schools.

Luckily for her, one of those schools just happened to be in Bartlet, a town only an hour's drive from the Dawson homestead. If she could get a teaching position there, she could live at home and keep a close watch on Charlie and the business.

She knew the real reason for Sam's visit now, could see it in his pompous pleased expression. He figured he was in the catbird seat, a position of power, and he intended to use it to persuade her to go out with him.

She smiled sweetly, but her eyes burned a bright green. She'd been manipulated by a pro—her ex-husband—and Sam Wooten was an amateur compared to him. "Thank you for coming all this way to tell me, Sam. But if you'll excuse me, we have guests."

"I thought you might like to have dinner with me tonight so we could talk about the meeting." Before she could answer, he rushed on, "You could fill me in on some of your other qualifications. After all, I know so little about you and I..." His voice trailed away when he saw her shake her head and give him a hard look.

She would have liked to introduce her knee to his groin. Instead, from a lifetime of putting on the face, as Charlie called it, for the paying guests, she just continued to stare. Movement at the corner of her eye caught her attention. They were no longer alone, and she knew without turning her head that it was Max Warner who had stepped out of the dining room and was watching and listening. "I'm sorry, Sam, but I really do have to see to the guests."

"But when they leave?"

With the smile still plastered on her face, she said, "That'll be a week from now, and that's too far ahead to make plans, don't you think? You never know what could happen."

"Well, maybe I could join you and your guests for dinner tonight."

She could feel Max's scrutiny. "Is there something you need, Mr. Warner?" she asked, her tone thick as honey.

Max brought the cold bottle of beer to his mouth, paused, then took a long slow pull. His eyes never left hers. Lowering the bottle, he gave her a tight smile, then turned on his heel and disappeared back into the dining room.

She'd been mesmerized by the intensity of those glacial blue eyes, and it took Sam's voice to bring her back down to earth.

"Who's he?" Sam wanted to know as he stood straighter and puffed out his chest.

Sighing inwardly, she said, "He's a guest, Sam. And I'm sorry, but I won't be here for dinner. I'm the guide for this trip." She almost laughed at his shock.

"You mean you're going to stay up there for a week with all those men?"

"Sam—" she grasped his arm and started leading him across the entryway "—it's my job. It's how Dawson Outriggers makes money." She opened the front door and waited.

"But...alone?"

"Thanks for coming by, Sam."

"Listen," he said, "what if I were to come along? Then we'd have plenty of time to discuss the job."

"Sure, you're welcome to come, Sam. The cost is four thousand dollars. Charlie doesn't allow any freebies." She waited a second, pretending to consider the situation, then said, "We're already one man over our limit. Still, if you want, I could ask if we could squeeze in another." She nudged him through the doorway, but Sam stopped her from closing the door.

"Four thousand dollars?" He was barely able to keep the gasp out of his voice.

"For a week of the best fly-fishing, food and lodging in Montana—hell, in the U.S. It's well worth it," she said.

"But four thousand?"

Struggling with a compulsion to laugh and barely managing to keep herself under control, Nicole said as she closed the door, "Why don't I just call you when I get back? How about that?"

At last he was gone. The effort to hold her tongue had been so overwhelming that she looked around for something to vent her frustration on. But the urge quickly died when she remembered the dining room full of paying guests. For a moment she tallied up the profits, knowing it was just barely enough, barring any unforeseen problems, to meet the mortgage and pay the three months of bills still owing.

She glanced around, feeling suddenly nostalgic, and swallowed the lump in her throat. This place—the ranch, the land and the mountain—had been in her family for four generations. It was more than a home. It was her lifeline, her heart. No matter how many times she'd left, she'd always come back. Now she was here to stay. Provided, of course, she could keep a tight rein on Charlie.

She loved her home and believed she'd do just about anything to keep it. But Charlie and his excesses were quickly running them deeply in debt. It was puzzling, for he loved the place as much as she did and knew the consequences of his irresponsible actions. Yet he continued to jeopardize their existence with his wild schemes. Their lawyer had advised her that, if Charlie kept up the drinking and gambling, maybe it was time to do something about it—take steps to safeguard her interest. The thought of taking legal action against Charlie was too much. If she could keep him out of trouble and get that permanent teaching position, they'd be okay.

She vowed she'd do whatever was necessary to ensure that.

CHAPTER THREE

IT DIDN'T TAKE much eavesdropping for Max to size up the situation. Bribery was an ugly word. He had the feeling this Sam character Sandra was talking with was trying, none too subtly, to pull a fast one. Anger, deep and primitive, rippled through him. At that moment he wanted nothing more than to wrap his hands around the man's throat. He even took a step forward before her soft-voiced question stopped him dead in his tracks. And that gaze. Those incredible green eyes, with all their soft sweetness, shouldn't be looking at him with such censure. Then he reminded himself that Sandra, for whatever reason, was masquerading as Nicole. Until he found out why, he would have to watch himself.

He stepped back into the dining room, but not entirely out of earshot. He was surprised at the finesse, firmness, even humor with which she took care of the situation with Sam. She'd grown strong since her disappearance. Capable. Those realizations made it all too clear that he and Doug needed a plan.

He intercepted Doug at the buffet table as he was making his way down the line of food with the look of a man who hadn't eaten in weeks. Max eyed the heaping plate—the thick sandwich, the mound of potato salad, plus a pile of chips and pickles. "What happened to your no-fat regimen?"

Doug pushed Max out of his way and began spearing green and black olives with his fork. "Mountain air makes me hungry."

"We're not in the mountains yet."

"Just the idea makes me ravenous." Doug ignored Max's hovering, set the plate down and dug through the cooler for a bottle of beer. He gestured at the one Max held. "Better not drink all that on an empty stomach. Eat something, Max. I understand the trek to the lodge takes a while." He popped a green olive in his mouth and watched Max chug-a-lug the remainder of his beer.

The cold hurt all the way down, a good hurt that forced his eyes shut on a sigh. When Max could talk again, he said, "You look like a walking advertisement for Eddie Bauer or Banana Republic. Did you buy all new clothes for the trip?"

"Yep."

Max grinned. "Now you're a true Westerner, a man of few words?"

"Screw you, Warner."

"We need to come up with a plan. And fast." He grabbed a potato chip from Doug's plate. "Both of us can't go off and leave her here. But it's going to look weird if we both decide not to go to the lodge. Any suggestions?"

When Max's hand snaked out in an attempt to pick up half his sandwich, Doug knocked it aside. "One of us goes to the lodge and enjoys his vacation. The other makes an excuse about needing a rest, hangs around here and works at finding out what she's doing in Montana." He glanced over his shoulder and studied the men seated around the table. They'd finished lunch and were having another drink as they listened to

Dawson discuss the trip. When Doug glanced back at Max, he found that half his sandwich was missing and at that very moment was being consumed.

Max swallowed, then grinned. "I think I should stay behind, keep an eye on Sandra and alert the office to what's happening, don't you?"

Doug agreed eagerly, as thought of being knee-deep in water, the sun on his shoulders while he cast into a clear stream, assailed him. But his bubble of happiness burst at the idea of leaving Max, knowing how he felt about Sandra. "I don't know," he hedged. "Maybe you ought to…" His voice was drowned out by laughter coming from the table behind them.

THE LOUD SOUND of male laughter jerked Nicole's attention back to the present and the problem at hand. She had seven eager so-called sportsmen to keep happy and busy for five days. As she headed for the dining room, she stopped beside the library table and flipped though the guest book, studying names. Then she collected the personal-liability-release forms that all guests were required to sign. She counted only five. The two late arrivals hadn't yet signed theirs. She fished out a couple of blanks, straightened her shoulders and entered the laughter-filled room.

As customary, Charlie was seated at the head of the long table, impressing the men with fish stories of the past. She had to admit he was a good storyteller, keeping his listeners fascinated. A perfect host, with charisma, wit and an abundance of welcoming benevolence that was hard to resist. He was indeed a charmer, Nicole thought with a warm rush of love.

The conversation petered out as first one then another of the men noticed her presence. She gestured at the ones who'd started to stand to be seated, then continued across the room to Charlie's side. Even though her attention was centered on the two men at the buffet table, she didn't miss a beat or a step as she helped her father to his feet. She knew what was coming and waited.

"Gentlemen, as you can see—" he tapped his cast with his cane "—I'm unable to do very much. But my daughter, Nick, has agreed to be your guide for your stay." Seeing a few disgruntled expressions, he hurriedly continued, "Now, before you moan and groan about Nick's being a female, let me tell you she's a better fly fisherman than I am, plus she knows all the prime spots to catch the big ones. Besides, she won't be fishing, only taking you and dropping you off and seeing to your needs."

He deliberately let his gaze linger on each man, showing them he meant business. Little did they know that he was only a figurehead outdoorsman. Nick ran Dawson Outriggers. He'd handed the business over to her years ago, and the only season she'd ever missed was the year she was married to that son of a bitch in Los Angeles. Nick was the one who took the tours out, and the repeaters knew that. They found they'd enjoyed themselves so much that, on successive trips, they couldn't have cared less that their guide was a woman.

Charlie was always the speech maker, figuring the men needed it. But he'd done it so many times that he told Nick she should record him on tape, then when he died she could have him stuffed, prop him up and just push the buttons. Nick didn't find the suggestion funny.

"Now, that's the way it's going to be, and I promise

you'll have the time of your life and catch more fish than you can tell tales about.'' This last bit of the speech was always the hardest, since he'd already deposited their checks with big plans for the money. ''But if anyone has a mind to kick up a ruckus over Nick's being your guide, get it out of your craw now. If that ain't possible, then I'll give you your money back and have one of the boys drive you, right now, back to Bartlet, where you can make arrangements to catch a flight to Missoula, Helena or Great Falls.''

Like her father, Nicole captured each man's gaze straight on, giving them a friendly but no-nonsense smile. When she reached Warner, her smile melted away, leaving her expression blank. What was it about him that bothered her? Better yet, what was it about *her* that brought on that angry stare? She thought she could actually feel his icy blue eyes boring into her. She shifted her own eyes away, shook off the uneasy feeling and glanced at her watch. ''If you're all agreeable, I think we should be leaving in, say, thirty minutes.''

One of the men cleared his throat, then asked, ''How long a hike is it to the lodge?''

Nicole met the man's gaze. She'd studied the personal-information sheets the guests had been required to fill out, and to which she or Charlie had added comments, so she would know each man by name. The comments included detailed physical descriptions and a rather fly-by-the-seat-of-the-pants personality profile. Charlie was very good at judging a person's strengths and weaknesses, and he'd taught her a great deal about observation. They'd only lost two guests over the years, and each time they'd had all the necessary information needed for the sheriff's office.

Now she smiled and replied, "If we make good time, Hal, it should take about three hours. It's a wonderful hike up the mountain, not too difficult but enough for a good workout and seeing some great scenery. If we leave soon, we'll make it to the lodge in time for everyone to shower and have drinks on the lodge's front porch to watch the sun set. Then our chef will serve you a fabulous dinner."

"What's on the agenda for, say, after dinner?" Hal asked, giving her what he no doubt considered his sexiest smile, his meaning thinly veiled.

Great, she thought, as if she didn't have enough problems. There was a familiar sinking feeling in the pit of her stomach. Now, besides the Warner-and-Hart duo, here was another one to watch out for. Though her father had always taught her to keep her public face, that the paying guest, no matter how obnoxious, was to be treated politely and with respect, there was a limit.

Another Dawson cardinal rule her father had impressed upon her was to never ever take the sexual crap men were so apt to deal out to females when they felt their domain or ego was being invaded or threatened. Any deviation from plain good manners usually got the offender one strong warning. If the guest transgressed again, he was escorted off the mountain and sent packing without getting his money back. She'd had enough, for one day, of men flexing their hormones and was about to give Hal her first and only warning when she was rudely cut off.

Max had stepped up behind Hal and given the shorter man a friendly, if somewhat hard, slap on the shoulder. "I think you'll probably be too tired for anything after dinner but sleep, don't you, Hal?" It wasn't what he said. Or that the friendly slap had made Hal gasp. It was the menacing tone Max used that caused immediate silence among everyone.

Confused by his automatic reflexive behavior, Max tried to cover up the stupidity of what he'd done. He even forced himself to smile at the group, Hal in particular, but found he could barely restrain himself from putting his fist in the man's face.

Doug, feeling obliged to save his partner's butt, said jovially, "I imagine we'll all be pretty bushed after a hike up a mountain."

There were a few weak laughs, then everyone started talking at once to cover the awkwardness. Nicole exchanged a pained look with her father and received what was meant to be a comforting grin in return.

"Instead of sending Reed with the truck this time," Charlie said, "Ash can go with the gear and supplies. Reed can tag along with you and the group." He pulled Nicole to one side. "Remember, Sweetpea, don't take no lip. If one of these city boys steps outta line, give me or the sheriff a call and we'll take care of it."

She stared at her father. From a lifetime of learning his habits, there was one that stood out. When he started calling her by endearing nicknames like Sweetpea, she knew something was wrong. He'd been acting strangely since breakfast. "Dad, please tell me you're not in trouble again."

Charlie's gaze shifted from her probing look as he pretended to check out each guest. "I resent the implication that I'm always in trouble."

"I don't care. Are you?"

"Pumpkin, don't you worry about a thing. I've

found a sure way out of our problems." His leathery face split into a cunning smile. "I need to find Reed and fill him in on the change of plans."

His reassurance struck fear into her heart. She would have demanded to know what he was up to, but as slick as an eel he slipped away, leaving her more worried than ever.

Max couldn't stop watching her. It took Doug's firm yank on his arm to drag his attention away. "Max, if you don't stop ogling her like that, Dawson's going to give us the boot-in-the-butt-heave-ho out of here."

"Sorry, but I just can't figure out what's going on, can you?"

"I think she doesn't know who she is. You know, amnesia?"

"Bull! This woman is Sandra. What I can't figure out is why Dawson and the others are so comfortable calling her Nick. Dammit, he even *treats* her like a daughter!"

Doug shrugged. "I guess it's something we'll have to find out. After all, it's what we do."

Max shot him a killing glance. "Fine. But plans have changed."

Doug sighed. He knew full well what was coming. "You want me to stay behind and keep an eye on Charlie, and you're going to the lodge with Sandra?"

"Sorry, but I have to do this, Doug. I have to find out what she's up to myself."

"It's going to cost you."

Max grinned. "I never doubted it for a moment." He was about to sneak a thick slice of pickle from Doug's plate when Sandra interrupted them. As he gazed at her, his heart was in his throat. Her short hair was still damp at the ends and smelled of gardenias.

The faded green-and-yellow-striped shirt was tucked neatly into the waist of her walking shorts, and her hiking boots were scuffed and well-worn. She couldn't have been more beautiful to him if she'd been wearing silk and pearls.

Nicole handed, first Max, then Doug, a single sheet of paper. "These are liability-release forms. I need you to read them carefully and sign them before we leave. She made herself look at Max, even contrived a tiny smile as her gaze ran over him from head to toe. He was wearing an expensive shirt, slacks and Italian loafers. "I think you'll have just enough time to change before we leave."

Max and Doug watched her walk away, followed her every movement until she was out of the room. "You've got to stop drooling and staring, Max. They're liable to think you're either a pervert or have some medical problem."

Max laughed, thumped his friend on the back and headed for his room. When he'd changed and returned to the dining room, it was to find it empty except for Doug.

"Everyone's outside and waiting for you." Doug fidgeted with his glasses, then ran his fingers through his hair and eyed Max's old jeans and polo shirt with distaste. When his gaze dropped to the hiking boots, he gave a nod of approval. "Did you put on two pairs of socks? You know how your feet sweat."

"Yes, Mother Hart. Listen, I'm taking the cellular phone with me, so I'll keep in touch. You call Ray and Tommy at the office and have them—"

"Already done."

"You told them not to let a whisper of this get out, didn't you?"

"Not a word."

Max glanced around for his gear. "And don't call Helen Applewhite, either. Not until we know what's going on here."

"How long have we been partners, Max?"

He was distracted by a thousand things and didn't understand Doug's question. "Seems like forever. Why?"

"Then don't give me orders like a rookie investigator, will you?"

"I'm sorry, pal. I just... Where the hell's my gear?"

"I took it out to the truck. You'd better get going."

"You're not pissed off that I'm going to the lodge, instead of you, are you?"

"Yes, but I'll get over it." Doug's answer was said with a smile and they both laughed. "Be careful. Something strange is happening around here. It could be anything."

Max was halfway out of the dining room when he remembered the form and dug it out of his pocket. Then he stopped and glanced over his shoulder. The retort on the tip of his tongue died as he saw Doug's worried expression. "You've heard something?"

"Just rumblings about things happening around here. Weird things I think I'd like to look into." He caught up with Max, slung his arm around his shoulders and escorted him outside. "By the way, Charlie was more than willing to let me have a room here for the week after I explained I was all strung out and needed the rest, quiet and relaxation. Too bad, I like the old guy."

They stood at the top of the porch steps and Max watched the scene below. Suddenly what Doug had just said sunk in. "Too bad about what?"

"Earth to Max." Doug's voice sounded like the hiss of a snake next to Max's ear. "Don't forget what and who brought us here in the first place. We do have a client—Carl Bedford, remember?"

Max nodded and started off down the steps. "Yeah. Sure. Whatever. I'll keep in touch. And, Doug, stay out of trouble."

Nicole eyed the lounging group of five men, half listening to what they were saying to one another, but catching the excitement in their voices that they tried to hide. Weekend fisherman, she judged. Forget the bragging. She figured none of them had ever been on a serious fly-fishing trip. She knew from experience that if they were true sportsmen, all that cockiness and chest-thumping would disappear in about a day or two. That was when they'd realize they were actually living their dream.

Five men, she thought, and tried to size them up individually.

Hal Overton, whom she'd dubbed lover boy, was thirty-two. He was a real California pretty boy, with that gilded hair, deep tan and a body that probably kept him in the gym more than he was in his Hollywood law office. She had an idea he was one of those spoiled, obnoxious, rich guys who thought he was an expert and seasoned outdoorsman. He'd bragged to Charlie, Reed, Ash and anyone else who would listen of the places he'd fished and hunted all over the world.

Hal's friend, Preston Waters, was the opposite: short, overweight, with visible "love handles" and a stomach that stretched the limits of his waistband and pulled at the buttons on his shirt. From watching and listening, she learned that Preston and Hal were childhood pals. She decided Preston was the one with the brains and manners, and he'd be the one to pull Hal into line. From long experience, she knew the mountain had a way of changing people for the better. She'd seen it happen too many times to discount the magic.

Clarence Wiltshire and George Morrison laughingly told her they were number-crunchers. Accountants and brothers-in-law from St. Louis, Missouri, and old fishing buddies who said they'd saved for three years for this trip to Montana. To Nicole, they even resembled each other. Middle-aged. Of average height with light brown hair and dark eyes. They were still pale from a long cold Missouri winter. She liked them immediately and smiled at their identical caps loaded with what she was sure were homemade fishing flies. These two would be easy to please as long at they had their lines in the water. She sensed the idea of a female guide didn't bother them a bit.

Larry Spell was the oldest of the group—sixty-five. His dark brown hair was heavily streaked with gray, his short legs were bowed, and his hands were rough and callused. He was also the only loner, and that was a little unusual. Most of their guests came in pairs or groups. But Larry was as comfortable with his solitariness as Hal and Preston were with each other's company. Larry had left the occupation portion on his form blank and named as next of kin his sister in Santa Fe, New Mexico, which he also claimed as his home.

Out of the seven paying guests, only six were going to the lodge. She raised her eyes when the sixth man, Maximilian Warner, came down the porch steps and approached. She wanted nothing more than to back away, but managed to stand her ground.

"I'm sorry to hold everyone up." He handed Sandra the form and watched as she gave it a quick glance, then passed it to Charlie. He arched a dark brow and said for her ears only, ''You're not the least bit interested in my vital statistics?''

Her emerald green eyes flashed. The corners of her sensuous mouth curled slightly upward. ''I think I know all I need to know without any help.'' Nicole turned to the group, and her smile was sincere and friendly. ''If you're all ready, I think it's well past time to leave. But first off, I'd like to ask that you follow the path and try not to lag behind, and if anyone—'' she cut a glance at Max ''—gets tired or the pace is too fast, let me know and we'll stop.''

Hal stepped forward and put on his most charming smile. ''What's the mule for? To carry the old-timers if they can't make it?''

Everyone turned to look at the sturdy brown animal with the two box-shaped canvas-covered packs strapped to his back. ''That's Pepper and he's carrying water and some refreshments. We'll be taking a couple of rest stops along the way.'' She frowned, looked around and was about to ask her father where Reed was when Reed and his brother, Ash, came racing around the corner.

Reed picked up Pepper's lead, stroked the short bristle-brush mane, then turned to face his audience. ''Sorry I'm late. But I had to call my dad about the changes.'' His younger brother elbowed him in the ribs and he cleared his throat. ''Is it okay if Ash comes up with the truck?''

Nicole bit her lip and looked at her father. The issue had been settled earlier between them, but she kept quiet, knowing how much of a kick Charlie got out of teasing the boys. As her father let the tension stretch, she studied the boys. Reed was thirteen and Ash eleven, and they could have passed for twins even though Ash was shorter. They both resembled their mother, Shannon Reed Bartlet, with her black-Irish heritage. Even the boys' five-year-old sister, Ginny, was fast growing into the same mold. Their father, Ash, Senior, with his blond good looks, had been left out of the gene-pool loop when the three were conceived.

"Oh, hell," Charlie grumbled, when all the while he knew he'd let the kid go. "I guess it's okay. Looks like everyone is running off on me, anyway." He glanced at Doug and his expression brightened. "You don't by any chance play poker, do you, young man?"

"My middle name's five-card draw," Doug said.

"Dad," Nicole warned, "you promised."

"No high stakes. Penny ante. Just a friendly little game or two." She shrugged and turned away, but the worry rode heavily on her shoulders. An unsupervised Charles Dawson was an open invitation to trouble. "Gentlemen, if you're ready?"

Nicole took the lead, forcing herself to keep her pace to that of her guests. They rounded the side of the house and strung themselves out in a long line, with Reed and Pepper bringing up the rear.

Two hours later, when they'd put the house and fenced pastures far behind them and had started up a gentle incline, Nicole headed for a grove of tall trees. The sizable boulders that had tumbled down the mountain had been strategically placed within the shady ring of trees in a circular seating arrangement around a bigger slab of rock, which could be used as a picnic table. She stopped to let everyone catch up with her.

The incredible beauty of the mountain was in front of Max, and he could only imagine what lay ahead.

The scenery was indescribable. "Breathtaking" was too cliché. With every step that had brought him closer to the mountain, he'd felt the tension in his body seeping slowly away. For a group of men on a dream vacation, they were strangely silent, he thought. Then Max realized why.

Like him, they were shedding their problems, responsibilities and worries the way a snake sheds its skin. He could not only feel the difference but see it. Hal's manic pace had slowed, and Preston was no longer sprinting to catch up with his friend. Larry's and Clarence's postures were more relaxed, and their arms were swinging in rhythm with their feet. And Larry's ramrod-straight back and military-squared shoulders looked rounded and at ease.

Max glanced back over his shoulder and was surprised at how high they'd already come. He could see the expanse of rolling meadows, squared off by fence lines. He could still see the slate roof and chimneys of the Dawson homestead. It was a magical sight, one that stirred something deep inside. Despite all that was on his mind, he felt the strength and peace of the land. A kind of homecoming he hadn't experienced since his childhood in Texas. He noticed that Sandra—he couldn't even begin to think of her as Nicole—had stopped, and he quickened his steps.

"Max?" Nicole raised her voice to get his attention and motioned for him to join the others. She recognized that look of awe, had seen it often in many other tourists and sportsmen. Their excitement and wonder never failed to touch her, and usually put her in a good frame of mind.

Today for some reason was different. When she'd turned to check on the others, she found her gaze drifting to the last guest in line. He certainly was good-looking. *Dammit, admit it,* she scolded herself. He was extremely sexy with his dark hair, rugged features and sky blue eyes. Although a New Yorker, he didn't have that pale city-boy elegance. Max Warner reminded her of the men of Montana, smart and strong, tough, sure of themselves, but gentle where and when it counted.

She gave herself a mental shake and a kick in the butt. She had to stop letting him insinuate himself into her thoughts, interfering with her job. "We're going to take a short breather here and have something cold to drink," she said. "If anyone has to converse with Mother Nature, trees make a great cover." She motioned for Reed to bring Pepper over, and as soon as the big mule butted her with his head in greeting, she and Reed began to untie one side of the canvas.

"Need any help?" Hal asked.

Nicole gave a start and spun around. He'd slipped up behind her, and was too close. When she attempted to step away from him, he grasped her arms. It would have been innocent enough if he hadn't let the back of his fingers brush the sides of her breasts. He smiled, all teeth and bright eyes.

The little slug, she thought, and slapped his hands away. "Don't—"

"Need some help with that?" Max asked, and roughly shouldered Hal aside, and in the process stepped on the man's toe. When he grunted in pain, Max leaned close, pressed down harder and whispered. "Don't play your games with the lady, pal, or..." He left the threat hanging.

Nicole figured she and Reed where the only ones to overhear what Max had said. Still, she was furious. But not with Hal. She knew she could and would handle him with a few chosen threats. Without thinking, she grabbed Max's arm and yanked, managing to throw him off balance and allowing Hal to get away. She brought her face close to his so their noses were almost touching. "I'm sure you meant to help, but don't," she said, her smile overshadowed by the sarcasm in her voice. Then her voice lowered and she all but growled, "I mean it. Don't *ever* do that. I don't need protecting."

"Don't ever?" Max repeated. He was puzzled by her anger. Sandra was too sensitive and too much of a lady to use that tone or manner with anyone.

Nicole dropped his arm as if touching him actually burned her fingertips. "Right. Don't. Stay out of my business." She motioned Reed, who was frozen with youthful admiration, to go ahead and untie the canvas.

"Listen, I was just—" Max began.

She flipped the cover off the cooler. "I know very well what you were doing," she snapped. "But I don't need your help. I didn't ask for it, and I don't want it."

"But—"

"No exceptions." She nodded for Reed to grab one end of the cooler and together they lowered it to the ground. "If they don't respect me, see that I can take care of myself in any situation, how are they going to respect my abilities to guide them and take care of them? So do us both a favor—back off and stay away from me." She spun on her heel and calmly joined the group of men. They were beginning to let down their guards with one another and discuss past fishing trips. She summoned a smile she was far from feeling.

"There's cold water or soft drinks," she announced. "We'll rest here about fifteen minutes, then push on."

She didn't want them cooling down and stiffening up too much.

Larry Spell touched her arm to keep her from leaving them. "How's the fishing this time of year? I wasn't sure."

Nicole relaxed. She was comfortable talking about what she'd known and done all her life. "We have a pretty long fishing season. And I guarantee you the trout in Dawson Mountain rivers are the biggest in Montana." She winked and smiled, then said seriously, "I promise you, you won't be disappointed."

"I bet it gets pretty cold here, doesn't it?" Preston Waters asked.

Max watched her laughing and talking with the men as he accepted the bottle of water Reed tossed him. He couldn't figure it out. For what he was sure was the first time in his life, he'd had all the finesse of a gorilla. He'd jumped into the middle of her problem like a jealous lover. Hal had touched what was his, and like a demented animal, he'd reacted.

"Better drink the water and cool off, Mr. Warner," Reed said.

He turned his head and looked at the kid. He was suddenly embarrassed by the amusement in the boy's expression. "Is she always so...self-sufficient?"

"You mean hardheaded? Yes, sir. And she can be dangerous, too, when she gets really mad. I once saw her lose her temper at a bear 'cause he was disturbing one of her guests while he was fishing. She screamed and cussed at that bear until he just up and ran off."

Max studied the serious young face and the sparkling forest green eyes. Still unsure how to react, he saw the way the boy's lips twitched. Suddenly they both started laughing. When he could catch his breath,

Max said, "You're the tall-tale teller of your family, are you?"

Reed placed his hand over his heart, but he couldn't keep a straight face as he said, "I swear it's the truth."

Here was a well of information, Max thought, just waiting for him to explore. He wanted to ask the boy more, but was stopped when Nicole joined them carrying an armload of empty cans and a couple of bottles. Stepping out of the way, he had time to get a closer inspection. He realized that maybe he was wrong, that there was no way this Nicole could be his Sandra. She didn't have the elegance or sophistication. And she certainly didn't have Sandra's sweet disposition. He watched as Reed pulled out a plastic garbage bag and held it open while she dumped the trash into it.

Nicole smiled at him, her anger in control, and said, "Are you through with your water?" She held the bag out to him, and he dropped in his bottle.

She was positioned directly in front of him, only a foot or so away, and there was a look about her, the way she gazed at him, that went straight to his groin. He fought the feeling by inhaling. A mistake. A fragrance, unidentifiable, nameless, that had nothing to do with manufactured perfume, filled his head. A scent that tantalized his senses and tickled his imagination.

Despite the coolness of the shade, he felt the heat of desire flash through him. The impact almost knocked him speechless. She leaned down and helped Reed lift the cooler back up so he could strap it onto the side of the mule. That one smooth move paralyzed him; his body was no longer on fire with passion but frozen like a block of ice. As she lowered and tilted her head, he'd seen the small dark crescent-shaped mole behind her left ear.

If he'd had any doubts about her identity, they'd flown away on the breeze that stirred her short hair and allowed him to see the distinct birthmark. He was looking at his Sandra. The only problem, he figured, was she didn't know she was Sandra Applewhite.

CHAPTER FOUR

THE GROUP had really loosened up. They talked among themselves more, trading stories, discussing jobs, homes, wives and girlfriends. Nicole deliberately tried to stay far enough ahead so they'd feel at ease about what they were saying, but still close enough to remain in sight. A couple of times she'd glanced over her shoulder to gauge the distance between herself and the men, and couldn't help but notice the way Max and Reed seemed to be becoming fast friends. That surprised her.

Reed was something of a loner. A self-contained thirteen-year-old who worked hard and kept pretty much to himself. She guessed she was the only one besides his family he actually talked to at any length. She wondered what a man of Max Warner's age and sophistication could possibly have in common with Reed.

Max had no idea how long he'd been walking, just putting one foot in front of the other, his mind overflowing with the vision of that crescent-shaped birthmark. There was only one—could be only one—explanation. Sandra was alive and well and living in Montana. But how could that be? For the first time since arriving in Montana and seeing her, he really doubted what his eyes and his heart wanted so much to be true.

He was tired. Tired of the way questions kept running over and over in his mind, tired of endless nights lying awake thinking about her. He was tired of feeling empty inside. *Oh, hell, admit it, Max, you're just tired of being alone.* Now, the endless turmoil of was she or wasn't she Sandra had to stop, or he thought he might go stark raving mad.

Concentrate on the differences, he told himself. Instead of being the sweet-natured uncomplicated Sandra he'd come to care about, she was an enigma. Like a jigsaw puzzle with the pieces altered only a fraction so they almost, but not quite, fit together. The pieces could be forced, but the finished puzzle would never look right. It would always be off-kilter.

His thoughts were pursuing each other like a dog chasing its tail. He'd maybe'd and what-if'd himself until he was almost cross-eyed. And still he had no real answers. He tried to clear his head by taking deep breaths and focusing on what was around him. The day was rapidly cooling now and a breeze had kicked up, shaking the leaves in the trees overhead.

Reed was keeping pace with him in companionable silence, breaking it only now and then to fuss at the mule. A good investigator always talked to friends and neighbors of the person being investigated. The boy could be a well of information just waiting to be tapped. But Max had a hard-and-fast rule—never use children in an investigation, no matter how overwhelming the urge. If he started breaking his own rules, then where would he be?

It didn't take but a moment to shoot down his every excuse. When had he ever let anything or anyone stand in the way of getting what he wanted? He tried to abide by a set of standards he'd set, and he did most of the time. A little voice whispered in his ear that this situation was entirely different. There should be no holds barred. Should be— Dammit, no one had ever called him a coward.

Once *coward* had been spoken in his mind, he'd have to face the truth head-on. He looked at the woman leading the way over the trail, around the twists and turns, in and out of the trees, and knew he couldn't retreat from his search for the truth. He had to know what and why. He had to start somewhere, and now was as good a time as any.

"Tell me something, Reed. How long have you known...Nicole?"

Reed glanced at the big man moving with easy strides beside him. He wasn't like the usual sportsmen from the city who bragged about their money and the other trips they'd been on, and were full of dirty talk about women. Max was different, and besides, he was dying to hear all about New York or any place away from Montana. Furthermore, it was as plain as day that this man was interested in Nicky, and Reed thought he might be able to strike up a deal, finagle a trade of sorts. He was about to answer Max when Pepper dug in all four hooves, pulling everything to a teeth-jarring stop, and began braying as loud as a diesel horn. Reed dived for the canvas cover.

When Nicole heard Pepper's braying, a chill of fear rippled through her. She swung around and headed back down the trail at a run. When she came level with Hal and Preston, she shouted, "Group together and freeze. Do it—now!" she snapped at them when they just stared. She told the rest of the men the same as she passed them and was pleased to see that they instantly obeyed her.

Skidding to stop beside Pepper, she ignored the ear-splitting noise. She shouldered Max aside just as Reed got the canvas untied, flipped the covering out of the way and drew a Browning .380 rifle from its scabbard. She double-checked to make sure it was loaded, then rushed back up the trail.

"Would you mind telling me what's going on?" Max demanded.

His voice, so close, startled her, making her already pounding heart beat faster. She hadn't heard him following her. "Get back with the others, Max. *Now.*" She kept her attention on the woods beyond, straining to catch a glimpse or a sign of what animal had set Pepper off.

"What're you looking for?"

"Do you *ever* do what you're told?" She could see by the way his eyes narrowed that he didn't like taking orders and certainly wasn't about to take them from her. Keeping alert to every changing nuance around them, she thought she caught a whiff of fear on the breeze.

"What is it?" he asked.

She kept searching the perimeter. "Bear. Mountain lion. Maybe a wolf."

Cautiously Max glanced around, trying to sense where the danger was coming from. His first thought was of Sandra. "Give me the rifle and get back down the trail." All his senses were attuned to the strangeness all around them. "Jeez, can you make that damn animal shut up?" As he was reaching for the rifle, his attention shifted back to her face. If looks had the power to turn a person into something loathesome, he would have been a slug.

Nicole stepped away from his outstretched hand.

She had no intention of giving up the rifle, but it didn't mean she wouldn't have liked to turn it on him. "You better thank your lucky stars for Pepper, Mr. New York," she ground out between clenched teeth. "He's an alarmist, sure. But he only acts like that when he senses danger." She swung around, checking out the men, the surrounding trees and boulders. "He'll stop when he feels safe and whatever spooked him is gone."

Instead of taking offense, Max laughed. "Mr. New York? I could tell you a thing or— Oh, never mind. Pepper's your watchdog, so to speak?"

"So to speak." She deliberately stepped around him so her back was to the rest. "Mr. Warner, I'm capable of taking care of myself against beast and man." She hesitated long enough to let the last of her sentence sink in. "I don't need or want your help or interference." She started to walk away, then paused and said over her shoulder, "And don't ever try and take anything away from me."

As abruptly as Pepper had voiced his alarm, he stopped, then everyone started talking at once. Max rejoined Reed, and through the barrage of excited questions, Nicole explained what had happened.

Hal demanded, "There're bears and wolves up here?"

Preston edged closer to his friend as the rest of the men moved together in a tighter group. Everyone was suddenly nervous.

She bit her lip to keep from smiling and said as seriously as she could, "This is the wilderness, Hal."

Preston quickly recovered and asked as he looked around, "But what about while we're fishing? Are we safe?"

"Of course you are. And you'll all be equipped with walkie-talkies. If anything should occur, and I doubt that it will, all you have to do is remember to never run and call for help." She tried to interject just the right amount of humor into her speech, and as she talked she noticed that Hal had half turned away. When he swung back, he had a small pistol in his hand. She felt a chill run through her, then forced herself to count to ten.

"I came prepared for something like this," Hal said. "Brought my own protection." He waved the handgun in the air.

Max heard Reed groan, the sound snapping him out of his shock. He started toward the idiot swinging the gun around as if it was no more dangerous than a glove. He was almost upon Hal when he was stopped dead in his tracks, not unlike Pepper, by Nicole's glare.

She'd wanted to flinch or duck at the way Hal was handling the weapon. Instead, she'd tucked the rifle under her arm, the barrel pointing down, and while Hal had postured and bragged to the others, she'd stepped over to him, which was when her angry gaze locked with Max's. Now moving with care, she calmly reached out and grabbed hold of Hal's wrist. Her fingernails dug into his flesh and pinched a nerve so that his fingers went numb. With her free hand, she swiftly twisted the pistol from his hand.

As she worked at unloading the weapon and controlling her temper, Hal moved as if to reclaim his property. She jabbed him in the stomach with an elbow hard enough for him to realize she'd done it intentionally. When she finished emptying and checking the gun, she said, "Follow me, Hal. You and I are going to have a private chat." She didn't wait to listen to his complaining, but headed back up the path. When she was out of the others' hearing, she swung around, waiting for him to catch up.

"I'd like my—"

He got no further. She was suddenly in his face, soft-spoken, but there was no doubt that she was furious. "Listen very carefully, Hal, because I'm only going to say this once. Dawson's does not allow guests to carry or bring weapons onto the mountain—period. There is no hunting on our property. You know that by the agreement you signed. You broke the rules."

"But you—"

"My weapon is used strictly for *your* safety." He opened his mouth to protest, but she didn't give him the chance. "You're this close—" she demonstrated a minute distance with thumb and forefinger "—to getting your butt kicked down the mountain and off the property. Think, Hal. Four thousand dollars apiece is a lot of money for you and your friend to lose.

"And yes," she said seeing the question and confusion in his face, "you go, then so does Preston, and you can explain to him why. Now if you two want to have the week you've paid a lot of money for, if you want to really enjoy yourselves, then I suggest you take stock of your situation and stop trying to play at being macho. Four thousand bucks apiece is a lot to lose over stupidity." She wasn't about to stop there. "And do us both a favor. Don't make any more passes at me. I'm not interested.

"As for the gun, you best just write it off as a loss, because I plan to turn it over to the sheriff's office for disposal." She watched as Hal struggled with everything she'd said. "There's no negotiating any of this, Hal. It's my way or no way."

She waited, calm but watchful. At last the tension seemed to seep out of him and she relaxed. But the problem wasn't completely over. She now had to do something so he could save face with the other men. When he turned and glanced at his friend and the others, she knew what to do. She held out her hand and smiled.

"You're a tough broad," he said, little by little managing to grin, then, after a brief hesitation, he accepted her handshake.

"I know." She patted him on the shoulder. "But the gun's a goner, so don't try and sweet-talk me out of it." He laughed and they started back toward the waiting group.

Nicole glanced around at the deepening shadows. "We've got about forty-five more minutes before we reach the lodge," she said to no one in particular. "If we hurry, we'll make it in time for everyone to clean up and have drinks on the veranda to see the sunset."

They resumed the hike. Max had no idea what she and Hal had said, but it looked as if she'd done all the talking. And he hadn't missed the fact that she kept Hal's gun and passed it unceremoniously to Reed to pack away as she addressed the group. He knew something else. Whatever she'd said to Hal had worked.

"Did you know that Nicole can stand in the middle of a stream and just by talking hypnotize those big old granddaddy trout to just jump right into her arms and beg to be fried up and eaten?" Reed asked.

Max did a double take as what Reed said sunk in, then laughed. "Where'd you hear that story?"

"Old Charlie. Says she has the magic touch. Knows

how to handle people *and* fish. She's a schoolteacher, did you know?''

"No, I didn't know, but that explains it, doesn't it? If she can control a bunch of kids, then six men oughtta be a piece of cake.''

Reed nodded. "Guess.'' He cleared his throat. "Where 'bouts in New York do you live? Charlie said you were something like a private detective.''

"Security consultant.'' Max bit back a smile.

"Cool.''

"The office and my apartment overlook Central Park. You ever been there?''

"Naw, but I'd like to.''

"What would a Montana man do in New York?''

Reed felt his chest expand with pride. He liked the way Max talked to him. As if he were an equal. "I'd want to be an actor—go to New York and take acting lessons. We do some stuff here, plays and things...'' He gave a long deep soulful sigh as if the weight of the world were on his shoulders. "But my dad wouldn't hear of it. He'd have cats and dogs if he knew. He says acting is for people without brain cells.''

"What about your mother?''

"She thinks I'm too young.''

"Well, Reed, she may be right. If you waited a couple of years, what do you think she'd say?''

"Probably be okay with it. Cry a lot if I left.''

They fell silent. Even with the span of years between them, they both had the same understanding of mothers.

It was an opening. For a brief moment Max let his gaze wander to the ghost leading the way up the trail. Birthmark be damned. He couldn't go on the way he was; he had to start his investigation somewhere. But from the first time he'd seen her alive and well, his heart had stopped and he'd thrown all reason out the door. If she truly wasn't Sandra, then he had to face the fact that Sandra was dead to him forever. And if Sandra was dead, then who was Nicole Dawson?

Reluctantly Max decided to hell with standards, scruples and rules. He took a steadying breath and repeated his earlier question to Reed. "How long have you known Nicole?"

Reed cast him a look of bewilderment. "All my life."

"You're sure?"

"Yeah, sure I'm sure. We've always spent a week at the lodge every summer. Have for as long as I can remember. Dad and Mom like fly-fishing. Nicole and Charlie always joined us. It's sort of like a tradition."

Four thousand dollars a week per person seemed a little extreme for a family holiday. Not for the first time Max wondered who Reed's parents were and what line of business they were in. But as the question formed in his mind, it just as quickly disappeared. They'd come around a bend in the trail and he'd almost bumped into the still group of men. Everyone had stopped to stare.

It was like walking head-on and wide-awake into another world. The sheer proportions, the gigantic scale of the setting, dwarfed them all. Like the rest of the men, he stood gaping. In the clearing ahead, beyond the neat curving flower beds and winding walkways, was the lodge. A huge two-story log structure on a massive stone foundation. The same light gray stones were used in the chimneys, and Max counted no less than six. A wide porch wrapped around the entire first floor and was dotted with groupings of rocking chairs and small tables. The multipaned windows on both floors were as tall as a man and caught the rays of the sun through the tree limbs, so it seemed as if the windows were winking at them.

The trees around them looked bigger, the clouds in the sky near enough to reach out and touch. Even the air was different. Sweet. Cleansing. Like a man in a dream, Max trailed behind the others as they moved forward. The closer he got to the incredible structure, the greater his astonishment. The logs of the lodge were enormous. As he gawked, he was reminded of the hasty history and background information Doug had gathered on the Dawsons. He wished he hadn't been so distracted on their flight to Montana by his heaving stomach and fear. He might have learned more.

But he knew that the land and mountain had been in the Dawson family for more than four generations. It was Nicole's great-grandfather who started the construction of the lodge and her grandfather who finished it and turned it into a business. Another tidbit of something Doug said came back to him. Teddy Roosevelt, the old Roughrider himself and twenty-sixth president of the United States, had spent time at the lodge on one of his so-called working vacations.

Whatever Doug had tried to tell him disappeared from Max's mind as something new captured his imagination. How in hell, he wondered, did men without the aid of today's machinery possibly move, notch, then lift these colossal logs, especially to a two-story height? With an effort, he brought his attention back to the real world and smiled. He'd always considered himself jaded; he'd seen it all and nothing could surprise him. Well, he'd been wrong, and from the looks of wonder on the others' faces, they were just as impressed.

He was the last to climb the steps to the porch, and like someone playing follow-the-leader, he turned to see what they were all staring at in such hushed reverence. He felt his own breath cut off in his throat. They'd trekked up the sloped side of the mountain, the side that looked as if Mother Nature had sheered the land off at an angle to make room for the thousands of acres of fertile valley below. But there was another side, and they now stared out at a panoramic view right out of every sportsman's fantasy.

About two hundred yards away was the river, shining like liquid gold in the dwindling daylight as it snaked its way down the mountain. Through the trees he could see where it widened, then narrowed, its banks forming a sandy pebble beach. In other places the course of the river was changed by huge gray boulders, smooth and shiny from the flow of the water. Just gazing at the water and the deepening shadows of the trees, Max sighed, feeling a true sense of tranquillity.

Nicole appeared beside him and leaned against the railing. Everyone else had gone into the lodge. Why she'd picked him to talk to was a mystery, she thought, especially considering the warning she'd issued him earlier. But she'd seen something in his face that drew her. Maybe it was the way he gazed out at the river and the land, something about the yearning in his eyes that whispered to her. Or maybe it was the way he moved, with such sureness and confidence.

It had been a long time since she'd been physically attracted to a man. And she admitted she was more than a little attracted to Max Warner. More than just a casual fascination bloomed in warm ripples inside her. She felt heat when he was near, and cold when he left. Her feelings amused and angered her, but she wasn't foolish enough to deny them. She wasn't one to run away from trouble, because she knew it usually caught up with her eventually.

"Takes your breath away, doesn't it?" she said.

"Yes. It's unbelievable. But you know that—you see it all the time. Right?"

"True. Still, I never get tired of being here, of seeing it. Even in the winter when everything is frozen and white under a thick layer of snow, it stirs my heart."

"Have you ever left?" His voice was raspy from the lump in his throat.

"Yes. College, then…" Her voice trailed away. She didn't like to think that far back and bump into too many unhappy memories.

"For any length of time after college?"

"A little over a year." She glanced at her watch, then pushed away from the railing. "You have time to clean up and meet everyone back here in thirty minutes for a predinner drink. The sunset is something you shouldn't miss, New York, not on your first trip here."

Max chuckled at the nickname she'd given him. He could have told her things, of places he'd been and things he'd seen, but he let her have her way. "All right, all right, don't nag me, Montana. I'm going."

She liked his smile. It had a quality, a depth, almost as if they shared an intimacy of some sort. She was being fanciful and shook her head. But she watched him walk away, noting his movements and the strength under the tight worn jeans. He had a way about him that sent her pulses pumping. Just then, he paused at the door, turned and caught her assessing him. Heat bloomed in her cheeks, but she refused to look away. He winked and grinned. And all she could do as he continued on in was sag against the railing. God, what a look he'd given her! She'd felt it right down to her toes.

"He's a looker, ain't he, Miss Nicky?"

Nicole jumped at the voice, then smiled. JD Weaver was the chef at the lodge. He and his wife, Penny, who was the housekeeper, had been working at Dawson's for more years than she could remember. She grinned as he walked toward her, then touched her lips to his scratchy cheek. JD wasn't a tall man—he stood eye to eye with her—but he was wiry and strong. His head was completely bald, and he was seldom without a baseball cap. Under the bill of the cap his dark eyes crinkled at the corners with amusement. His face, from endless hours in the sun, was deeply grooved and lined. If JD wasn't in the kitchen, everyone knew they could find him at his favorite fishing spot, and God help the person who disturbed him.

"What you grinnin' at, girlie?"

"You. Did Ash and the truck arrive all right?"

JD nodded. She didn't fool him. He'd seen the way her eyes had followed that man. "Henny-Penny's been in hog heaven, cleaning and putting their gear in their rooms. The kid helped her."

"Ash?"

"She made him scrub toilets, too, and I'm gonna make him peel the taters later. Thinks he's goin' fishing with me in the morning."

Nicole bit the inside of her cheek to keep from smiling. "He's pretty good for his age, JD. You better watch out."

"When a snot-nosed, fuzzy-face baby of eleven—hell, he ain't even got all his good teeth yet—can outcast and outfish old JD is when I hang up my rod." He glanced around furtively, then leaned closer and whispered, "Did you bring me my ch*w?"

"I shouldn't have." Since Penny had made him give up chewing tobacco, he usually had a wad of bubble gum in his cheek, just to fill in the empty space, he told her. Now the craggy face split, the seams parted, as he smiled. She dug a small bag with a hard square of tobacco out of the pocket of her shorts. For a second she hesitated. "You promise—just a tiny sliver once a day and only while you're fishing?"

JD laid his hand over his heart. "Swear on my sweet mother's grave."

She handed it over, watching as he stuffed it into the back pocket of his jeans. "You know what Penny'll do to me if she finds out."

"Ain't no reason for Henny-Penny to know, now is there?"

Nicole shivered dramatically. "I'll pray she doesn't." Penny Weaver was a small round grandmotherly woman with dark sparkly eyes, and she could be a formidable ally or foe. Nicole had been lashed by the sharp edge of her tongue enough in her life to dread a repeat. She'd also been held in Penny's loving embrace.

Nicole watched JD beat a hasty retreat so he could hide his treasure. Anyone looking at or talking to old JD would immediately think he was just a typical cowboy. Certainly no one would ever dream that his culinary skills had been finely honed in Paris, or that he spoke French like a native-born Frenchman. When their guests left, they didn't know whether to brag about the fishing or rave about the food.

Glancing at her watch, she cursed under her breath, then headed to her room for a fast shower and change of clothes. The first night for the guests was the most significant. It was the time to make them feel welcome and comfortable and still set down the rules they'd have to follow for the week.

She was all too aware that some guests balked at the restraints put on them, but once she made them see that they were deep in the wilderness and not at some fancy resort, things usually settled down. Dawson Mountain wasn't predator-free. There were dangers everywhere—the four-legged kind, as well as the two-legged variety. Thinking of predators immediately brought Max Warner to her mind's eye.

CHAPTER FIVE

MAX WAS AS IMPRESSED with the interior of the lodge as he was with the exterior. The soaring heights of those massive log walls and the oversize stone fireplaces were almost overwhelming. A wide staircase divided the first floor, with the dining room and what he assumed was the kitchen area on one side and the lounge on the other. At the top of the stairs, the second floor formed a U-shaped gallery leading to the numerous guest rooms. In his rush to get cleaned up, he barely had time to notice much about the room other than its comfort and unostentatious luxury. Mainly he was pleased to see that with six men showering there was plenty of hot water.

He was obviously quicker than the others and had time on his hands—time he needed to put to good use, but privately. He explored the porch, and as he turned another corner, he was pleased to find himself back where he'd started. The porch really did wrap around the entire lodge.

He continued his casual stroll, once accidentally bumping a chair and sending it rocking violently. When he rounded another corner, hidden from sight, but still within the hearing of anyone who ventured outside, he stopped. Leaning against the railing, he pulled the cellular phone from his shirt pocket and dialed. After ten rings, agitated and frustrated, he was about to hang up when Doug finally answered.

"What the hell were you doing—taking a nap?"

"Hello to you, too, Max. I wasn't exactly in a position to answer right away."

"Why?" There was no need to take his short temper out on his friend.

"If you must know, I was attempting to draw to an inside straight. I lost, and Charlie's gone to get us beer and another family album. Max, she's not Sandra. No way in hell, partner. I've seen pictures of her naked on a bearskin rug, her first time on a horse, first day at school, first date, her high-school prom and all the summers and vacations in between. She's not Sandra."

Max didn't want to hear it, but listened nonetheless. "She has a crescent birthmark behind her left ear identical to Sandra's. Explain that, will you?"

"I'm beginning to believe that saying about everyone having a double somewhere in the world. I think we've just witnessed the truth of the statement."

"You're saying it's one of those weird happenings, like UFOs, alien abductions, ghosts and Bigfoot?"

"You don't believe in UFOs? Did I ever tell you—"

"No, and don't do it now." Max was suddenly worried about his partner. When Doug was on a job, he was usually the serious one, all business. Time was money in his pocket. "What the hell have you been up to, besides playing cards and looking at old photographs?"

"Having a damn good time. Charlie Dawson is a real character, and I've nearly laughed myself silly.

Why, the wily old coot's won three hundred bucks off me.''

Max couldn't believe what he was hearing and was about to voice his concerns when the amusement in Doug's voice died completely away. ''The office's come up with a few things. Charlie's been in some questionable business deals lately. He managed to lose a lot of money recently because of bad judgment or bad advice. Add to that the fact that he loves gambling, women and liquor...well, it's taken all of Nicky's savings to pay the taxes and pull them out of the hole. Right now they're riding on what's being made off the outrigger and guide business. And they'd be doing okay if Charlie could stay away from the liquor and the cards.''

Max thought he heard the sound of voices coming from around the corner and said, ''Keep digging into his daughter's past. There has to be a logical explanation.''

''And if there isn't? If it's just what I said—look-alikes—what then?''

''I become a UFO watcher and an instant believer in all the other things.'' Doug laughed. Max hadn't heard that wild cackle in a long time, and it brought on his own genuine smile.

''Max, wait. One more thing. There've been some strange things happening around here. Seems there's been a rash of thefts, like missing machine parts. Then there were a couple of small unexplained fires that could've been disastrous if they hadn't been caught and extinguished in time. A lot of the animals have got sick, and the vet had to be called. Plenty of other peculiar things, too, but you get the drift. Individually not much, but put them together and they add up to some hefty expenses. It all has the earmarks of intimidation, and I think it's just another thing on Bedford's agenda for getting Charlie to sell.''

Max was sure he'd heard a door slam and footsteps. ''You're more familiar with him than I am. Is that his style?''

''Oh, hell, yes. Carl Bernard Bedford is far from being born with a silver spoon in his mouth. He came up hard and rough. I think he's made his wishes known to his men, given them a free hand at being creative.''

Now Max was sure he heard someone on the porch. ''I have to go, Doug. Keep things rolling there and I'll do the same. I'm going to have the answer I need by tomorrow, then we'll go from there.'' He cut anything Doug might have said off with a press of a button, then stepped around the corner, smiling as he watched his hostess.

It hadn't taken her long to shower and dress. Dawson's was a vacation lodge; casual attire for dinner was not only acceptable, but mandatory. She was wearing a pair of chocolate corduroy slacks and a heavy cable sweater of a lighter shade of brown. It seemed evenings on the mountain were surprisingly cold as the wind shifted and blew down from the snowcapped Rocky Mountains. Max stepped out of sight.

A puzzled scowl settled between Nicole's eyes as she glanced up and down the length of the deserted porch. She could have sworn she'd heard a voice. Then she noticed the gentle movements of the empty rocking chair and began looking around. But her concern was immediately forgotten as she started checking the hors d'oeuvres, the platters of a variety of cheeses, crackers and fruit. JD and Penny had set up the bar beside the door, and the crystal glasses caught the light and flashed a prism of colors.

The first night and last night were toasted with champagne, and the dark bottles were iced and waiting. She gave another quick glance around, checking to make sure she was alone, then stuck her finger in the iced bowl of caviar, popped the gob of glistening black beluga in her mouth, then closed her eyes and savored the rich salty flavor.

"Why is it, I wonder, that something snitched tastes so much better?" Max grinned as her eyes widened in surprise.

Swallowing hard, she said, "Jeez, you scared the...you scared me to death. Where did you come from?" She noticed the cellular phone in his hand and couldn't help her look of disgust.

"Be still a second." He reached out and lightly touched her lip, showed her the black bead of roe, then, as she watched, he slowly licked it off the tip of his finger.

Nicole opened her mouth to speak, but nothing came out.

Max didn't miss her reaction. It amused him to see how he'd thrown her off stride, and now he watched as she struggled to regain her voice. She wasn't going to admit it yet, but he knew she was attracted to him. He fully intended to use that attraction for his own purposes.

He'd also noticed her look of disgust, and now he realized it was directed at the phone he held in his other hand. "Are these forbidden?"

With a shake of her head, she finally found her voice and said, "No, but I wish they were. Some of the guests come here, and for whatever reason, feel they can't be out of touch with the world for a week. As if everything revolved around them.'' Like her father, she cursed the invention of the cellular telephone.

"Up until ten years ago we deliberately didn't have a telephone at the lodge. Just a shortwave radio so we could stay in touch with the ranch. But with the increasing popularity of the portable phone, we were forced to buy and install our own tower and microwave dish. Then we had to camouflage the ugly thing because the very guests who insisted we install that convenience bitched about the eyesore in paradise.''

With an effort she forced herself to shut up, pressing her lips together. She couldn't figure out what it was about him that had sent her off on her nervous tirade.

Max slid the small phone into his shirt pocket. "It does seem a sacrilege doesn't it? But I needed to check on my partner.'' He accepted the icy glass of pale champagne. "Doug hasn't been himself lately.''

"I'm sorry. I don't usually go off like that. Of course you have every right to bring your phone.''

"You look beautiful this evening, Nicole.''

She was taken aback by the compliment and the way he looked at her. As if they were lovers and he wanted nothing more than to take her in his arms and kiss her senseless.

She dropped her gaze. "Thanks.'' It was all she could think to say.

"What's your favorite color?''

"Yellow. Why?''

"What's your favorite flavor of ice cream?''

"Vanilla. What is this—twenty questions? And why do you want to know?''

"I'm just trying to get to know you, that's all.''

"Why?''

"Because I like you."

"You don't *know* me."

"That's what I'm trying to remedy."

"Again, why? You're here for a week and then you're gone. We'll never see each other again."

"Maybe. Maybe not."

Nicole ran a nervous hand through her hair. "Let me tell you what I told Hal. We have rules. Come on to me or get out of line, and you're off the mountain." But Max wasn't like Hal, and so wasn't the least bit put off by her manner.

"Haven't you ever broken the rules?"

She wasn't about to tell him that was how she ended up married to a man to whom fidelity was a foreign word and he didn't speak the language. "No." He brought his face close to hers, but she refused to back away.

"Never? Well, I don't give up easily." When her lips parted for a quick comeback, he said, "We'll have this conversation again soon, when we're alone. Now, one more question." Her expression told him she was about to walk off, and he touched her shoulder before she could move. "Just out of curiosity. What's your favorite perfume?"

It was easier to ignore the implications behind his words and answer his questions. "I don't wear it out here, New York. The fish and wildlife wouldn't appreciate it much."

He loved her sass. "Humor me. If you could have your pick of any kind, what would it be?"

She sighed and gave him a look that would have stopped a lesser man. "Look, perfume costs money and I don't have it to spare."

"Okay, if not perfume, then what's your favorite flower?"

He wasn't going to leave it or her alone without an answer. "Gardenias," she said after a moment.

He was chilled to the bone by her answers. They were identical to Sandra's choices.

Nicole realized that suddenly he was no longer gazing at her like a lover but an enemy. How could the mention of flowers bring on such a drastic change? She would have asked him if the rest of the group hadn't joined them. There was that first-night excitement in the air as they were introduced to JD, and glasses of champagne and plates of food were passed around. Then, as the sun began to set, one by one they stopped talking.

Nicole was amused and touched by the silence. The men were mesmerized by the sunset, and though she, too, had seen it countless times in her life, she wasn't ashamed to admit it still moved her.

Max was as impressed as the others. The sun hung low in the sky like a ball of molten fire, washing the land and trees with a vibrant glow. But it was the twisting turning ribbon of river that seized his gaze and left him drunk with the wonder of the scene. It was a vision dreams are made of. As he watched, the wind kicked up, agitating the surface into rippling waves. The tips of the waves caught the light and burst into flames that danced playfully on the surface.

It must have taken twenty minutes for the sun to set and the growing darkness to blend in with the shadows. With a collective sigh, everyone on the porch began to move about, migrating toward the bar for something stronger than champagne. Nicole had seen it happen before, grown worldly men struck speechless by something so beautiful.

It was entertaining, though she hid her amusement, to see the emotion they tried to hide behind with their drinks, silence or sometimes bluster. As always, it was her job to bring them back to the present and take away any feelings of discomfort. "If you want to bring your drinks in, I believe Penny is ready to serve dinner."

She couldn't have asked for a more perfect dinner. The men raved about JD's orange-glazed quail served on a bed of cherry-and-pecan cornbread dressing, tiny buttered new potatoes dusted with fresh parsley, a choice of three other vegetables and Penny's homemade yeast rolls. When groans met the offer of seconds or thirds, she told them that dessert, coffee and, if they wished, after-dinner drinks were going to be served in the lounge.

After they were settled there, Nicole took up a position directly in front of the fireplace. She saw the way amusement crinkled the corners of Max's eyes as he strived to keep his smile in check. Nor did she miss the way Larry ducked his head so she wouldn't see his grin. She'd always used the position as an ice breaker, and it never failed to work. The fireplace was so massive she almost could have stepped inside, stretched out her arms and still had room to spare. The picture reinforced the idea that everything at Dawson's was bigger and better than anything they'd ever seen. "Welcome to Dawson's, gentlemen." Her standard welcoming.

"There are just a few rules that need to be discussed before I leave you to enjoy yourselves." At the word "rules," she had their undivided attention. She also hadn't missed a couple of scowls. As predictable as ever, she'd hit a nerve. Men didn't like women laying down rules or giving them orders. She picked up a contraption from a table and held it up. It was a small black box about the size of a two-inch cube, with a couple of elastic straps riveted together. She held it up, leaving the straps dangling in the air.

"This is a radio with two buttons. The green one will reach me no matter where I am. Press it and talk. The red button is for emergencies only. When you press it, it admits a shrill noise, and that's for two reasons. Gentlemen, first let me impress upon you that this is your vacation. I want you to enjoy yourselves and have the time of your life. But remember and never forget that this is the wilderness. There are bears, mountain lions and wolves on the mountain."

Preston looked ready to faint and Hal was suddenly pale. "We've only had a couple of incidents, and that was when a black bear wanted a prime fishing spot one of our guests was working. As fishermen, I'm sure you know a good spot is worth fighting for—but not with a bear." There were a few chuckles and she continued, "That's what the red button on the radio is for. It not only warns me, but the sound usually scares off the wildlife. The radio is light and easy to wear." She showed them how to put it on by slipping her arms through the straps, then adjusting the box so it rested high on her shoulder.

"No guest leaves the lodge, whether fishing or hiking, without one. They'll be waiting for you by the door as we leave in the morning. Break the rules, and you'll find yourself in the truck heading for the ranch—where you'll have to deal with Charlie." She deliberately shivered and grimaced. Her actions got a laugh.

Nicole moved toward the door, then stopped and said as a parting shot, "Have a nice evening. Just keep in mind we get going early in the morning. Breakfast is from six to seven-thirty, and we leave around eight-thirty or nine."

MORNING, THOUGH IT WAS anticipated with eagerness, came much too early.

When Max finally stumbled downstairs, still half-asleep, and met the rest of the group at the breakfast table, he laughed. Then wished he hadn't. His head felt as though it had been filled with rocks, and every movement sent them crashing together.

Like a pack of teenagers left on their own for the first time, the men had refused to take Nicole's good advice. They'd stayed up late, getting to know one another over a few drinks too many. And from the woeful looks Max got, he knew they all felt as lousy as he did. He nodded and grunted a good-morning to everyone and no one, then poured himself some coffee and took stock of the others.

Hal, his pasty skin lightly tinted green, was valiantly attempting to eat some toast. Preston made no bones about how he felt and sat with his head in his hands, moaning. Clarence and George stared into their coffee, managing every now and then to lift red-rimmed eyes. Larry, the oldest and probably the wisest, was the only one who didn't look as if he wanted to curl up like a wounded animal and die. But everyone was too damn stubborn, himself included, to admit any weakness.

Nicole bounced into the dining room, all smiles. She knew from experience what to expect and wondered how many would back out and opt for a morning in bed. Her smile widened when everyone made it clear they were stronger than they looked. "Good. Now, if you'll get your gear and pick up your radios on the way out, the truck's ready to take you to the river."

She desperately wanted to laugh. They were moving slowly, but they were moving. "A couple of things I forgot last night. We've put together a lunch, snacks and cold drinks for each of you in individual coolers. But if you get tired or want to come back to the lodge at any time, use your radios to call me. Never remove food from the cooler, then leave it sitting out.

"Lastly, and most important. I don't mean to sound like a nag, and the chances you'll cross paths with a bear are slight. But if you do, please, please don't run. Freeze. Use the alarm on your radios. If the worst possible scenario happens and the bear charges, drop to the ground, roll your body into a ball and wrap your arms around your head. Don't forget the alarm, though." She looked from one to the other and smiled, trying to reassure them.

"Has anyone ever been attacked?" Preston asked nervously.

"Yes. About six years ago. We hadn't had a lot of rain and food was scarce. One of the guests left his half-eaten lunch on the riverbank, and then when the bear showed up, drawn by the scent of food, he tried to chase him off." They waited for the ending, and she sighed inwardly, knowing a lie could easily be found out. "Because he didn't follow the rules, he was mauled to death."

There was a collective swallow. Max was the last one to file out of the room. He said to Nicole, "I hope you slept soundly."

"Of course I did."

"I didn't."

She grinned and shook her head. "Alcohol isn't a good sedative, New York."

"That wasn't my problem. I couldn't get you off my mind, Montana. What am I going to do about it?"

"Lose lots more sleep. Excuse me." She turned to go, but was stopped by his next comment.

"I think you're lying," he whispered. "I think you had trouble getting to sleep, too."

"In your dreams, New York. And I don't lie." *Not very often.* But she wasn't about to let him see he was right. "Get your gear or you'll be left behind."

"Yes, ma'am." He gave her a salute, then strolled away with a bounce to his step, knowing her eyes were following him. He didn't feel even the least twinge of guilt for planning to get his information one way or the other.

The guests were left on the river, each at a different site. The last was Larry, and as they dropped him off and watched him trudge happily toward the water, Max slipped into the front seat of the Jeep. "What special place have you picked for me?" He glanced at her as she started the truck and pulled back onto the bumpy track. "From that scowl you keep shooting at me, maybe I'd be better off back at the lodge."

"What? Sorry. I was thinking that Larry doesn't look well." The fact that he was the oldest of the group and alone also concerned her.

Max turned to look straight ahead. "He's okay."

She slowed the truck and said, "Maybe you should team up with him. Just for the morning, and I'll come back at noon and see how it's going."

Max laid his hand over hers on the gearshift.

"Leave him be, Montana. There are times a man just needs to be alone with his thoughts."

"Not if I think he's sick."

"He *is* sick. Larry has cancer and about six months left to live. Let him enjoy himself. I promise he'll be fine. He's well aware of his limitations."

"How did you know?" she whispered.

"He told me last night. I'm the only one who does know, and he only told me after I saw and recognized the painkillers he was taking."

"I should tell Dad. There could be trouble if anything happens."

"Just keep it under your hat, will you? This is the trip of a lifetime for Larry. With the help of his sister, he just barely managed to afford it."

"Oh, hell." She blinked rapidly to clear her vision, then tugged down the visor of her baseball cap. "I wish you'd never told me."

"But—"

"Oh, shut up." She jerked the Jeep into gear, and they bumped along awhile before she said, "I'm sorry. My mother died of cancer. Fortunately or unfortunately, depending on which way you look at it, she died very quickly after she was diagnosed. She didn't have time to suffer too much."

It was an opening he wasn't about to pass up. "How old were you when it happened?"

"Ten."

"That's tough. Any brothers or sisters?"

"No. Just me." She took her eyes off the rutted road for a second. "You're very observant," she said. "I mean, the way you noticed Larry's painkillers."

"That's my job," he said. She'd tried to hide the fact that she knew very well what he did for a living.

He wasn't about to let her off the hook, though. "You read the form you insisted I fill out, so you should know."

She refused to look at him, sure he would probably read something significant into her guilty expression. She'd been far too busy checking out where he was from, if he was married and other vital statistics and had only glanced at occupation. She deliberately kept her gaze on the road ahead. "You and Doug are private detectives."

Max chuckled. "We prefer 'security consultants.' A nice term to sum up a multitude of job descriptions without making anyone nervous."

"Well, let's see how good a P.I. you are. What about Clarence and George? What do you make of them? Are they gay?"

"No. I'd guess they've been friends since childhood. Grew up in the same town, went to the same schools and college, then started a business together. Married sisters."

Nicole laughed. "You're a cheat. There's no way you could know all that by just observing them."

He had to struggle to keep a straight face. "I swear."

"And you're a big liar."

"Okay, so sue me—they told me last night."

"What about Hal and Preston?"

"That's easy. They both work for the same law firm. Hal's a flamboyant pretty boy who draws business like a magnet. Preston has all the brains and does all the real work. Hal knows he needs Preston to stay on top, and Preston likes the limelight and the women Hal attracts."

She gave a very unladylike whistle, making him

laugh, then said, "That's about what I figured. Preston's the stable one and probably keeps Hal in line and gets him out of trouble."

"Very good. Now, what about you?"

She suddenly had that uneasy feeling again. "What *about* me?"

"Want me to turn my expert powers of observation on you?"

"No. And stop staring at me." She steered the truck over a couple of deep potholes, which shut him up, but only briefly.

He decided now was as good an opportunity as any to start his inquiry, but he knew he had to keep it light and fun. "I'll tell you what, ladies and gentleman." He made his voice sound like a carnival barker's. "I bet you I can amaze and astound the young lady with my mysterious talents. I can tell her things about herself only she would know. Come on, take a chance and make a bet."

"What does the winner get?"

Max tapped his fingers on his thighs like a piano player warming up. "If I win, you spend the day with me." He held up his hands, forefingers making a cross as if to ward off the evil look she gave him. "Fishing, just fishing, and you'll talk to me. No silent treatment."

"And if you lose, what do I get?"

"I'll spend a whole day helping you with your work. I'll be your slave." Any way he cut it, he came out the winner.

"You'll do whatever I want?"

"Your wish will be my command."

A little voice in her head warned her, but she couldn't pass up the challenge. She loved winning.

She nodded. "Okay, you're on. What do your powers of observation tell you about me?"

Max closed his eyes, then made her laugh when he pressed the tips of his fingers on his forehead. "I'm beginning to see. No, wait. Is it? It can't be, but yes, here it comes. You love chocolate, anything chocolate, but it gives you a headache."

Nicole felt a whisper of a chill slide up her back. Without thinking, she began to slow the truck. "What else?"

"I think I'm getting something.... Yes, here it comes. You're fond of cats, but you're allergic to them."

Stunned, she stopped the truck. How could he possibly know that about her? "What else?"

"Let's see. You love horses, are an accomplished rider and have been riding since you were a kid."

"That's easy. You saw me when you arrived." But although she dismissed it, she felt goose bumps rise on her skin.

"You're a strong swimmer?"

She nodded. "That's not hard to figure out. We live and make part of our living from the river. I was raised around it and help with the white-water rafting."

"You only eat vanilla ice cream."

"I already told you that."

He glanced at her, then dropped his hands with a sigh. "That's all." Turning in the seat, he smiled. "I win, right?"

She was having trouble finding her voice, but managed a whispered, "Yes."

"I think we should start out with a question first, don't you?"

She hadn't recovered from the shock of not only

losing, but the fact that he knew entirely too much about her for a complete stranger. Maybe he was psychic. Whatever it was it intrigued her. "What did you say?"

Max turned so he was facing forward and he could hide his amusement. Then he motioned for her to drive on, which she did. "Nice morning for fishing, isn't it?" he said. "Remember, I like a little conversation. First question. Tell me, what made you leave Montana for a year?"

She pressed her lips together and scowled at the road ahead.

"You're not a welsher, are you?" He gave her one of his charming smiles. "I'm just trying to get to know you better."

She wasn't about to fall back into his trap of asking why, then end up saying more than she intended. Instead, she deliberately steered the truck through a particularly nasty piece of road that sent him bouncing toward the roof and grabbing for something to hold on to. She'd always found it hard to talk with clenched teeth and figured he wouldn't be any different. But eventually her innate sense of fairness won out.

"I was married and living in Los Angeles for a year."

For a moment he felt like he'd been punched in the gut, then he realized she'd said *married,* past tense. "Divorced?"

"Yes."

"Why?"

She couldn't help or stop the escaping chuckle. Now it was his turn to ask why. "Roger taught European history at Berkeley. He didn't think marriage should put a crimp in his inexhaustible supply of adoring females. I disagreed."

Her explanation told him more than she'd put into words. He decided not to pursue it and changed the subject. "What do you do up here when winter sets in?"

"The lodge is closed, and unless it's an emergency, anyone with half a brain stays away from the mountain."

Damn, getting her to open up was proving more difficult than he thought. "What about at the ranch? Isn't it hard there, too?"

"Very." She could see he wasn't going to let it go. "There's the cattle to take care of. The ones we've kept from the summer sales. And school—I teach first grade—but when the roads are inaccessible and the chores are done, Dad and I read a lot or watch old movies."

Sandra read a lot and loved old movies, especially comedies. Max forced a smile, but he was shaking inside. If this woman wasn't Sandra, then...? A more appropriate question—how was it possible for two women who were identical in appearance and had the same likes and dislikes not to be the same person? He hated to admit it, but she scared the hell out of him. Even though she looked like Sandra and had all the right answers, his worst nightmare was that she wasn't Sandra. All he could do was continue with his less-than-subtle interrogation. "I bet I can guess what type of movies you prefer," he said.

Nicole pulled the truck under a shady spot between two trees and turned off the engine. Silently she cursed herself for deciding to take him to her favorite fishing spot. It was farther away, and now she was saddled with his company and his curiosity. He made her uneasy, and not just because he was obviously interested in her. There were too many conflicting signs, not to mention the feeling she was being manipulated, but for the life of her she couldn't figure out the reason. The warning bells kept ringing, but she seemed determined to turn a deaf ear.

"That's not much of a stretch, is it, New York? I mean there can only be two guesses, comedies or drama."

"Chicken." He opened the door and got out, then walked to the rear of the truck and picked up his fishing gear. "I'd have thought you were a better sport. I tell you what. If I lose, I'll help you do your work for a full day."

"And if you win and I lose, what do I have to do?"

"Have a picnic lunch with me tomorrow."

The odds were in her favor either way. She didn't trust him, but she couldn't see what harm another bet would do, either. "Okay. What kind of movies do I like?"

He couldn't decide whether he wanted to spend a whole day working for her or have an intimate picnic lunch. His instincts told him he'd be better off if she thought she was in control. "Drama. Probably those action/adventure things with Bruce Willis or Arnold."

"Wrong. Comedies, and I win." The flush of victory was short-lived. She had a moment of uncertainty, wondering if indeed she *had* won, and if so, why she felt as though *he'd* actually won. Then she reminded herself that he was, after all, a charming devil. It was hard to resist trouble when it was cloaked in such a sexy package.

CHAPTER SIX

STREAMS OF LIGHT, tinted red and orange with the on-slaught of morning, slipped inch by slow inch across the bedroom ceiling. Max lay with his hands tucked behind his head watching the changing colors, count-ing the passage of time in his head. He knew the exact moment the light reached the overhead fan. Any way he cut it, it was just too damn early to even think about getting up. Especially for a man who'd spent the last three days vacillating between heaven and hell. Peace of mind was like sleep, and both eluded him.

He was drowning in his own uncertainties. The doubts ate at him. His dream of Sandra's still being alive diminished with each passing day. He'd grabbed at more straws than could fit in a broom. One moment he thought he was right: Sandra was alive and suffer-ing from some form of amnesia, and everyone at Daw-son's was in on the conspiracy to hide her true iden-tity. Of course, after a deep breath and the return of his sanity, he knew how ridiculous that theory was.

For three days he followed Nicole around, fulfilling his commitments after losing his wagers. He grinned. Staging bets so he was always the loser, yet the win-ner, was taxing his creative resourcefulness. Still, he was too damn butt-headed to give up or give in. He'd had time to talk to JD and Penny, Reed and his little brother, Ash. He'd grilled them all about Nicole without them being the wiser—except maybe Penny. No matter how charming he was, she always gave him a long look before she responded to any of his subtle quizzing.

He had to face the truth. As hard as it was to admit, Nicole was not Sandra. There was no grand scheme. No lies. No cover-ups. There were no conspiracies, and there most certainly was no amnesia. The only answer, as much as he hated to believe his partner was right, was that everyone must have a double. He knew he had to accept it, but there were still unanswered questions—the likes and dislikes the women had in common and, lastly and most importantly, the shared birthmarks.

Questions be damned. In his head he knew he was right—they were doubles. It was his heart that was giving him trouble. He felt a deep well of sadness creeping up from the depth of him to sit heavily on his chest. He sighed long and loud in the serenity of the quiet room. Underneath the melancholy and feeling of loss, a germ of an idea was fermenting and growing in strength. He'd made promises to himself and to Helen Applewhite. Maybe there was a way to keep them. What he needed was a solid plan.

Max kept vigil on the rays of light, watching the once brilliant colors bleach into shades of pastels as they fanned out across the ceiling. When they reached the end and started to slide down the wall, he realized it was close to five o'clock. Why should he be the only one to suffer? He rolled over and picked up the cellular phone from the bedside table. After he punched in a number, he waited...and waited...and waited. He was about to hang up when the instrument clicked in his ear and the ringing stopped.

"Doug. Doug, I know you're there. I can hear you breathing. Where the bloody hell have you been? I've tried to reach you for two days." He thought he heard a muffled groan, or was it a moan? Concern for his friend brought him to a sitting position. "Doug, is something wrong? Are you okay?"

"No. If you must know, I'm dying."

Max heard the rusty tone in the voice, and his anxiety leaped with the pounding of his heart.

"Max? Max, please come get me. Take me away from here."

The pathetic timbre of the voice snapped Max out of bed and onto his feet. He started grabbing for clothes. "What's happened? Tell me what's going on."

"The old fart is trying to kill me, Max. I swear he is." The rusty voice grew rougher, deeper with distress, as if he was whispering so as not to be overheard. "I've tried to do as we discussed and keep Charlie under close surveillance. Dammit, Max, we've been going flat out for two days and nights. He's hauled me around to every honky-tonk within a hundred-mile radius. We finally ended up at a place called the Golden Spur, a country-western dance hall, where I got drunker than Cooter Brown."

Doug's voice dropped lower. "I was line dancing, Max. Me! After that, all hell broke loose. Charlie was trying to pick up a couple babes for us. By then, age, looks and marital status didn't matter—anything looked good to us. Hell, the condition I was in I thought they were Hollywood starlets. Later Charlie told me they were ugly enough to make a snake slither away. Max, are you laughing?"

"No." He wondered how he managed to say a word

as he collapsed onto the side of the bed, struggling to keep silent.

"Well, you better not be. Charlie and I got the crap beat out of us over those two women. We were jumped in the parking lot by the ladies—and I use that word loosely—but we were ambushed by their husbands.

"I think that was two days ago, Max, but don't hold me to it. Since then, I've been in three poker games, dropped a grand to a couple of crafty cardsharps who lost their teeth and hair when we were still in diapers. I've been drunk and sober a couple times. I've eaten fried mountain oysters. I've faced the humiliation of being sick as a dog on the side of the road with the local sheriff—who, by the way, is the size of a grizzly bear—looking on. And if all that wasn't bad enough, Charlie hauled me out to watch a couple of his cowboys while they did some ungodly things to poor little boy cattle. I can't take it anymore, Max. Charlie Dawson has the stamina and libido of a thirty-five-year-old. He's going to get me killed. Even worse, one evening I'm likely to weaken and take the ladies up on their offer, and Sara will kill me, instead. You're my friend, my pal, my partner. You have to help me."

Max didn't, couldn't, stifle his laughter. It felt so damn good he just kept it up until Doug's outrageous story and pleas ran out, and he joined in. Finally sober enough to speak, Max wiped the tears from his eyes and said shakily, "I take it you haven't had much time to find out about Nicole, have you?"

"What the hell do you think I've been doing—enjoying myself? She's not Sandra."

"I know." There was a long somewhat pregnant silence from the other end and Max waited.

"When, might I ask, did you find that out?"

Max chuckled. "A couple of days ago. I've been trying to call you, Doug, to tell you."

"Charlie picked my pocket and confiscated my phone. I'm not exactly sure when. But back up—how long have you known about Nicole?"

"Long enough to have to eat crow." Max was trying to dress one-handed while he held the phone to his ear. "By the way, I now believe in UFOs, alien abductions, Bigfoot and things that go bump in the night. Nicole isn't Sandra, but I tell you, Doug, she's not only a dead ringer, she has the same likes and dislikes as Sandra. It's unearthly. Supernatural is the only word to describe it."

"Maybe not," Doug said. "Nicole was adopted, Max."

For a second Max didn't see the connection. "So? Sandra wasn't."

"How do we know? Did you ask? I don't think it was a question that ever came up with Helen."

"You think since Nicole was adopted, maybe Sandra was, too. And if that's the case, they could be twins? Identical twins?" In his excitement he almost tripped as he stepped into his jeans. But Doug's theory had the impetus to charge his sluggish movements like a jolt of electricity. He started rushing around the room, hunting for his shoes and shirt. "Identical twins. Jeez, it could be, Doug. It could very well be."

"It's the only logical answer except—" Doug hummed a few bars of the theme song from the old Twilight Zone series while Max laughed. "…except for reincarnation, doubles, or maybe invasion of creatures from another planet who snatch bodies and steal their victims' identities. Have you checked around for some empty pods?"

"Stop it, Doug. This is serious. I'll call Helen." He fell silent for a second, then, "No, you call Helen, but don't tell her anything about Nicole. Nothing." He wouldn't let Doug get a word in. "Don't ask questions. Just do it, and call me back as soon as you talk to her and have anything."

"Fine," Doug said. "I'll do that, but why the urgency? We know Nicole isn't Sandra and we'll find out if they're related, but dammit, Max, it's over. Right? I've found enough about Charlie and the financial trouble he's in. Enough to satisfy Bedford. You do remember our client, don't you? I want to come up there and get some fishing in before we leave. Plus, I've got something I think we need to discuss about Bedford and his methods."

Max was too caught up in his own scheming to listen. "Stay put, Doug. I'm working on a plan, but I need to flesh it out first."

"What are you cooking up, Max?"

"When I figure it all out, you'll be the first to know." He hung up before he could be deluged with more questions, then finished dressing and headed downstairs. Unlike the other guests, he'd explored the lodge, been in the kitchen and deliberately made friends with the help. He knew that JD and Penny had a log cabin about a hundred yards behind the lodge and that Reed and Ash were staying with them. Nicole stayed in a suite off the kitchen that was originally the Weavers' quarters until their cabin was built. He also knew that Nicole was an early riser.

NICOLE STOOD directly in front of the coffeemaker, staring at it, keeping vigil, a sentry in the dawn hour. Her shoulders were hunched and her arms were wrapped around her waist. Suddenly she gave a body-shaking shiver, curled her bare toes away from the cold of the kitchen floor and hugged her old pink chenille robe closer. It was the only sign she was alive and fractionally awake as she stood spellbound by the sounds and smells of the seeping coffee. Her mind was just beginning to kick in, but her body hadn't caught up yet.

With a passion that bordered on hatred she despised getting up early. There had been times in her childhood when her parents had had to literally drag her out of bed to get her up. They'd tried everything from the sublime to the ridiculous. Like turning on the overhead light, opening the blinds, dousing her with ice water. In the winter they'd opened all her bedroom windows. It had been a constant fight. Adulthood had made many changes. She still hated the early morning, but she managed to get herself up. Nevertheless her family and friends had learned to tread lightly around her until she'd had her first cup of coffee.

"Good morning, sunshine," Max sang out. "It's a wonder—" His words were cut off when a mug crashed to the floor. She stood staring down at the broken pieces. Slowly she turned her gaze to him, and he visibly flinched under the fierce glare.

He forced himself to keep a straight face. "Oops. I take it you…" He shut up as he watched her fingers curl around another mug. She was adorable, barefoot and wearing the raggedy old robe, her sleep-tousled hair flattened at the back and sticking up in all directions everywhere else.

Nicole turned heavy-lidded belligerent eyes back to him. "It's not even six yet. What're you doing down here?"

He figured since she was talking to him, it was safe to answer. "I was..." He figured wrong. She cut him such a look that the rest of the sentence dried up in his throat. He fought to keep from laughing and leaned against the counter, waiting and watching as she continued to glower at the coffeemaker.

When the brewing did its last spitting and gurgling, Nicole tossed out the grounds and filter, then poured herself a large mug. Without a glance his way she picked it up and headed back to her room. The door slammed behind her.

Max poured a cup and took a sip, paying little notice other than it was hot. His attention was on the closed bedroom door. He gave a mental shrug, figuring he might as well chance having something thrown at him or getting his head bitten off. He pushed open the door, then hesitated, unsure of his decision to intrude on her private sanctum.

Nicole heard the creaking hinge and glanced up. She was curled up on the sofa in the sitting room, her hands wrapped around the half-empty mug. "It's safe now. I'm awake."

Max eased inside, closing the door and glancing around curiously. The room was unmistakably hers with its bright floral chintz-covered sofa, chairs and window treatment. There were pretty crystal vases of fresh wildflowers on the fireplace mantel, bookcases filled to overflowing. In one corner was a large television, a stereo, VCR and stacks of movies. He took all this in, then he joined her on the sofa. "I take it you're not a morning person."

"What gave you the clue?"

He laughed. "Visions of a black eye or broken nose. I imagine you've got a nasty right."

"I live and work, most of the year, in a man's world. Something about the wilderness gives them ideas. My left's pretty good, too."

"I've watched you handle the men just fine. Hal hasn't even looked at you crosswise."

She was feeling Max's nearness and sipped her coffee to cover her nervousness. "It was nothing I did or said. Usually after the first day, everything settles down and they realize they came to fish. They're distracted by the allure of Mother Nature and the river, instead of me." It wasn't right that one man should be so damn attractive. Sometimes she found him looking at her and would feel her insides tighten in response.

Max frowned at the thought of what she might have to put up with from members of his sex. He found it totally captivating that she made no attempt to tidy her hair or try to rub the sheet imprint from her cheek. Then he reminded himself that she was not Sandra, nor was she like any other woman he'd ever met. She was straightforward and as honest as the day was long. He found that exciting. "Does it happen much—the passes and harassment?"

"Often enough that there are three dead bolts on my door."

He glanced at the door and smiled. "Yeah, those'll keep 'em out."

"What are you doing up so early and in my room, Max?" She hated the way her heart was slamming against her ribs and wondered if he could see the pulse racing in her neck. She pulled the collar of her robe higher.

He finished his coffee and set the cup on the table.

"I wanted to take you up on that offer of a picnic today."

She laughed. "My offer. I don't think so. The deal was a picnic if I lost the bet. I didn't lose. You did."

"But wouldn't a picnic be nice?"

She gave it some thought. After the first day, as usual, the men had worked out their own schedule. Most preferred to fish early in the morning, have lunch, then rest during the warmer hours. A couple returned to the river in late afternoon, stopping only when it was getting close to dinner. The guests either spent their leisure time playing cards, sitting on the porch, as did Larry most days, or hiking with Reed and Ash. All in all, it worked out that she had a couple of free hours to herself. She guessed a picnic with Max couldn't hurt—much.

"Come on, we can do a little leisurely fishing ourselves. I'll even put the lunch together. You won't have to lift a finger. Just enjoy yourself." She looked torn between duty and the desire to have some fun. He rushed on, "I bet I catch the biggest fish."

She had a knack or maybe luck for catching the big ones. She struggled to keep her expression serious. "What's the bet?"

"Five bucks says I win?"

Nicole shook her head. "I don't gamble."

"What?"

"I don't gamble."

Max couldn't help but laugh out loud. "What do you think we've been doing for the last couple of days?"

"Those are bets for services. For fun. I don't gamble for money—ever."

"Ah, I see. You split hairs for your own purposes."

"You got it." He was too near, making her uncomfortably aware that she was naked under the robe. If he made a pass at her, she doubted she'd have the willpower or the inclination to resist. She quickly stood up and he did the same, leaving them closer than ever. She cleared her throat, took a step back and repeated her question. "What's the bet?"

"A walk in the moonlight this evening if I win, and if you win, I'll personally serve you dinner."

There was a catch somewhere. She just couldn't see it yet.

He'd learned a valuable lesson that first morning fishing. Watching her cast, to quote a cliché, was like poetry in motion. Her movements were smooth and graceful, her aim as accurate as a sharpshooter getting a bull's-eye. Max realized that winning this particular bet wasn't going to be easy.

But again, either way he was a winner. He'd prefer an evening gazing at the moon with Nicole in his arms, but if he lost and had to serve her dinner, more than likely he'd be eating with her, too. Somehow he'd have to make it an intimate meal, just for two. He was mentally planning ways to keep those two young big-ears, Reed and Ash, away. "Sorry, what did you say?"

"And I thought I was the only one with cobwebs for brains this early in the morning. I said, if you'd leave, I could get dressed."

"I'd be more than willing to stay and help. You know, do up a few hard-to-reach buttons. I'm even pretty good with a comb and brush."

"I'm sure you are, but no thanks." Nicole ran her fingers through her hair, still not in the least embarrassed by her appearance. "Go away, Max." She watched him leave, and when the door shut behind him, she sighed with relief. It wasn't wise to flirt with the devil, but for the life of her, she couldn't seem to keep away from him.

As Max left her room, he felt an unexplainable pang of regret. It was too damn easy. For a second he even felt guilty. The fact was, though Nicole wasn't Sandra and didn't have her exceptional qualities, he was fascinated, maybe even infatuated, with her just the same. Then he reminded himself that he had a promise to keep and plans to finalize. He could ill afford to let emotions, recriminations or his personal feelings get in the way.

Nicole found it didn't take long to shower and dress. If she lingered longer over her makeup, she tried not to think of the reason why. And if she rushed around her room, discarding one pair of jeans for another newer pair, or a tan knit shirt for a yellow cotton shirt, she tried to deny she was excited about the picnic.

When at last she yanked open her door, she almost screamed with surprise at seeing JD standing there with his fist raised to knock.

"Jeez, you scared the hell out of me," he said.

"You didn't do my heart a lot of good, either. What's wrong?"

JD stepped back and out of her way. "Nothing's wrong. That good-lookin' fellow told me you and he was gonna have lunch together. A picnic. He asked if he could put it together. Is it true?"

"Yes." She wouldn't look away from his probing gaze. "Is there something wrong with that?"

"Naw. And don't go gettin' your dander up at me. He's spent time here talking to me and the missus. No fancy airs with him. I like him."

"I hear a 'but' in your voice, JD. Spit it out."

He quickly filled the commercial coffeemaker with water and fresh-ground coffee. "Ain't got nothing against the young man, and I think you need some fun." He gave her a rough pat on the shoulder and cleared his throat. "Oh, hell and damnation, you know what a fussbudget Henny-Penny is. She just doesn't want you gettin' your heart broke like the last time. You be careful."

"I'm smarter and a lot wiser now. It'll take more than a pretty face to turn my head, make an ass of myself or generally screw up my life. As for my heart, I'm not sure I have one left to break. So you don't think I should go on the picnic?"

JD slipped the apron over his head, turned the bill of his baseball cap to the back of his head, then securely tied the apron around his waist. "I ain't said that." He gathered the ingredients for his cloud-light biscuits together in a bowl and began mixing them together. "I like him. Honest, I do. Me and the missus think you deserve some fun. Just walk careful, that's all."

She didn't know whether to laugh or cry. "I'll tiptoe."

"Ain't no use you poking fun at me." He tossed flour on the glass-smooth wooden table in the center of the kitchen, scooped out a huge clump of sticky dough and slapped it on the table.

"I'm sorry, JD. You know I'd never make fun of you."

"Don't know no such thing. But since you come home, you've changed. Gotten harder. Cynical."

"You think so?" Nicole followed him as he slid a pan of biscuit dough into the oven. "Dad said the same thing a couple of times. I thought he was just being his ornery self.''

''Never known Charlie to be far off the mark when he's callin' a spade a spade. Have you?''

''No. I guess not.'' She watched as he pulled a slab of bacon from one of the refrigerated lockers, slammed it down on another table and began slicing it into thin strips.

''Well, my advice, whether you want it or not, is to shake off the anger over Roger. Get back to the girl you was. You can't be thinkin' every man is like that bastard ex-husband, 'cause that just ain't so. Go on that picnic today and find the old Nicky. Be yourself. Don't take things so seriouslike, and for heaven's sake have fun. Laugh. And if that blue-eyed man kisses you, give him back as good as he gives. Just remember to be the one to walk away smilin'.''

Nicole laughed as she checked the biscuits in the oven, then began washing the fresh strawberries. Of course JD and her father were right. For a year she'd been moping around. In her heart she knew she wasn't responsible for her marriage failing. Yet, alone at night, she rehashed and examined every detail, trying to find where *she'd* gone wrong. The problem, she realized, was that she was still angry—at Roger and at herself. She'd been made to look the fool, had been lied to and deceived—and it damn well hurt.

JD shoved another pan of biscuits into the oven, then glanced at the big kitchen clock over the doorway. ''Better get movin'. Henny-Penny and the boys'll be here, and you ain't got the coffee urn filled or nothin' set out yet.''

She'd carried the weight of guilt entirely too long. It was time to stop whining and feeling sorry for her-

self and get on with her life. She was sick of being
angry with the world for something she had no control
over. Damn tired of living like a nun, too. It was time
to move on with her life, forget Roger Seevers.
"Thanks, JD."

He scratched a place over his right ear, then reset-
tled the baseball cap. "Fer what?"

She kissed him on the cheek. "For reminding me
I'm still alive and kicking and it's okay to do crazy
things again."

"Is that what I done? Guess I'm smarter than I
thought, after all."

CHAPTER SEVEN

SHE'D RUSHED through the morning, dropping off the guests along the river, constantly checking her watch. She couldn't understand it. She was as excited as a teenager anticipating her first date. A couple of times she'd tried to enter the kitchen, but was shooed away by Max and an amused Penny. They were cooking up more than food in there.

At noon the morning cycle was repeated, only in reverse. She picked up the fishermen and returned them to the lodge for lunch. Then she waited again, but this time she had company. Reed and Ash, full of excitement for real adventure, paced the front porch, waiting for Hal, Preston, George and Clarence to finish lunch.

Finally the men left with the two boys. Larry, who preferred evening fishing, would spend the afternoon resting on the porch with a pair of binoculars, gazing at the birds and the wildlife. Without considering how eager she'd appear, Nicole raced through the lodge, shoved open the kitchen door and skidded to a stop when she saw only Penny. "Where's—"

"He's waiting for you by the Jeep."

As Nicole passed her, heading for the back door, Penny said, "You've got the color back in your cheeks and that gleam in your eye. Have fun, child."

Nicole winked and kissed the older woman on her

softly wrinkled scented cheek. "Thanks. Call me if anyone needs me."

"Go have fun, Nicky, and stop worrying. Everything has a way of working out."

Nicole sailed down the steps and across the yard to the garage. She spotted Max leaning against the side of the Jeep, waved, then hastened her steps. As she drew closer, she couldn't help but notice how snug his jeans were or the way his knit shirt pulled across his chest. *Calm down, Nicky. He's a guest, here to have fun.* Damn, she could manage that. Just as she reached him, she laughed out loud at her own thoughts.

"What's so funny?" Max asked. Something seemed different about her, but he couldn't figure out what it was. He liked the way she moved, her long legs reaching out and eating up the distance between them. As she rounded the Jeep and climbed into the driver's seat, he didn't try to hide the way he scrutinized her from head to toe. She didn't have that graceful hip-swing motion most women had. Nicole moved with an aggressive stride that brought to mind strength and self-assurance—attributes he'd never thought of as alluring, but they fit her and were damn sexy to him. He strolled around to the passenger side and climbed in.

Nicole started the Jeep, then twisted in the seat to see where she was going before she backed out. She knew he had never taken his eyes off her and felt the flush of heat in her cheeks. No. He was not going to make her feel awkward again. Shifting her gaze from the driveway to his face, she stared back. Those blue eyes never wavered from hers, but changed from curiosity to something stronger. It was like a current of electricity shooting through her, leaving her a little breathless. She didn't know if it was desire or anger that caused her reaction. Or maybe it was the crystal-clear message she read. He wanted her. Though unspoken, she knew.

Responding to pure instinct at what she saw, she grabbed the material of his shirt with both hands, jerked him to her and planted a kiss on his lips. It was supposed to be a quick hard kiss to let him know she was well aware of what he was trying to do and that she wasn't one to be teased or taken lightly. The kiss was supposed to send him a message that she wasn't a pushover and was up on all the moves. The kiss was supposed to be a lot of things, but not deep and wild with such a rush of emotions. It wasn't supposed to make her hot or have him breathing hard as he wrapped his hand around the back of her head to keep her mouth from leaving his.

She realized whatever the kiss was meant to be, it hadn't made the statement she'd intended. Or had it? Nicole pulled her head back, keeping their lips only a hairbreadth apart. "That's what you wanted, wasn't it?" she asked.

"Partly." She'd taken him by surprise, a lovely one, but he hadn't expected it or seen it coming, and was having trouble separating his thoughts of Sandra. But Sandra would never have been so bold. Sandra was shy and sensitive, not at all the reckless type.

"You've been eyeing me since you arrived. Watching my every move, haven't you? I haven't missed the way you looked at me, either."

"Like how?" He couldn't ever remember being called on eyeing a woman. Confrontation wasn't one of Sandra's strong points. She never would have challenged him. "When?"

His fake show of confusion made her smile and give a husky laugh. "Like this morning in my room. Don't tell me you weren't thinking about kissing me then."

"I won't." Her curly hair, so unlike Sandra's, felt like silk slipping through his fingers as she pulled farther away. "I wanted to do a lot more than kiss you this morning. Do you know you have a very sexy mouth?" He'd been thrown off guard by her boldness but recovered quickly. "The rest of you looks pretty tantalizing, too."

She chuckled as she reversed the Jeep down the drive. "You don't scare or back off easily, do you?"

"Ah." He watched the rise and fall of her breasts. "Is that what this is about? Was that kiss meant to be a deterrent?" He shook his head, smiled, then leaned a little closer, letting his breath tickle her ear as he said, "I hate to tell you, but you only whetted my appetite for you." He doubted if Sandra ever would have entered into that sort of banter with all its sexual undercurrents.

A thrill of danger sizzled through her, making her nerve endings jiggle to life. There was an edge of sexual tension between them. She felt the soft inner shudder of excitement, something she hadn't felt in ages, and savored it.

He was disappointed when she didn't have a quick comeback. Instead, she turned her attention to where they were going. His pulse was racing, his finely tuned senses alert to every nuance in her voice. He wasn't ready to drop the subject. The fact that she wanted to linger over her victory excited him and delighted him. She was not a novice but an experienced player in the game. He leaned back and relaxed.

Nicole decided to take him to her special spot on

the river. They were quiet during most of the drive, each lost in thought. It was Nicole who broke the silence. "What's your life like in the big city, New York?"

He'd been mired down in his plans, and it took a moment to grasp what she'd asked. "Boring. I work and go home."

"Yeah, sure. With all the wonderful theaters and plays, restaurants and nightclubs, to say nothing of the excitement of—what was it you called your company and what you did—a security consultant?"

He realized he'd made one fatal mistake. He'd misjudged her intelligence. It wasn't that she knew what his company was; it was that over the past couple of days, she'd let him dance around her pointed questions when all the time she was wise to what he was doing. "We do private investigations, surveillance, offer bodyguard service and consultations for security."

She didn't know what had come over her. Playing with fire, and taking unnecessary and dangerous chances was out of character. She'd always been straightforward in what she wanted. At first Roger had loved what he called her bawdy sense of humor and her sexuality. His opinion seemed to change when he achieved tenure. Her outspokenness embarrassed him. As did her casual taste in fashion. The most humiliating incident was when he told her that her sexual aggressiveness turned him off. That announcement had cut deeper than all the rest. It had made her unsure of herself. Now, of course, she realized that Roger was a self-indulgent control freak. Her gut reaction said Max was an eager sparring partner, but her logical side, the doubts Roger had planted, made her hesitate.

Maybe she'd come on too strong and needed to back off a little for a while.

"Do you enjoy your work?" she asked, hoping to steer them onto neutral ground.

Max became aware they'd turned off the main track that passed for a road and were on what appeared to be a less-used path. They were also on an upward slope. "Not anymore. I'm sick to death of it." The feeling behind his statement surprised him.

"That's why you and your partner came to Dawson's?"

"To relax and fish, yes." He was suddenly suspicious of the line of questioning, wondering if she knew more about them than she was letting on. Maybe she knew about Bedford. Then he dismissed his concerns. There was no way she could know about their client, and there sure as hell wasn't any way she knew about Sandra.

Nicole had always been good at judging people, except for Roger, and felt that Max was being very careful of what he told her. She let it pass and pulled the Jeep off the path and under a stand of trees, turned off the ignition and climbed out. She eyed the big picnic basket in the back. "I'll get the gear and rods. You get the food."

Looking around, he saw the place was totally different from the other locations he'd fished. She was sharing something special with him, and as he followed her through the forest of trees and undergrowth, his heart raced with excitement. Then he could hear the river, a soothing sound, the splash and slap of water pouring over rocks. As they came out from the thicket of trees, she stepped aside. He could only stare.

A cascading waterfall seemed to sprout from the

center of a fern-covered rocky cliff. Trees and more ferns clung to the banks of the river, tinting the water emerald green. Max looked into the depths and could see the dark shadows of fish swimming around the rock-strewn bottom.

A light breeze caressed his skin. Gazing down, he watched shadows from the overhanging trees move on the surface of the water. There was a strong scent of damp earth and an unidentifiable sweet fragrance in the air. It whirled around him, and he felt a tug of longing to be one with the land. The desire to lose himself and let his worries fly away on the breeze overcame any other needs real or imagined. He dropped the picnic basket on the bank, then took his waders and rod from Nicole.

KNEE-DEEP IN THE RIVER, feeling the gentle tug of the current, Nicole figured from the way her stomach was growling that they'd been fishing for about two hours. She reeled in her line, removed the fly and stored it away on her vest pocket, then shouldered her rod and headed for the bank. "I'm starving, New York."

He glanced over his shoulder, surprised to hear a human voice. "San—" He caught himself just in time. But for a second his eyes had played tricks on him. The sun had caught her blond hair and highlighted her face in a way that made him think he was seeing Sandra. "Montana. You quitting?"

Shaking her head, she couldn't hide her smile. She'd seen that disoriented lost-in-another-world look too many times not to recognize it. "I'm going to break open the picnic basket and see what you threw together." She slipped out of her waders and stored her gear, then returned to the riverbank, squatted down and washed her hands and face in the cool water. She hadn't thought to bring something to dry off with, so she pulled her shirt from the waistband of her jeans and patted her face and hands. Max was suddenly beside her, washing up, too, and she smiled at him.

"I'd go fishing with you any day, any time, any place," he said.

She nodded, at a complete loss for words. He'd just given her the greatest of compliments. "Same here." She'd fished with him the first day, but he'd seemed nervous, distracted, his movements clumsy. Today he was in top form and she'd had to work to outcast him. Only a true fisherman understood the need for quiet and inner reflection while fishing. It was more than just casting a line in the water, catching a fish. That was the easy part.

Fly-fishing was an art, almost a religion. It was mental strategy, cunning and the determination of the fisherman to pit his knowledge against nature. He had to read the river, study the current and the way the insects swarmed over the surface. It was the way the fish were swimming that counted. She'd met few serious fishermen who liked to hold a conversation with another while plying his art. They were sportsmen of few words, prone to converse in hand signals, grunts and nods.

Max made a production of spreading out the blanket Penny had packed. He motioned for Nicole to sit, then did the same. He kept the basket between them and started handing her wineglasses, plates, napkins and a couple of forks. At last he took out the sealed containers. "I hope you like red wine with chicken."

"Sure." She tried to peek into the basket, but Max

quickly closed the top, so she jerked away. "What kind of chicken?"

"Fried, and some special Warner potato salad."

"Yours? Did you actually make it or did Penny?"

"I want you to know I made everything. Fried the chicken like my dear old Texas grandmother taught me." He laughed at her look of surprise. "You didn't really think I was actually a New Yorker, did you?"

"Well, yes. Though I did wonder about the accent. It's not exactly Eastern, but neither do you have a Texas drawl. I never would have guessed. Where are you from? Houston? Dallas? Some other big city?"

"Try a dinky dusty hick town. I joined the service and saw the world. I guess I lost the accent somewhere along the way." He took her plate from her and began to fill it. "What about you? How much of the world have you seen?"

She was so hungry she didn't even stop to think what she was saying as he placed a crispy brown breast and a wing on her plate. "Outside of Montana, I've been to Berkeley and a few other towns in California."

"From your tone of voice, I take it you weren't impressed?"

"You're right. It was made perfectly clear to me that I was a country girl and should stay where I belonged."

"That's rubbish."

She took a bite of the crunchy chicken, savored the moist meat. Once she'd swallowed, she smiled. "I believe your chicken's better than Penny's. Did she ask you for your recipe?"

"No, but she watched me like a hawk eyeing a field mouse. I don't imagine she missed a thing." As he took a forkful of potato salad, he suddenly realized what it was about her that bothered him. Rarely did she talk about herself. She was usually too busy asking questions.

He knew everything there was to know about Sandra, believed he knew her better than anyone, including her mother. That knowledge made him see for the first time just how little he knew about Nicole. Though not for lack of trying. He'd come to learn something important in the past couple of hours. She was as private a person as he was. But his secretiveness was from too long in his line of business and knowing others' dirty little secrets. Her reasons, he suspected, were from being deeply hurt.

The best way to disarm someone, he believed, was usually the direct route. ''Penny mentioned that you'd had a pretty bad marriage. She didn't mince her words—called him a bastard. How did you meet him? At college?''

Nicole took a sip of wine. ''No. He and a couple of his friends were here for a week. Like you're doing.'' It still angered and embarrassed her to realize what a fool she'd been, and she spoke more to herself than to Max. ''I was blinded by a pretty face and a glib tongue. I guess since we owned a ranch, a mountain and a business, Roger thought he was getting a bride with money in the family. We were both dead wrong.''

Glancing around, he could see how an outsider, especially a sportsman, would immediately have visions of wealth. But an abundance of real estate didn't necessarily mean a large cash reserve. Usually, in fact, it was the opposite. It didn't take a genius to see that she blamed herself for the breakup, and the pain he saw had nothing to do with being swept off her feet followed by the realization that she'd been married for reasons other than herself. He sensed something deeper. "Is that what ended it, when you found out he thought you were rich?"

Nicole set her clean plate down, took the last sip of wine. When Max made to fill it again, she shook her head. She surprised herself by saying, "Actually I found out all too quickly that I didn't fit in with my husband's life. That whole back-stabbing social culture made me uncomfortable."

He could still see the hurt in her eyes. It surprised him that he had to swallow around a lump in his throat. "It was their loss, wasn't it. I mean, how often do you think they get to meet someone with your looks and brains?"

She laughed. "You mean an oddity? Not nearly enough from the amusement I brought them."

"They hurt you. I'm sorry."

"Thanks." She dabbed at her mouth with the napkin, then wiped her hands, amazed at how relaxed she was with him. Suddenly she wanted to let go of all her anger about the past and laugh. "It's sort of funny, you know. Me in my denim and boots, talking about ranching, river rafting, fly-fishing and the mountain, while the other women discussed the rigors of doing anything and everything necessary so their husbands would receive tenure. Or they chatted incessantly about where to shop for the best clothes, whose homes were the biggest and whose children were the brightest and cutest. You could say I was way out of my league."

Max packed away the leftover food, then stretched

out on the blanket and closed his eyes. "I've been there and it's no fun."

"You?" He looked so comfortable. She joined him, but made sure there was enough distance between them so he wouldn't get any ideas.

"You didn't think I was always so witty, intelligent, handsome or had such a winning personality, did you?" Her laughter had a light tinkle to it that made him smile inside and out. "Losing that small-town imprint was like changing my genetic makeup." He rolled onto his side so he could look at her. Nicole raised her arm and glanced at her watch. "Do you have another appointment, or am I boring you to death?" he asked.

"Neither," she said. "I was wondering how Reed and Ash are coping with the terrible foursome."

Max grinned. "I can't believe you let those two kids take the four guys hiking."

"I'm not that crazy. All they're doing is taking the men on a one-hour hike down a well-traveled path to the launching area for the white-water rafting trip." She glanced at him, then tried to hide a huge yawn. "They'll be met by Joe and Bobby Carlson, our rafting guides."

"What about Larry? When do you have to get back to the lodge to take him out?"

"He and JD have struck up a friendship. JD's going to take him to his special fishing hole." She paused. "Is there some reason you wanted to know all this?"

"I was just wondering how long we had."

She yawned again. "Bull. You want to know how much fishing you can get in between now and then."

Her lazy manner was contagious. He settled on his back and closed his eyes. "Guilty."

She grinned. "You won't get much fishing done looking from inside your eyelids."

"You'd be surprised what I can do with my eyes shut."

"No," she murmured, "I wouldn't, and I'm not going to ask, either."

"Damn. You're sure? I could explain in great detail."

"You probably have a vivid imagination," she said. The tone of their conversation had changed. Though the words were innocent enough, there was an underlying crackle of tension that slowly sizzled between them. But it seemed they were just too comfortable and content to give in to their desires.

Nicole felt the warmth from the heat of the sun on her body, took a deep breath and for the first time in a long time totally relaxed in the company of a man. Her eyelids began to grow heavy. "You better pack the remainder of the food and put it back in the Jeep." She smiled, listening to him grumble about being just as comfortable as she was.

SHE DIDN'T KNOW what had awakened her. Maybe it was the movement of the sun through the trees and the deepening shadows, or the way the afternoon had cooled down. Or it could have been that inner alarm that warns a person when something is different. Maybe it was the confusion of sensing she was tangled in a man's arms and wrapped around his body. For a second she couldn't think who it could be. The heaviness of sleep lifted from her mind and she remembered.

Two things were becoming clear: Max had his eyes open and was staring at her, and there was no mistaking the evidence of his desire pressing against her thigh. She bit her lip to keep from laughing.

"You find the state I'm in amusing?" he whispered. He'd awakened from a disturbing dream where he'd been making love to Sandra who had suddenly become Nicole. And if that wasn't disturbing enough, suddenly there were both women with him and his prowess failed him.

Nicole rubbed her face against the crook of his arm like a lazy cat. "Not amusing exactly. More like intriguing. Do you usually wake up with your kickstand at the ready?"

"Kickstand?" He grinned. "That's not very flattering, but no, not since I was a teenager." At first when she'd opened her eyes and gazed at him, all he could see was Sandra looking at him. She was as alive to him now as she ever would be. He lowered his mouth and kissed her softly and a little hesitantly. He didn't want to scare her off. Under the gentle but persistent invasion of his tongue, her mouth opened. Initially she only teased and tantalized him, then everything changed. She was the seducer, her mouth suddenly as hungry as his, and he found himself plunged into an abyss of desire. It hit him in the gut with a force that stunned him, like a jolt out of the blue. His kiss deepened and roughened. One hand tangled itself in her hair while the other found the soft mound of her breast.

Nicole didn't know who was trying to consume whom. It was as if a dam too long contained had been opened. All she cared about was his mouth and the way his hand gently kneaded her breast. She tugged at his shirt, yanking it free of his jeans, and ran her fingers up his back, then down and under his waistband. His skin was smooth and hot. She caressed the taut muscles of his butt, then dug her fingers into the hard flesh and pulled him against her.

Max gave a gasp of surprise. His senses reeled and he kissed with wild abandon, forgetting any attempt at being gentle or thoughtful. All he could feel was the magic of her fingers and the way she rubbed up against him.

She had no idea how or when her shirt had come loose and unbuttoned, or how her bra had become unhooked. What she did know was the way his talented fingers made her breasts feel as if they were on fire. There were no coy overtures to pull away, slow down or stop. Her mouth and body made it clear she wanted him. She let her hands slowly glide under his waistband and around to the front of his jeans. Her nimble fingers quickly yanked the snap apart and were working on pulling the zipper down when she stopped, every muscle suddenly frozen. She forced her lips from his mouth, tried to focus on his face as she struggled to catch her breath and calm her hammering heart.

Max knew what was going on and said, "You wouldn't have any suggestions about how to solve this little problem we seem to have gotten ourselves into, would you?"

"Only if you carry something in your wallet or tackle box."

"I'm afraid not. How about you?"

Nicole shook her head, her confused and disappointed expression mirroring his. An instant later they were both laughing.

Max rolled onto his back, covered his eyes with one arm and continued to laugh. "Serves me right. Mom always told me to be prepared—or was that the Boy Scouts? Anyway, I never once gave it a thought. Who would even think about condoms when you're going on a fishing trip with a bunch of men?''

He glanced at Nicole to make sure she wasn't upset, and lost his train of thought for a moment. Like him, she was on her back, her clothes in total disarray. Her jeans were undone at the waist and her shirt was parted and hanging from her shoulders. The waning afternoon cast a luminous light across her small round breasts and down her flat stomach and narrow waist. She had the same bone structure as Sandra, but where he'd imagined Sandra was soft and delicate, Nicole was fit and firm.

And where his dreams had been of a sweet seduction, he'd been seduced. Visions of tenderness, even tears of shyness, had turned into raw passion. When he thought of Nicole, he was filled with lust. The kind that had the power to rip away all reason. And humor? He never expected to laugh at himself or with her over their aborted attempt.

Her body was still humming with desire. She ached from it. "I don't know about you—" she jumped up and began stripping off the rest of her clothes "—but I'm in need of a cold shower." She glanced at him and shivered at the way he was watching her disrobe. "Want to join me?"

He didn't need a second invitation and was soon running after her as she headed down a narrow path through the trees. The grass was soft and cool under his feet, and the warm breeze against his skin began to calm his appetite for her. She was lovely to watch, naked, running through the forest like a wood nymph.

He realized he was captivated by her lack of embarrassment about her desires or her nudity.

Just as she reached the edge of the river, she stopped and looked over her shoulder. Damn, she thought, if the man wasn't gorgeous. It was obvious he made a point of keeping in shape. She hit the water before him and was coming up for air when she felt his arm encircle her waist. She gave him credit for speed, enthusiasm and a sense of humor. Not many men in their situation would have stopped so easily and gracefully. She twisted in his arms, pressed her body against his and laughed. "You know we have a big problem?"

"I'm all too aware of it, and if you don't stop rubbing against me, Montana, I just might forget."

As he moved into deeper water and Nicole was unable to touch bottom, she managed to keep her arms wrapped around his neck yet keep the rest of her body out of contact with his. The deeper the water the colder it became. She gave a shoulder-shaking shiver and he found he was suddenly fascinated by the way the chill tightened her nipples, which showed just above the surface of the water. When he lifted his gaze to hers, she was smiling, knowing all to well what the sight of her naked breasts was doing to him.

Her eyes danced with mischief. "I don't think you truly understand how serious the problem is. I have nothing at the lodge." She laughed again. "Since you didn't bring anything with you, what would you suggest?" She couldn't resist his mouth and kissed him softly. "I want you, New York. I want to make love to you and know what it feels like to have you inside me." She swiped back her wet hair and grinned. "We're in an awful fix."

Any verbal response he might have given stuck in

his throat. His only answer, despite the cold water, was showy and physical, and she didn't miss the display. "*Damn*, Montana. You absolutely take my breath away. You make me weak in the knees." So saying, he held on to her, then plunged them both beneath the surface. When they came up, she was smiling, knowing full well that dunking his head had had little effect on his physical condition. "We could always take matters into our own hands—so to speak." Steadying his footing on the rocky river bottom, he pulled her against his chest. "I take you in hand," he whispered against her lip, "and you do the same." He slid a hand between them, down her stomach, then between her legs.

Nicole gasped and tightened her arm around his neck. Determined he wasn't going to be left out in the cold, she followed his lead. He was hard and smooth in her hand, and the more he moved his hips against her, the more difficult it was to concentrate on her efforts. Then her mouth found his.

If she'd been on fire earlier, his clever fingers quickly had her ready to explode. Suddenly she shuddered against him and at the same time lost her breath in his kiss. Before her grip slackened, she felt his entire body stiffen, then he gave a deep moan against her lips.

The strength of his release knocked him off balance and sent him stumbling backward. Frantically he tried to regain his footing, taking her with him as he staggered over the rocks. He lost the struggle to stand and they hit the water with a great splash and came up sputtering.

In more ways than one, he'd been knocked off his feet. But his first thought was Nicole. When he saw her dazed satisfied expression, he laughed. "That was a surprise."

"Wonderful." She shook the water from her hair and cobwebs out of her brain. "You know, of course, that you only whetted my appetite for the real thing."

"God, I know." She took hold of his hand and led him out of the water where they collapsed on the grass of the riverbank.

He knew damn well he couldn't stay another night under the same roof with her and not make love to her. "I think there just might be a solution. Surely one of the men brought something. Ha! Hal. He'd never leave home without condoms. I bet I could lift a couple without him being the wiser."

"You'd ransack another guest's room? You'd steal for me?"

It took a second to realize she was teasing. "Nicole, I think at this moment, I'd kill for you."

CHAPTER EIGHT

HE FELT LIKE A TEENAGER with rampaging hormones. He was having delicious visions of Nicole while trying to hold an intelligent conversation, act interested and make appropriate comments, and so had no idea what he was saying. Lust, pure and simple, was what he was feeling. It amused, disturbed and frightened him to realize that all his energy, his thoughts, were focused on making love to one woman. The idea almost made him laugh. He'd become sexually obsessed.

Men were notorious for picking up on the slightest tremor of sexual tension in the air. He would never subject her to the looks and comments that could spring up if the men caught the smallest hint of interest between them. If they did catch on and a crude remark was made, he'd just have to tear their tongues out. He couldn't subject Nicole to that sort of embarrassment. But he was having a difficult time keeping his eyes off her. Every time he glanced her way, he felt electrified. Flushed and ready. There was a lot to say about expectation making the reward sweeter.

As for Nicole, it didn't take a mind reader to know what Max was thinking. She was having trouble keeping her thoughts in check herself. Worse still, she was the hostess and had to relive with the men every thrill they'd had white-water rafting down the river. She was glad they'd had so much fun, glad they had nothing but praise for Reed and Ash.

JD's wonderful meal had been overshadowed by the excited and lively conversation. That enthusiasm continued when everyone moved out to the porch for after-dinner drinks and coffee. Even the glorious display of the setting sun was ignored, and Nicole found herself stuck between Hal, Preston and George. She listened with half an ear, torn between boredom and amusement, as they rehashed every dip, rough rapid and bend in the river. Her gaze kept sliding to Max. His face was in shadow and she couldn't see his expression, but she knew he was as eager to resume what they'd started in the afternoon as she was.

She leaned her shoulder against the porch's rough-hewn log column, nodded and tried to look enthralled with what Preston was saying. Just as she and Max had returned to the lodge, the men had been coming up the trail from their outing. From then on she hadn't had a chance to talk to Max. But she hadn't missed the fact that he'd been late joining everyone at the dinner table. She wondered if he'd been room-raiding, Hal's suite in particular. And if he had, had his thieving foray been rewarded?

All Max could do was wait and pray the evening would soon be over. He glanced at his watch and stifled a sigh of exasperation. Would these guys never wind down and go to bed? He'd always been a past master at hiding his feelings. Mr. Stoneface, Doug had dubbed him. Now he had to keep to the shadows in hopes no one looked at him too closely and saw the signs of a man in sexual pain. Sometimes he envied the animal kingdom. It would be a wonderful release to yell, scream, stomp around or even head-butt a tree. Hell, he felt downright primal.

He had to hand it to her. She'd hooked him as effectively as a trout. What impressed him most was that she made no excuses for her desire and passion. There were no apologies or shocked words about what had happened between them. She hadn't used that old line that she'd never done this before—taken a guest to her special place and made love. As he sat slowly sipping his drink, he realized something important. Nicole was totally honest and straightforward. She didn't lie. She didn't try to mollycoddle anyone's feelings, either.

What suddenly hit him and stopped the glass halfway to his mouth was that Nicole was everything Sandra was not. And that wasn't necessarily a bad thing. A delicate, sensitive and trusting person like Sandra couldn't hold up to what he had planned. He only wished... Max stopped, telling himself not to go there, that it was too damn dangerous to compare the two women.

Nicole tapped him twice on the shoulder to get his attention. "Where were you?"

Max glanced around and felt a profound sense of relief. The porch was empty. "In your bed with you," he whispered just in case someone was within hearing. "Where is everyone?"

"They're all tuckered out and finally decided to turn in. JD, Penny and the boys have left, too." She tried to sound surprised, but the mocking smile that tilted the corners of her mouth belied that. "We're the only two left."

Max glanced at his watch and pretended to yawn. "I think I'll turn in."

"Me, too."

"I'll give everyone time to settle down, make sure they're all asleep and come to you."

She nodded and bit back a smile. "By the way, how did your pillaging and plundering go? Any luck?"

His grin was so wide it hurt his face. He felt like the proverbial Cheshire cat. "God bless Hal. He came through. But we have a minor hitch."

Nicole leaned over, close enough that a breast brushed his shoulder. Her breath, when she spoke, caressed his ear. "I don't want to hear problems. You have the goods?"

"Yes." He felt like a spy in some bad B-movie.

She smiled, then deliberately blew softly in his ear. "Then be in the appointed place in, say, an hour."

"That place being your bedroom, I hope?" Now he found himself talking out of the corner of his mouth like an actor in that same bad B-movie.

His teasing was contagious. "You got it, kid. See you there."

Max twisted around in the chair and watched her stroll off, her hips swinging like a fancy street tart. "Whew!" he exclaimed quietly, but loud enough for her to hear. "Hot mama." Sitting back, he let out a long unsteady breath, then murmured to himself, "Body, don't fail me now."

IT WAS THE LONGEST hour of her life.

She bathed, powdered, perfumed and primped. She combed her hair one way, then another and finally ended up ruffling it with her fingers. She applied three different shades of lipstick, then wiped each one off. She was as nervous as a schoolgirl on her first date. What would she say? What could she talk about?

Nicole laughed. Who the hell wanted to waste time

talking? For the hundredth time she glanced at the clock over the fireplace in her sitting room. When a light tap came on the door, she jumped as if she'd been shot. He was fifteen minutes early. As she opened the door she was laughing.

Max's knees went weak at the sight of the oversize T-shirt. The worn-thin white material did little to hide the treasures underneath. If she'd been wearing silk or satin, she couldn't have looked more alluring. "What's so funny?" he asked, his voice raspy with desire.

Nicole triple-locked the door. "I was laughing at myself." He slipped his arms around her waist and drew her to him. "I found it amusing that you were fifteen minutes early, until I realized I'd been waiting for you for the last thirty."

He nuzzled her neck. God, she smelled sweet. "That's reassuring." Placing his hands on her shoulders, he held her away from him and slipped one hand into his shirt pocket. "I've got good news and bad news." He pulled a mangled foil package out and waved it before her eyes. "One. I only found one."

She gave another laugh. "Then...then we better make it unforgettable."

"Hell, we better make it last all damn night. I'm not going around tomorrow feeling the way I did this evening."

She couldn't stand the distance between them any longer and sank against him, shivering as her breasts touched his chest, then turned her face up and met his mouth with her own. Thoughts of being naked together, of rubbing their bodies together, were enough to send her hands diving to his waist.

Dexterity had always been one of her strong points.

With a flick of her fingers his jeans pooled around his feet just as he was stepping out of his shoes. For a moment the kiss deepened, making it as intimate as sex itself, and she lost her train of thought. Then the buttons of his shirt easily gave way and dropped to the floor. Her hands seemed to have an agenda all their own. They ran lightly over his body, caressing, touching, as if memorizing every curve, every angle.

As much as he wanted to feel her naked flesh, to tear the T-shirt off her so he could caress and kiss her everywhere, he couldn't stop kissing her mouth. He was as dry as the Sahara and she was like his first sip of water. It was nectar sweet and opened up a craving he'd never known before. His knees were actually shaking, weak in fact, as she touched him.

He let his hands slide down her back and over her buttocks. Then he grabbed a handful of her in each hand and lifted her into him, pressing her hard against his erection. He moaned as she moved her hips slowly back and forth.

He kept hold of her, lifting her until she was able to wrap her legs around his waist and her arms around his neck. Only when she was secure in his arms did he stop kissing her, get his bearings and head for her bedroom. As he lowered her to the bed and followed her down, they were all arms and tangled legs. He'd managed to yank the T-shirt over her head and pitch it across the room.

He hovered above her, studying her kiss-swollen lips, the blush of her cheeks and the way the pupils of her eyes dilated. He knew he was out of control and struggled to restrain himself, slow down. But all he could think about was being inside her. He lowered his head and caught a nipple between his lips. Her body arched and at the same time her hands grasped him, guided him toward her heat. "My expectations of a long night was wishful thinking, a pipe dream. I want you so damn bad I can't hold on much longer."

Nicole gave him a dreamy smile and waved the foil-wrapped package at him. "I think we put too much stock in our willpower. Would you hurry up and put the thing on? I'd do it, but I'm afraid I'd be all thumbs. What if I punched a hole in it?"

"God, don't even think that!"

Nicole watched the way he looked at her, realizing she couldn't judge his emotions by his expression. All she could see was the hard edge of desire. It had changed his eyes, intensifying the color until she felt pinned to the bed. When he lowered his body onto hers, she trembled, every nerve jumping to life as he slid deep inside her. A soft groan escaped her lips, a sound she was barely aware she'd made as an assortment of emotions rippled through her.

Her warm wetness, the way she tightened around him, almost made Max lose control. Then he lowered his mouth to hers, nudged her lips apart and slipped his tongue inside. The rhythm of the kiss, the in-and-out motion, mirrored the movement of his hips and had Nicole clutching at his shoulders, digging her fingernails into his flesh. Max gave a low rumbling sound. He felt the strength of her body, her strong legs wrapped around his waist, the tangle of her embrace. He was lost in the heat of her desire and his own.

Nicole could feel their sweat-sheened skin rubbing together as they rocked together. She wrenched her mouth from his and struggled for a steadying breath, but her heart was thumping much too fast and her pulse racing wildly. She was on fire and icy cold at the same instant. Suddenly her body shuddered and trembled with such force that she threw back her head and gasped. The unexpected power of the release shocked her, leaving her panting as her lungs grabbed for air.

"Hold on, Nicky," Max managed through stiff lips. She slid her legs lower, across his buttocks, and anchored him to her while he thrust deeper and deeper. Suddenly he stiffened, made a soft sob of a groan, then collapsed against her.

Nicole didn't move, enjoying his weight on top of her, as she tried to remember if a man had ever made her feel like this before. She was limp and exhausted and exhilarated at the same time, more satisfied than she'd ever believed possible. That sense of peace and fulfillment both frightened and thrilled her.

Nothing ever lasted, she reminded herself, not for her. She'd learned that sad fact firsthand a long time ago. There were promises made to herself when she'd come face-to-face with the heartbreaking truth of infidelity—she would learn to enjoy what there was of love but guard her heart. Her lashes fluttered down, closing access to her emotions. She'd never let him see the hunger of a tender heart in her eyes.

Max gazed at her, amazed and dazed. Something inside him shifted out of kilter. She was so damn beautiful. He wanted to make love to her forever. He put the brakes on his drifting thoughts. "Well, I guess we blew our all-nighter in one shot."

She could still feel him inside her and wrapped her arms around his shoulders to keep him from moving. Then she whispered, her lips beside his ear, "What a shot."

He was concerned he might be too heavy for her,

but she'd proved her agility and strength. It was new for him to be able to lie, still deeply embedded in that warm place, quiet, peaceful and be allowed to drift away.

When he awakened, he was curled around her, sheltering her body with his. He moved and she quickly turned over to face him. "I'm sorry, I fell asleep," he said. He started to rise, but she held him back.

"I took care of things."

For a second he just stared at her, then pulled the sheet back and looked. He was a little embarrassed. He'd never had a woman do that for him, but then he'd never dropped off so quickly afterward.

She could have sworn he blushed, then decided she must be wrong. But it didn't stop her from having fun. "You know, my ex always said it wasn't quantity that mattered, but quality. Man, was he ever wrong. Quality can be faked, but not quantity." He *was* blushing! She could feel the sudden change of heat in his chest.

Nicole rolled onto her back and stretched lazily. "I never knew being so bad could feel so good." It was the only excuse she was willing to give for her outrageous behavior. "Did you search everyone's belongings?"

"No. I gave our dilemma some rational thought. Clarence and George are happily married men. I knew they wouldn't bring any protection with them. And Larry...well, sex is probably the last thing on his mind. Preston's the type that doesn't have many women in his life. They're not on his mind day and night like Hal. Plus, he's too wrapped up in his vacation with a bunch of men to care about women. Hal was the only logical one, and I didn't rifle through all his belongings. I checked his wallet, and when I came up empty, I went straight to his shaving kit. Knowing Hal, I wasn't surprised, but I was deeply disappointed to find only one.''

"What would you suggest we do for the rest of the evening? I've got some wonderful old movies we could watch.''

Max closed his eyes and shook his head. "I don't think I could concentrate with you so near. Why don't we do something novel, like talk?''

"About what?'' she asked.

"You and me. I'd like to get to know you.''

"Why? You'll be leaving in a few days, and this little interlude will be just a memory.''

"Maybe. Maybe not,'' he said cryptically. "How long have you been divorced, Nicky?''

She liked the way he said Nicky, instead of the more formal Nicole. "Almost two years. Why?''

"Don't snap. Play along. Maybe you'll enjoy opening up. I'm just curious about your life. You seem so cut off from everything out here.''

"Cut off from what?'' She turned on her side and propped herself up on her elbow. "If you mean men, I haven't had much use for them lately. But if you think just because I live in Montana, and on a ranch, that I don't have the opportunity to date, then you're very much mistaken.''

"Hold it. I didn't mean that. What I was trying to say was you seem isolated out here.'' Max sighed inwardly. His ploy wasn't going as he'd hoped. "I mean, this isn't exactly a beehive of activity. Oh, hell.'' He'd probably do better if he shut up.

"I get by, thank you very much.''

"Like that Sam character back at the ranch,'' he

said irritably, "who was trying to bribe you for a date. Or was it a date he had in mind?"

She chuckled. "Sam? I'm nice—*only* nice—to him because he's the principal at the school where I've been teaching, and he's also on the school board. I could use his vote, though, mind you, I don't have to have it. I've contacted each of the members and talked to them."

"Sweet-talked them, you mean?"

"Whatever it takes."

Max slipped his arm under her shoulders and pulled her close. He wanted more than anything to go back to sleep and awake in the morning with her beside him. But he knew he was going to have to leave soon. He couldn't take the chance of any of the men finding out and embarrassing Nicole.

"What about you?" she asked. "All I know about you is that you live in New York and are partners with Doug in a security-consultant business.

"What do you want to know?"

"Oh, come on," she said with the same tone of irritation he'd used. "Now who's being close-mouthed?"

Moonlight streamed in through the window at the head of the bed, highlighting her skin and making it glow like silver. More than anything he wanted to make love to her again, but... "I'm divorced, too."

She waited. "Well, don't stop there. How long were you married? Why did you split? Jeez, it's like pulling teeth to get anything out of you."

He hadn't realized how much he disliked talking about himself until now. "Two years. I've been single for five."

"And glad of it, from your tone of voice."

"I don't know," he said. "Lately I wonder. If she'd been the right woman, it would have been different. That claim is a big jump for me. Until lately, I pretty much let my bitterness override any other feelings I might have."

She stroked his chest, teasing at the sparse dark hair until he grasped her hand and stilled it. "What happened recently to make you question yourself?"

He almost said Sandra's name, but caught himself in time. "Coming face-to-face with the reality that I'm not going to live forever. Life slips by too fast and it's best not to spend a lot of time waiting for things to happen. You have to make them happen yourself." He chuckled. "God, now I'm getting gloomy. I'm sorry."

She could tell he was talking about two separate but related events. She'd done the same herself before. It surprised her that she recognized what he was trying to convey. "What brought you to Montana?"

"Mostly boredom."

"Expensive cure for the blues." The way he shrugged, she realized money was not a problem for him. It also told her something else. He was cynical and didn't care deeply about much at this point of his life. She thought it a sad testament to his thirty-two years. "What about your company? The people who depend on you?"

He shifted his position so he could look at her. "I'm sick of my life. Tired of being alone and unsettled."

"Maybe you're having a midlife crisis?"

"Kind of early, but yeah, maybe." He cupped her cheek, then kissed her lazily. When their lips parted, he slid his arm out from under her and sat up. He closed his eyes for a moment in an effort to reclaim his good intentions. "You know I want to stay with you tonight, but if I do, I'll make love to you again—and that's something that's going to have to wait. It's time I went back to my room."

Nicole sat up, too. She smiled at the way his gaze lingered on her breasts. "This is the last time, New York." She tried to keep her voice light, teasing. "You only have one more day here." She glanced at the clock on the bedside table and saw it was after one in the morning. "Actually, this full day, then we'll be heading back to the ranch tomorrow. You'll be going back to your own life and I'll continue mine."

He slipped out of bed and began dressing. "Things have a way of changing, Nicky, when you least expect it."

"What's that supposed to mean?" She threw back the covers, then laughed when he groaned and pretended to cover his eyes as he handed her her robe.

"I'm not a strong man tonight, Nicky. Don't tempt fate." He gave her a quick kiss, then pivoted and strode out of the bedroom.

She listened to the door quietly shut and sat on the side of the bed. What had he meant? She almost let herself hope.

A HEAVY MORNING FOG hugged the ground and the surface of the river, like thick white frosting on a cake. It was a beautiful, ghostly sight. But it made visibility impossible for the fishermen. The Jeep was ready, packed with the men's gear and parked in front. They were all congregated on the lodge porch, drinking coffee and discussing the problem that was delaying their early-morning start. This was the last day, and everyone was anxious to be on the river.

Everyone, that is, except Max. He leaned comfortably against the railing, his back to the river and the magnificent view, and watched Nicole. The morning air was crisp and had a bite to it. She was wearing jeans that fit her like a glove and a yellow-and-white plaid flannel shirt. He was sure every lustful thought he was having was in his face and had to remind himself to be careful. Staring would only attract the interest of the others. But it was damn hard to keep his eyes off her as she moved from one man to the other, laughing and talking.

When she'd finally worked her way over to him, she grinned and paused. "As soon as the wind picks up, the fog will begin to dissipate."

"Thank you, Montana. How many times have you said that this morning?"

"Five. You make six. But it's true."

She was so damn beautiful his throat suddenly closed on him and he could only stare and nod. Bright pink stained her cheeks and he smiled. She was being as careful as he was and had started to move off when his next words stopped her. "How about dropping me off last and stay and fish with me this morning?"

"Okay. I'll even have JD put something special in your lunch."

"You're enough for any man."

She walked away on unsteady legs. It wasn't so much what he'd said, though heaven knew that was enough to send her pulses racing. But it was the way he looked at her. The way his eyes roamed over her, undressing her as if he'd never seen her before and was savoring every imagined detail. Taking a deep breath, she headed for the kitchen.

"Cripes, Nicky, are you coming down with something?" JD asked. "You look poorly. Flushed."

"I'm fine," she said.

Penny poked him in the ribs. "What's wrong with you, woman?"

"Do you have any of those fresh strawberries left?" Nicole asked.

JD and Penny both stopped what they were doing and stared. "Maybe," JD said. "Why you askin'?"

She loved them dearly and knew they were fully aware something was going on with her and Max. But there were times when their teasing got the better of her. "Because I want what's left."

"Don't go gettin' that snippety tone with me," JD said as he disappeared into the refrigerator locker and came out with a pint of plump ripe strawberries.

"You hush up your leg-pulling, you old coot," Penny said as she took the fruit from him and carefully wrapped it in a dampened paper towel, then put it in a small cooler with an ice pack. "Are you so senile you've forgotten what it's like to be bitten by the love-bug?"

"I'm not in love," Nicole said in swift denial.

JD nodded, agreeing with Nicole. "Looks like somethin' else to me. Somethin' hot." He gave Henny-Penny a loud smacking kiss on the cheek. "Gives a fellow ideas seein' all those looks no one's supposed to be seein'."

She wasn't going to dignify them with another denial. It was just what JD wanted so he could keep it up. She scowled at them, picked up the cooler and turned to leave. He stopped her with a firm hand on her arm.

"I cleared it with your daddy."

For a second she blanched, and while she waited for her heart to calm down, she caught the sparkle in his eyes. "One of these days, JD."

He chuckled. "Okay. New subject. Henny-Penny and me, well, we've come to think a lot of Larry. I asked him to stay on for a couple more days as our guest. Charlie says it's fine by him, and Larry'll be staying at the house with us. What do you say?"

She knew that JD had found a fishing buddy and that Larry had spent his evening with them. "I think it's great. You know he's very ill, don't you?"

"Told us." JD looked away, his eyes shiny with moisture. He had a soft heart and hated for anyone to see his weakness. "Me and Henny-Penny thought a couple extra days of my cooking and the outdoors would be real good for him."

"I agree." She heard the wind crackling the tree limbs by the kitchen window and quickly kissed his cheek. "I'll see you later. If you need me, give me a call."

"Be careful, kiddo."

His tone made her stop and turn around. She looked at Penny, then JD. "Is there something I should know?"

Penny answered for JD. "Just remember, he's leaving tomorrow."

"I love you both, but you worry too much. I promise I'm never going to let myself be hurt again."

CHAPTER NINE

AFTER SHE'D SETTLED Hal and Preston on the river, Nicole dropped Clarence and George off at their favorite spot and was driving back up the path when Max leaned over and kissed her. She'd always boasted that she'd driven the river road so often she could do it with her eyes closed. But this time she did slow down, then brought the Jeep to a stop.

Max smiled, but didn't move away. "I didn't get much sleep last night—or what was left of it."

"I slept like a baby."

"And you're a liar."

"Well," she said grudgingly, "maybe I tossed and turned a little." His eyes were that intense sky-blue shade this morning, mirroring his emotions. She felt the heat of his nearness, and desire bubbled up inside her. The way he kept looking at her was unnerving and unsettling. She shifted in the driver's seat, twisting so she was facing him. "Do you want to go back to the waterfalls and fish, or are you feeling adventurous?"

"Adventurous is putting it mildly. I'm feeling downright desperate for a distraction this morning."

His gaze ran over her in a way that left little doubt he had just stripped her naked. She shivered, laughed, then shifted the Jeep into gear. "You have to stop looking at me like that, Max."

"Why? My imagination's better than nothing at all."

They bumped along in silence for a while, then Nicole turned the Jeep off the road and they started a steep climb. She shifted into four-wheel drive and headed between a thick row of spiny trees. Bushes scraped the sides of the Jeep, and overhanging limbs slapped at the windshield. She made a sharp turn and steered into an opening in the trees. "The river is fed by the melting snows." She opened the door and slid out, remembering to grab the small cooler. "I haven't been up here in a long time. I hope... Come on, New York. I promise the trees don't bite."

He had a morbid fleeting thought that the area, with its isolation and cover, was an ideal place for disposing of a body. Then he snapped out of that train of thought, telling himself it was his guilty conscience bedeviling him.

"Where are you taking me, Montana?" he said as he hurried to catch up with her.

"Just follow me and don't be so suspicious."

The overgrown path led them to a deep cut in the mountain and a narrow cliff ledge. He was wise enough to keep his mouth shut and set each foot in exactly the same spot she'd placed hers. They edged around a boulder that looked as if it had been thrown into the side of the cliff and stuck there.

He was about to suggest they stop so he could catch his breath when Nicole turned and held out her hand. He grasped it firmly, joined her on a ledge, then gasped. The cliff gave way to a flat open space about the size of a tennis court. The small field was thick with lush green grass and a profusion of wildflowers, bringing to mind a Monet painting. In the center was a small crystal-clear pool of water being fed by a stream from the cliff that babbled and splashed softly over the smooth rocks.

Nicole tugged at his hand, and he trailed along. The air was colder, and he glanced around for the source. Then he realized the air was coming from the top of the snowcapped mountain. "How long does the snow stay?"

She didn't answer, merely let go of his hand and sat on the ground by the edge of the water. She took off her boots and socks, then pulled up the legs of her jeans. "Come on, New York. Let's see how strong you are."

He sat down beside her with a laugh, watching as she gritted her teeth, took a breath, then plunged her feet into the water. He flinched and shivered. "Frostbite isn't on my agenda for today."

"Chicken!" She lay back on the grass, folded her arms behind her head and smiled. "I never would have thought it of you. No guts."

"Right, and I'm not a sucker. I don't fall for insults or taunts to my masculinity." He watched as she lifted one very shapely foot out of the water and wiggled it in the air. She was much too smug for her own good. He kept his gaze locked with hers as he yanked off his boots and socks, then rolled up his jeans. Holding his breath, he clenched his teeth and shoved his feet into the water. His breath shot out in a hiss of words. "So you like to tease, do you?" The water was warm and soothing, and after a moment he relaxed and sighed. "I don't understand. We're so close to the snow."

"I don't, either. We had a guest who was a geologist, and I told him about this place. He said something about thermal warming of the rocks, underground hot springs, anomalies and freaks of nature. Nothing he said really explained it. So I just call it Dawson Mountain's gift." She gazed at the sun, then closed her eyes. "It's the most relaxing place in the world, and when I'm upset or worried, I always come here."

"Have you ever been up here during the winter?"

"No one comes up this far on the mountain in the winter." She gave him a look that spoke volumes about what she thought of his knowledge of Montana. "Sometimes we can barely get out the back door of the ranch house. Trying for the lodge up here in the dead of winter could be suicide." She shook her head at the thought.

"But you did come here once, didn't you."

It was more than a guess, and she wondered how he knew her so well. "Once, a long time ago, although it was actually in the fall. The weather here can be crazy. We'd just had our first snowfall, and then the temperature rose, so it felt like summer. As wonderful as it was to see the field covered with ice and the steam rise off the water, I'd never do it again. I got caught in a sudden snowstorm." She didn't tell him that Charlie had warned her of the dangers and the changing weather, but she'd made up her mind. "That was one trip that scared the hell out of me."

"You're a risk taker. You'll probably do it again someday." The realization bothered him, yet at the same time pleased him. He needed to know she was willing to gamble, take chances and keep a steady head in the face of danger.

Nicole opened the small cooler and pulled out the chilled fresh strawberries. "JD usually likes to dip them in Grand Marnier, then roll them in powdered sugar or chocolate.''

"But you like them like this. Me, too.''

She studied the deep red berries before she bit into one. "I would have brought champagne, but I know you're not fond of it.''

As he munched on the strawberry, he filed away the fact that she was observant. The more he tallied Nicole's strengths and compared them to Sandra's, the more convinced he was his plan would work. There were going to be some major hurdles to overcome when they got back to the ranch, but all in all he was pleased with himself.

"You're awfully thoughtful," she said.

"It's the warm water, the sun, the scent of fresh earth and strawberries. It's a turn-on, and I'm trying to ignore the temptation of having you so close to me.''

"Is that all you think about?" She sucked juice from her fingers.

"When I'm with you— Dammit, don't do that.'' He grabbed her hand and began licking her fingertips.

She closed her eyes, letting herself drift on the sensations rippling through her. "You better stop," she said, her voice barely audible, "or you might start something you can't finish.''

He kissed the inside of her wrist, pushed the shirt-sleeve back and began working up her arm to the bend in her elbow. "Think of it as a challenge. We'll have to find a new way to—''

He was interrupted by the sharp sound of gunshots. Before he could comment or question Nicole, she was on her feet. He quickly got up and stood beside her.

"Rifle shots," she said.

He looked grim. "Two."

"Three. Two were fired at the same time. Come on." She jammed her feet into her boots, then took off for the Jeep. "It's not far from here. I think I know where."

"Nicole." He hopped on one foot at a time as he pulled on his boots, then grabbed both his and her socks. "Dammit." She didn't wait, and he raced to catch up with her. At the Jeep, he said, "What the hell do you think you're going to do?" He grasped her shoulder with one hand, then tossed the socks in the open window of the Jeep with the other.

She twisted out of his grip, reached into the back of the Jeep and pulled out her rifle. Double-checking that it was loaded, she tucked it under her arm, grabbed some extra bullets, then picked up her cellular phone and shoved it into her back pocket. She looked at Max. "There's no hunting on the mountain. Everyone knows that. No one is supposed to be this far up but us."

"They're poachers, Nicky, and could be dangerous."

"You're right."

He visibly relaxed.

"Why don't you stay by the Jeep while I check it out?" she said.

"What?"

"I'll take one of the walkie-talkies and let you know what's happening."

She started to walk off. He grabbed her arm and yanked her back. "Wait a damn minute. You're not going alone!"

Nicole sighed. "I'd never have taken you for one of those macho types." She opened the driver's door and pulled a .357 Magnum from the pocket flap. "This is loaded. Do you know how to handle it?"

"Absolutely," he said. He had to hand it to her—she came loaded for bear. The gun in his hand was lethal by anyone's standards. It was also big, heavy and the meanest son of a bitch he'd ever held. He had a feeling Nicole could handle it as easily as he could.

"Don't pout. I'm more than able to take care of myself—and you," she said. "You can come along for window dressing."

"Dressing? I..." There was no use arguing. He couldn't win if he tried, and there were warning bells going off in his head about quarreling with a woman who was carrying a rifle the size of a cannon. So he quickly checked the safety of the gun, tucked it into the back of his waistband, then took off after her.

It didn't take long to see she was half mountain goat and as agile as a cat. She held the rifle in both hands, using it like a balance pole, as she ascended the steep incline, knowing instinctively where to place each foot. He grabbed at anything and everything to pull himself along and keep upright.

When Nicole reached level ground, she turned and waited for Max to join her. She was impressed he'd managed to stay so close behind her. "Where'd you learn to scale a mountain?" she asked.

He was struggling not to breathe hard and give away that his lungs were in dire need of air. "The Navy." It was all he could manage and still sound normal, but he wanted to laugh at her surprised expression and the oxymoron of his statement.

"There's a clearing not too far from here. I'm sure that's where the shots came from." She started to move out, and once again he stopped her by grabbing her arm.

"Don't you think a plan of action would be better than just rushing in?" The look of disgust she gave him made him wish he'd kept his worries to himself.

"I never do anything rashly, New York." Anger made her green eyes flash. Then she sighed. "Look, Max. I know this mountain better than anyone. Just follow me, do as I say and don't get in my way."

He didn't like being considered so inept. And taking orders from Nicole stung. He tamed his misgivings and followed, noticing she was making a special effort to move quietly. Her steps were light and studied, and she was careful not to step on a branch or slip on a moss-slick rock.

At last she stopped and listened. She put a finger to her lips and pointed to her right. Then she cupped her ear, signaling him to listen.

It took him a moment to block out the sounds of the forest and his own hammering heart so he could hear the voices. They were far enough away that he couldn't make out the words, but it sounded like two men. Loaded guns and poachers were a deadly combination.

Nicole eased forward, taking extra precautions to be silent as she closed in on the clearing. The voices became louder and clearer, and she dropped to the ground in a squat. She realized she'd been so sure of Max and his abilities that she never once gave him a thought. He was where she knew he'd be—right behind her and following her lead.

With the barrel of her rifle she parted the branches of the thick bush. "Two of them," she whispered. "They're looking at something on the ground." She didn't want to give Max time to demand a discussion for a plan of action. Before he could react or try to stop her, she stood up, brought the rifle to her shoulder, aimed and fired, putting two quick shots between each man's feet. "Drop your rifles. Now! Or the next shot will be in the kneecaps." She was still and focused until she saw their rifles hit the ground and their hands in the air.

She moved so fast Max didn't have time to do more than gawk. When her rifle went off, he'd nearly lost his breakfast. When he saw where the shots had hit, he felt immensely relieved. He followed her out into the clearing, pulling the gun from his waistband.

"I know you two," Nicole said as she examined their trophy kill. She struggled for control over the hot surge of rage that almost swamped all her reasoning and rational judgment. When she was calm enough to think without wanting to pull the trigger again, she glanced up from the dead gray wolf at her feet. "You're from the Circle C. I've seen you around. In places you shouldn't have been."

Max glanced from one man to the other, noticing the scraggly beards and dirty clothes. They might be unkempt and scruffy, but their clothing, boots and rifles were top of the line.

"I don't know what you're talking about, lady. We've lost a couple of cattle—" he gestured at the wolf "—and thought he was a wild dog."

Nicole lifted her weapon and pointed at the speaker's head. "Get on the ground, both of you. Put your hands behind your head."

"Listen," the younger of the two said. "We made a mistake. But it's only a wolf." When the rifle turned in his direction, he paled, cursed and dropped to the ground like a stone beside his partner.

"Only a wolf," she said between clenched teeth. "You bastard, you just shot a federally protected animal. A minimum of six months in prison and a hefty fine. And don't give me that crap about dead cattle. You're not on the Circle C now. You're on my mountain. You were warned by the sheriff a couple of weeks ago about coming on Dawson property." She was so angry she could have spit nails. With no other outlet for her temper, she tucked her rifle under one arm and childishly kicked dirt in their faces, damning them to hell and back. Once she'd let off a little steam, she pulled the cellular phone from her back pocket.

"Jeff, this is Nicky. I've got a couple of Bedford's men in the clearing near the warm spring. They've killed a gray wolf." She listened to what the sheriff was telling her and watched Max as he kept a close eye on the poachers.

At hearing the name Bedford, Max nearly jumped out of his skin. For a second he could see all his plans being flushed down the tubes, but quickly recovered as he realized no one in Montana knew he and Doug were connected with Bedford.

When Nicole replaced the phone in her pocket, he relaxed. She looked very pleased with herself. "What's happening?" Then against his better judgment, he asked, "Do you know these men? Who's Bedford?"

"You're busted, boys," she said with such relish that Max's serious expression changed to a smile. "The sheriff will be here in about fifteen minutes." She glanced at the beautiful gray wolf and sadly shook her head. "Those two," she told Max, "work for Carl

Bedford. Bedford thinks just because he has money and power he can buy anything. That everything and everyone has a price. He wants the ranch and the mountain. As if twenty thousand acres aren't enough for him.''

"I take it you and Charlie don't want to sell?"

"You take it right. But Bedford plays dirty when he doesn't get his way. There've been a lot of unexplained accidents and mishaps at the ranch lately. I caught these two cutting fences."

"We were fixing them."

"Shut up," Max ordered. "Go on, Nicky."

"I caught them red-handed and called Jeff Hall."

"Ah, the sheriff. How's he going to be here in fifteen minutes?"

"He's flying in on Ash Bartlet's chopper." She shifted the rifle but refused to put it down, even with Max's weapon trained on the men. "Jeff arrested them for cutting the fence, but Bedford and his lawyers had them out in. an hour. Then about three weeks ago, some of our cattle started getting sick. I found tainted feed pellets in the pasture—feed no one at Dawson's had laid out. There were tire marks outside the fence line, and they matched the tires on a truck from Bedford's place. Then there's the couple of cardsharps Bedford imported to get in poker games with Dad and some of his gambling cronies."

She wasn't about to tell Max just how much her father had lost. Just thinking about it sent a sick feeling to the pit of her stomach. She knew her father was worried, though trying to hide it, and she was too scared to ask. "Bedford is a man who never gives up and won't take no for an answer. Jeez, I hate him."

The younger of the poachers cleared his throat and said, "Look, Miss Dawson, Mr. Bedford said—"

"Shut your trap, Andy," the other poacher snarled, effectively stopping the flow of words.

Max grinned at Nicole. "They seem to think this Bedford fellow can get them out of a federal rap. I have news for you boys. U.S. Fish and Wildlife has taken a strong stand against killing federally protected wildlife. They like to make examples of offenders as a deterrent. If I were a betting man—" he winked at Nicole "—I'd lay my money on each of you looking at a year in prison at least. Of course, if you were ordered to do it and you admit it, then maybe a judge would ease up a little. Think about it."

Nicole bit her lip to keep from smiling. He'd planted the seed of freedom, and if they did finger Bedford, maybe the press coverage would be enough to make him back off badgering them. She was about to show Max how much she appreciated his efforts when the sound of a helicopter coming in at treetop level had them all looking to the sky.

When the big white machine with the Bar B brand blazoned on the side like a coat of arms landed, Max whistled in admiration. It spoke volumes of Reed and Ash's family's financial situation. They waited as the blades wound down enough to calm the hurricane they'd whipped up. Then his attention was caught by the bear of a man who squeezed out of the pilot's seat. "Bear" was a good metaphor, he thought. The man even lumbered a little as he came toward them.

There wasn't a pistol on his hip nor a weapon of any kind. He wore no uniform, just jeans and a denim shirt. The only thing that proclaimed the man was the law was the bright silver star pinned to his shirt pocket. Max frowned. This wasn't his idea of a small-town sheriff at all.

As the man drew closer, Max got a better look. There were three long white scars across one side of his face. Only a fool would buck a man wearing such a badge of courage. He had a set to his mouth and a look in the bottomless pit of those dark brown eyes that could make a mountain lion turn tail and run.

Nicole kissed the big man on the cheek and accepted his smothering hug before introducing him to Max.

"You that friend of the guest Charlie's dragging around?" Jeff asked, his gaze steady.

"That's the one," Max said. "Who should I feel sorrier for?"

"I'd say your friend," Jeff replied, walking around the dead wolf, still ignoring the poachers. "Charlie's a wild man, always has been. By the way, your friend can't hold his liquor."

"He's from New York and had three wives. What do you expect?" That earned a laugh from the sheriff.

Jeff stopped beside the men on the ground. "Well, boys, I'd say you stepped in a deep pile of crap this time. There'll be no whitewashing or prettying it up. And your boss's money and fancy lawyers won't be worth all their hot air. Judge Harrison is a dyed-in-the-wool environmentalist and a staunch backer of the gray-wolf reintroduction program."

As he spoke, he pulled out a couple of pairs of handcuffs, then poked the men in their sides with the toe of his boot to make them sit up. "You boys have anything to say for yourselves?" Neither spoke and he shrugged. To add insult to injury, he handed each a pair of cuffs and let them handcuff themselves.

"Now, pick up the wolf. Put it in the back of the chopper, then get in and behave yourselves." He watched while they did as he'd ordered, then picked up their rifles and tucked them under one arm. "What are you doing up here, Nicky?" He eyed Max like a brother eyes his sister's first boyfriend.

Nicole watched them size each other up before she said, "I wanted to show Max the warm spring."

"Did you now?" Jeff's interest sharpened on Max.

"How're Jeri and the children?"

"Jeri's fine, but two of the girls have got chicken pox. They're on the mend, though." He seemed reluctant to leave. "You want me to take Max down with me?"

Max bristled like an irritated porcupine but kept his mouth shut and a smile on his lips. He didn't need an overprotective sheriff nosing around in his and Doug's business, especially if those questions were aimed Bedford's way. The last thing he needed was Carl Bedford telling the sheriff, who was obviously a close friend of the Dawsons', that they were working for him.

Nicole grinned. "No thanks. New York handles himself pretty well."

"For a foreigner?" Jeff added, his interest tweaked.

"Yes." She winked, and she and Max watched as Jeff lumbered back to the chopper and climbed in. The wind settled and the craft was out of sight before they headed back down the mountain.

The descent was much easier than the climb. Max blindly followed Nicole's lead, paying little attention to where he was going. Fears of his own kept racing through his mind. The sheriff was no fool; he hadn't missed the fact that something was going on between

Nicole and him. Friends and do-gooders were the worst possible denominators in an investigation. Of their own volitions and purposes, usually for the good of their friends, they generally stuck their noses in and managed to stir up trouble.

The sheriff had access to information a civilian didn't. It wouldn't take Jeff Hall long to dig up enough to become inquisitive. All Max could think about was getting back to the lodge and putting a call in to Doug. Until this moment he'd been so preoccupied with Nicole that he hadn't given his partner a thought. Now he was worried because Doug hadn't tried to contact him.

Somehow he managed to keep his footing and not fall on his face. When they reached the warm spring, he knew that, even if he suggested they pick up where they left off, it wouldn't be the same. Nicole was as distracted as he was. He was relieved when she dumped the remaining strawberries on the ground for the animals and birds and gathered up the cooler.

"You don't mind if we go back to the lodge, do you? I'd like to tell JD and the others what happened and talk to Dad."

"No, of course not." If he hadn't been concerned about how it would appear, he would have sighed with relief. When they reached the Jeep, he watched as she stored the pistol and rifle. "How badly has this Bedford character been harassing you and your father?"

Nicole started the Jeep, made a tight U-turn through the stand of trees, then headed back the way they'd come. "Seems forever, but I'd say over a year. The last six months have been the worst." She debated confiding in him, but then relaxed. After all, he'd be gone by the next day and she'd never see or hear from him again.

"There have been things I haven't told Dad about." She maneuvered around a boulder as she drove through the crushed grasses and broken bushes.

"What things?"

"Sam Wooten—"

"The principal of the school?" He hoped he got to see old Sam just once more.

"Yes. Sam told me that Bedford wanted to make a generous contribution to the school district for some computers and books."

"But there were strings, right?" Max gave a snort of disgust.

"Aren't there always? Yes. He wanted a voting position on the board. Thankfully the Bartlet school district is made up of locals with a lengthy history and a dislike for outsiders coming in, buying up land, making their taxes soar and trying to take over. Lastly there're the Bartlets—Ash and Shannon Reed Bartlet. Believe me, they are forces to be reckoned with."

"Those are Reed and Ash's parents and the owners of the Bar B and that chopper the sheriff used?"

"Jeff's, also—he's Ash's brother-in-law. There're always rumors circulating about them, stories about their past. One thing is clear from the history of the family—few buck the Bartlets and Jeff Hall."

"Sometimes money has a way of transcending and destroying a close-knit community."

"Oh, the Bartlets have more money in the bank than Midas—they're certainly as wealthy as Bedford, and they're the biggest landowners in Montana. What's more, they're cash rich."

Max mulled over what she'd told him and filed it

away. He realized he and Doug had been lured too quickly into working for Bedford. They should have checked out the local feelings and viewpoints first. He saw the lodge come into sight and was antsy to get to Doug for some answers.

As she pulled to a stop in back of the lodge and they were walking toward the kitchen door, he stopped her. "Tell me. If the Bartlets are so powerful and your families are so close, why don't you just ask them to either give you the teaching position or vote you in?"

She looked as if he'd sprouted horns. "Have it handed to me, you mean? Never! I don't want anything given to me I didn't earn."

Her statement said more about her character than any investigation could. He suddenly felt the weight of what he wanted on his shoulders. How, he wondered as he slid down into the black hole of his own doing, was he going to explain everything and make her understand?

CHAPTER TEN

JD MET THEM at the kitchen door. His inner alarm for detecting trouble had been going off all morning. One look at Nicky's face and he knew he was right. "What's happened?"

Nicole joined Penny, Reed and Ash at the kitchen table while Max took up a position behind her. She sneaked a potato chip from Reed's plate, then quickly filled them in on their encounter with Bedford's men.

Wide-eyed with excitement, Ash asked, "Was my dad with Uncle Jeff?"

The question set off a lively argument between the brothers, and JD and Penny demanded more answers from Nicole. Max felt it was as good a time as any to slip away. He touched Nicole's shoulder and whispered, "I have a couple of things I need to take care of. I'll be back in a little while." She was so wrapped up in relating what had happened that she absently acknowledged Max's departure with a wave of her hand.

But a minute later, she suddenly stopped talking, pushed the chair away and stood. "I've got to go call Charlie and tell him before Jeff does."

As soon as Max reached his bedroom, he locked the door, then picked up his cellular phone from the bedside table. He dialed Doug and was surprised when his partner answered on the second ring. "Why the hell haven't you called me back?" Max demanded.

At the same time Doug said, "Where the hell have you been?"

"I've been right here," Max growled. "Where have you been?"

"Let's don't play this again, Max. I tried to call you all day yesterday, half the night and this morning. You never answered."

Max realized he'd turned the cell phone off and apologized. "It's gotten complicated here."

"Well, if it's complicated there, it's downright chaotic here. Matt, Sandra *was* adopted."

"I'm not surprised. Are you? We kind of figured that's what it had to be." At the moment he was more concerned about filling Doug in on what he'd found out about Bedford. But his partner was wound up tight and wasn't about to let him get a word in. The phone began to crackle and buzz. Doug's voice started sounding like he had the hiccups, then faded out all together. Then, abruptly, it blared back.

"Helen said she never told us because she stopped thinking of Sandra as being adopted when she was a baby. As far as she was concerned, Sandra was her daughter. When I asked her if there was another baby, if Sandra had a sister, a twin, the old gal was positive there wasn't."

The phone hissed in Max's ear. "I thought... Can you hear me, Max?"

"Barely," Max said. "But go on, anyway."

"I thought, for reasons known only to her—you know, maybe guilt—she was lying, and so I kept pressing her. Remind me never to even hint that Helen's a liar. I don't remember ever being so politely told what dark place to put my questions. But I'd piqued her interest. I had to fill her in about Nicole—everything from the same birthdays to the identical birthmarks.

"She was shocked, Max, flabbergasted. Then something really strange happened. Her vehement denials drastically changed and she started asking more questions about Nicole, wanting to know all about her. Then just as fast as they came, her questions dried up. She got real quiet and couldn't get me off the phone fast enough. Said she was going to make a personal visit to the law firm and the attorney who handled the adoption for them. From what little she was willing to tell me, the lawyer was an old personal friend of Helen's husband. She said she'd get back to me, but Max—"

"That's all great, Doug," Max interrupted. "If you hear from her today, let me know what she has to say. Otherwise, I'll be back at the ranch tomorrow. But listen, we've got a problem." He filled him in on what had happened on the mountain and Bedford's men. "I'm working out a plan, but we'll never pull it off if the Dawsons ever find out we're working for Bedford."

He could hear Doug talking, but the volume kept cutting in and out, and he couldn't make out what was being said any longer. "Doug. Doug. We'll be back at the ranch around noon. I'll fill you in then." He turned off the phone and tossed it into his duffel bag. Then he decided to spend some time getting his gear together.

He felt better after talking with Doug and realized it was because he'd dumped some of his guilt on his partner. Nicole was a reasonable woman, he told himself. Back at the ranch, when they were alone and he had time to explain everything calmly and rationally, she'd understand. And he'd have Doug to back him up. He was sure once Nicole learned about Sandra and heard all the facts, she would see the genius and brilliance of his idea. He was sure she'd be more than willing to go along with it.

He was halfway down the stairs, feeling good about everything in general, when he stopped. Somewhere in the house a door slammed, hard enough that it echoed like thunder. He gave a dismissive shrug and continued, crossed the entry and strolled into the kitchen. Silence met his entrance. Conversation ceased, and eight pairs of eyes bored holes in him. For one fleeting moment he thought if looks could kill, he'd be dead meat. "Where's Nicky?"

JD turned his back and refused to answer.

Reed and Ash stared at the tabletop, looking as if they wished they were anywhere but the kitchen.

Penny was the only one to speak up. "She's gone out." When he started toward the door, she stopped him. "Young man, I don't know what your game is or what you've done, but Nicky's very mad at you. Let me give you a little warning for your own good. I'd watch my step, if I were you."

"Mad? At me?"

"Yes, you. She wouldn't say why, just that you were a stinking polecat, and that was the nicest of the things she said."

He headed for the door. "I can't imagine what she's upset about."

"Best you find out—" JD faced him armed with a cleaver "—and make it right. We don't take kindly to Nick gettin' hurt."

Now he was worried. These people were serious. "I don't blame you. I wouldn't, either. But I swear I've done nothing." It took him fifteen minutes to find her. He searched the area where the Jeep was parked. Even the garage and barn. He called her name as he jogged around the side of the house. Then he saw her sitting in a rocking chair.

"I've been looking for you everywhere." He took the porch steps two at a time. "JD has this crazy idea…" He saw the cellular phone gripped tightly in her hand and had a gnawing sick feeling in the pit of his stomach. "Nicky—"

"Tell me something, Max. What possible use would seducing me be for your client, Bedford?"

"Listen, Nicky. I know it looks bad, but…" He was a professional, dammit. He should have known better. Cellular phones were not, by any stretch of the imagination, secure lines. Transmissions were iffy in the city, cutting in and out, and when directional signals happened to get crossed, conversations could be picked up and listened to by anyone with a cellular phone. Why had he thought the mountains would be any different? That was the problem. He *hadn't* thought.

"If the two of you believed a sex scandal would embarrass me or Dad, then let me remind you that I'm a grown woman. If I want to screw around with every guest that comes up here, that's my business." She watched him flinch but pushed on, oblivious to anything other than her need to strike out against the cause of the ache in her heart. "Don't tell me it's not what I think, either. Are you working for Bedford?"

"Yes. But it's really not what you think."

Her smile was knife sharp with disgust. "You're trying to weasel out of it."

"I swear. It's not what—"

She cut off anything else he might have said. "Let's see. I believe it went something like…you're working on a plan. But you'll never pull it off if Dawson ever finds out you and Doug are working for Bedford. That's right, isn't it? That's the way it went, wasn't it?"

"Yes." He started to hunker down in front of her, but she jumped up and moved out of his reach so fast he was almost knocked over. He stood up and took a couple steps back so she wouldn't feel threatened and bolt. "I don't give a damn about Bedford and never was really working for him, not after I saw you." He knew he wasn't making any sense and figured his best out was to come totally clean. Now was as good a time as any to tell her about Sandra.

"You're a real pistol. After you saw me? Don't you dare start spouting some bull about caring for me or about our being instantly attracted to each other. Especially not after today. You saw firsthand what Bedford's men are like and I told you what he'd been doing, and you just stood there like a…like a…

"Dammit to hell, New York, I liked you. For some odd reason I even trusted you. You're nothing but a lackey for an unscrupulous greedy man." She spun around and headed for the door.

Max reached out and grasped her arm, pulling her back a step. "I didn't mean to hurt you. If you'll just stay and listen, I'll try and make some sense out of all this. Nicky, there *was* something between us."

She twisted her arm free. "Yes, indeed. Sex." She punched his chest with her finger to drive home her meaning. "Don't try and put any other name to it. You were handy and I was horny. That's it, pure and simple." She could tell by the intense deepening blue of his eyes that he was furious. "And don't try and fancy it up."

She started to leave and stopped again. "Stay away from me, Max. I don't want to see you or talk to you unless it's business and has something to do with you and your friend being a guest."

He watched her until she'd disappeared through the door, then sat down in the nearest chair. He'd had plenty of dealings with angry women before. But the cold unfeeling delivery that belied the hurt in her eyes tore at his gut. *Well, pal, you've really stuck your foot in it now.* What he needed to do was figure out how to make amends. He rested his head back and thought of Sandra.

THE TREK DOWN the mountain was always faster than the ascent. Nicole told the guests they'd be back at the ranch for lunch and have plenty of time to clean up, get their gear together and make the trip to the airport in Bartlet to catch their connecting flights out.

It was one of those beautiful mornings that come only to the mountains. The sun shone brightly from a sky dotted with cottony clouds. But Nicole wasn't fit to appreciate it. Lack of sleep and anger had taken their toll. She trudged down the path, and with every step, her head pounded like a jackhammer.

She was amazed at how she'd managed to get through the farewell dinner last night with the men. At first all she'd wanted to do was hide and wallow in self-pity. But she wasn't about to give Max the satisfaction of seeing her like that. Instead, she'd laughed and talked, eaten dinner with them and choked down champagne as she made a farewell toast.

Everyone had been in good spirits and no one seemed to notice that neither she nor Max had laughed at the jokes and fish stories that were passed around. They'd never noticed that she only pushed her food around and never once lifted her gaze to the big man sitting across the table.

She put one foot in front of the other, keeping ahead of the others as they strung out in single file behind her. She couldn't face their conversations and laughter. If only she could turn back time and make it stand still, she might have done things differently. Or would she?

Once more she'd been a fool. For some reason, the hurt she was feeling was more painful than when she'd found her ex-husband cheating on her. She should have known better. One thing was sure, she'd learned she was becoming an expert at hiding her feelings.

With every step she tried to figure what it was she'd done wrong. Thinking back, seeing what had happened in the clear light of reason, she came to the stunning realization that she wasn't the one at fault. Not for what happened to her marriage or with Max. Shrugging off the Roger fiasco, she thought of Max. So she was attracted to him from the start. That was human. Being impulsive and rash, even reckless, wasn't wrong. She wasn't the one who'd lied.

Damn him. It was all his fault. He'd brought out the worst in her. Sidestepping a protruding tree root, she continued down the trail. More than anything she wanted the day to be over and Max out of her life.

"Nicole." Hal sprinted to catch up with her and was grateful when she slowed.

"Hi. Are you and the others getting tired? We can take a rest stop anytime."

"No. I wanted to tell you how much I've enjoyed this week. This place..." He seemed at a loss for words. "This place does wonders for a person, doesn't it? I think it's magic."

Nicole shared his smile. How many times had she heard that, maybe not the same words, but the same sentiment? Too many times to remember. The men and women who came to the mountain brought more baggage with them than gear and clothes. But she'd never failed to see a change, as if the mountain and river somehow healed their turmoil.

"I'd also like to apologize for the way I acted on the trip up."

Nicole was touched. Hal was not the type of man to face, much less admit, his faults. She laughed and told him, "All the sweet talk in the world won't get your gun back."

"No, no. I wasn't..." He saw she was teasing and grinned. "This place has been good for me. I'm coming back next year." He gave her a cocky smile. "Maybe you'll take me on then." They both laughed.

Max trailed along at the rear of the line beside Reed and Pepper, the pack mule. He'd kept a close watch on Nicole and hadn't miss Hal making another move on her. What surprised him was hearing their laughter. His scowl gathered into a stormy frown. He started to pick up speed to catch up with them, but was stopped by Reed.

"You know," the boy said, "my dad says when a woman is madder than a wet hen, it's best to let her be, let her feathers settle before you say anything."

Max shook his head ruefully. "Your dad's a smart

man. Do he and your mother argue much?'' he asked absently, for he was only half listening, his attention riveted on the two people in the lead.

Reed nodded, his face as wise as an old sage. "She doesn't let him win many arguments. When he does, he pays for it later. So, he says, it's always best to let women think they're right. Easier on the nerves." He cleared his throat and switched Pepper's reins to his other hand. "JD said you hurt Nicky. Did you?"

"Yes, but I didn't mean to." Max tried to smile, but failed miserably. "I'm going to take your father's advice and let her cool off some before I explain."

"Might be the thing to do. I've seen Nicky lose her temper at a hired hand, some dweeb who was mistreating one of her horses. It was awesome."

There were a million things to think about and figure out about his plan, so Max let the conversation die naturally. The more distance the group put between themselves and the lodge, the less, it seemed, they cared to talk. Maybe they were reliving the past week. He tried not to. The problem was, the harder he tried to think only of the fishing and the men, the more he kept seeing Nicole as she'd walked away from him. It bugged him that he couldn't shake the picture of her on the bed, either. If he didn't know better, he'd think he cared about her. But he didn't, he told himself. She was the means to an end, a closure that was long overdue.

When the ranch house came into sight, he realized what his problem was—guilt. It lay in his stomach like a heavy stone. Suddenly, despite Reed's wise advice, he was driven with the need to try to clear the air between Nicole and himself before they reached the house. *Admit it,* he thought. The cold shoulder she was giving him was getting to him. He picked up his pace, passing Clarence and George, then Preston.

He reached her side just as they stepped onto the driveway that curved around to the front of the house. He waited for Hal to get the hint and fall back before he said, "Nicky. Nicky, would you slow down a second and let me talk to you?"

"Why?" There was a look of determination in his eyes and a set to his jaw that made her think of a dog with a bone. He wasn't going to give up, and she wasn't about to let any of the men overhear them. She stopped to let the group pass by them. "Why?" she said again.

"So I can explain, dammit."

"I think all that's necessary has been said. It's simple. You're a weasel and I'm a fool."

He would have replied, but as he glanced toward the house and the people standing on the porch, the words stuck in his throat. Charlie was holding the door open, motioning the guests through. Doug was talking to an elegantly dressed older woman. Max closed his eyes. He'd wanted to be alone with Nicole and smooth things over before springing the past on her. But Helen Applewhite's presence was going to put a wrench in the works and foul up all his plans.

Nicole sensed a change in Max, saw the way his body straightened and his attention swung from her to the people on the porch. It was a good time, she figured, to escape. She began walking toward the house. As she bounded up the steps, she glanced at her father, then at Max's partner. For a flash she thought it was her imagination that everyone was mimicking Max's watchful demeanor. It was as if they were all waiting and holding their breaths. She looked to the only person she didn't know and stopped.

There was something in the way the woman's hand clutched at her throat that made taking another step forward impossible. Or maybe it was the mesmerizing way the nickel-size diamond on her finger rained fiery sparks over the pale lined face.

The woman was about her father's age, with short silver hair, stylishly cut in a free-moving swept-back fashion. She was wearing a simple white linen dress that screamed money and black-and-white spectator pumps. It was the woman's expression, the initial stunned shock that had quickly melted into a look of deep abiding pain that held her frozen in place.

Nicole saw her lips move but couldn't make out what she'd said. Then the whisper came again. A little stronger this time, and she thought she'd been called Sandra. Suddenly the pain and the light and life went out of the blue eyes. They fluttered closed and the woman went limp, falling sideways and into Doug's arms.

It was the catalyst that got everyone moving at once. Nicole bounded up the remainder of the steps but was outdistanced by her father as he hobbled to the woman's side. Taking a step out of the way, she bumped into Max and would have said something when he placed his hand on her shoulder, but suddenly the woman was awake and talking.

"Her name's Helen Applewhite," Max whispered.

Helen brushed off Doug's and Charlie's hands with a shooing motion and stood, a little unsteady on her feet. She stared at Nicole. "Even after all the pictures Charlie showed me, they couldn't have prepared me for how much alike you are." Helen fought for control. She stood straight and proud, composed her face and her voice. "We're confusing you, aren't we, Sandra...Nicole?" Just saying her daughter's name, seeing her double alive and standing in front of her was too much. Fat tears squeezed from her eyes and rolled down her cheeks. Praying for strength, she said softly, "I'm Helen Applewhite. Your sister's mother."

Now it was Nicole's turn to stare in stunned disbelief. "My sister? Dad, what's she talking about?"

"Nick," Charlie began, then cleared his throat. "Sweetpea, we...I just found out yesterday. Helen arrived and Doug told me the whole sorry tale. They thought I should be the one to tell you— Oh, hell and damnation, this is harder than I thought. Pumpkin, you had a twin sister named Sandra. This brave lady is her mother." Suddenly at a loss for words and unsure what to do, he made a rumbling helpless sound. "Reed and Ash are helping Prissy with the men's lunch, and I think we should go in and have a talk."

"Twin sister?" Nicole allowed Max to guide her into the house. But she quickly pulled away when they reached the living room. If Doug had something to do with what was going on, then in all likelihood Max had his hand in the turmoil, too. "Dad, these two—" she shifted her gaze between Max and Doug "—are working for Bedford."

"Don't worry, Plum-lump. It's all taken care of."

She scowled, suddenly more disturbed by her father's use of the three terms of endearment in such quick succession. And the fact that his eyes wouldn't meet hers. He was in trouble again, and she would have called him on it, but Helen captured her hands, intent on steering her toward the sofa.

"Nicole, please sit down and I'll tell you all you

want to know. Oh, child, if you only knew how just looking at you fills my heart with happiness.''

Nicole glanced at her father for help, but coward that he was, he was backing toward the doorway. ''Dad!''

''I know it all,'' he said, ''and we have a houseful of guests to attend to.'' With that he was gone, closing the door behind him with a sigh of relief.

''I'm sorry.'' She looked at Helen. ''What did you say?'' Max and Doug had made themselves comfortable on overstuffed chairs directly across from her and Helen. Max's smile was meant to reassure her, but it didn't. Nothing was making sense. She'd lost control of the situation, and all she could do was wait it out.

''I guess it's hard to understand,'' Helen said. ''But here, let me show you.'' She picked up a thick photo album, one of several on the coffee table.

Nicole gazed at the heavy book in her lap. She'd always known she was adopted and had been satisfied with her parents' explanation. She'd never been curious about her birth parents. It never crossed her mind that she might have a sibling. Now she was faced with the disturbing idea of having a sister. A *twin* sister. ''Mrs. Applewhite—''

''Helen, please.'' She flipped the cover over. ''That's your sister.''

Nicole felt the stirrings of uncertainty and doubt, and was reluctant to look at the album. She continued staring at Helen as if waiting for a sign. She had a feeling her life was about to change forever. Slowly she dropped her gaze. The face in the color photograph was her face, the same green eyes, her mouth and smile. She had her chin, even down to the faint cleft and ghost of a dimple in her right cheek. Nicole studied the smile again and swallowed hard. It was weird seeing herself and knowing it wasn't.

"Uh, the hair's different. Blonder, longer and straight." It was the only thing she could think of to say.

Helen dabbed at her wet cheeks and managed a chuckle. "She hated her curly hair and worked hard at keeping it that style. The lighter color is thanks to her hairdresser." Without thinking, Helen raised her hand and gently stroked Nicole's short wavy curls.

Nicole sat very still. For a moment she was a child again, and her mother was stroking her hair. It had been her mother's way of getting her to sleep at night. Between the years of childhood and growing up she'd forgotten what it was like to be touched in that special way. She felt the ache of memories as they crowded in on her, the good mixed with the pain of losing her mother when she was just ten.

Abruptly she jerked her head away from Helen's touch, then immediately saw the confusion and hurt in her eyes. "I'm sorry. My mother used to do that to get me to sleep at night."

Helen pressed her lace handkerchief to her lips, struggling to regain her composure. "I did the same with Sandra. Especially when she was sick or just wouldn't settle down."

Nicole smiled. "Did you sing to her, too?"

"Oh, Lord, no. Never. I can't carry a tune in a wet paper bag."

"Neither could Mom, but she sang to me, anyway." Nicole felt better, ready to take another look at her sister.

As she started to turn the page, Helen stopped her by placing her hand over hers. "I had to come. As soon as Doug told me about you, I just couldn't stay away. If I'd known about you, I swear I would have adopted you, too. Never, never would I have allowed sisters, twins, to be separated.''

"Why did it happen? Do you know?"

It was only natural that Nicole would ask. Helen had no choice but to answer. "You have to understand. Harry, my husband, didn't really want a child. He was set in his ways and we traveled a lot with our Thoroughbreds. He knew a child would change our lives, but he loved me and finally agreed only because I wanted a child so badly. Never think that he didn't come to love Sandra, though. He doted on her.

"When Doug called me and told me about you, that you had to be Sandra's twin sister, I made a visit to the lawyer who handled the family business and the adoption. Nicole, I just learned that the firm knew there was a twin sister and so did Harry. But he only wanted one child, and the private agency handling the adoption was willing to split up the two of you. They had a family to place you with. Please understand that Harry was older and used to having his orders followed. He wanted me to be happy, but he was selfish and possessive of my time, and he didn't want his life or routine interrupted. Two babies, even with nannies and nurses, would have taken more of me than he was willing to give. I'm sorry for that. I loved my husband, and even though he's passed on, I don't think I'll ever forgive him for what he did." She leaned back and sighed. "Things might have been so different if you'd been with us."

There was so much pain in Helen's voice that Nicole grasped her hand. "When can I meet this sister of mine?" She shifted her position so she was facing

Helen. There was something very wrong. She'd felt it the minute the question was out of her mouth. She saw the looks Max and Doug traded and wondered what the two men had to do with anything. Then she realized she'd missed an important clue. Max, Doug and Helen were all acquainted.

Helen squeezed Nicole's hand, holding on to it like a lifeline. "Sandra's dead, Nicole, murdered by her husband."

Nicole was taken aback, stunned. More, she was confused. She looked at Max and voiced her troubled thoughts. "What does this have to do with you? With Bedford?"

Max always liked a dramatic exit. He figured it was as good a time as any to leave the women to get acquainted and for Nicole to learn all about her sister from Helen. He motioned for Doug to come with him. "With Bedford? Not a damn thing."

CHAPTER ELEVEN

NICOLE WAS LOST in a bizarre vacuum of time, talking and listening to Helen reminisce about Sandra. A peculiar kind of heaviness settled over the room, making her think her mind was playing tricks on her. It was downright spooky looking at the pictures, examining the life of someone from a tiny baby to a grown woman, when all the time she kept thinking it was herself. There were times, seeing Sandra smiling and relaxed or laughing with friends, that she'd even crazily found herself struggling to remember where she'd met those strangers or when she'd ever been to that particular place.

By the time they'd turned the last page in the last album, she was exhausted. She'd tried several times to find out about her sister's marriage and her death. Every time she broached the subject, Helen promptly deflected her question by talking about some other adventure of Sandra's.

"This is all too much for you, isn't it?" Helen asked finally. She wanted more than anything for Nicole to show some real feeling, but knew the more she talked the less the young woman listened. She patted Nicole's hand and politely lied. "To tell the truth, I'm a little frazzled myself. Seeing you...well, never mind. I think I need some fresh air, then I'm going to my room to lie down." She tried not to be so disappointed as she set the last album she'd been clutching to her chest on the table and stood.

Nicole watched her go, her heart heavy with pity and guilt. She rested her head on the back of the sofa and closed her eyes. What was she expected to feel for someone she'd never seen, met or even known about? She supposed there should have been some psychic or spiritual connection to her sister. Maybe clairvoyance, shared feelings, but there'd been nothing. She'd never felt weird or disoriented. She'd never felt sharp pains without a reason for them, and there were no unexplained dreams of a link to someone else. She'd certainly never had an out-of-body experience.

Nicole laughed. Now she was making herself crazy trying to figure out if there were clues she'd simply overlooked because she didn't recognize them. She sat up, suddenly disgusted and tired of the strain. She didn't need another problem added to her list. Max would soon be gone and that was almost a relief. That left her father to deal with.

Dammit. She sat up, startled by a jolt of unpleasantness when she thought of the way Charlie was acting. She suddenly remembered the guests and jumped to her feet.

WHEN HE AND DOUG left the women in the living room, Max glanced around, realized that the men were in the dining room having lunch and turned toward the front door. "We need to talk, Doug."

They went out onto the porch. Max rested against the railing and shut his eyes. For a second he was back at the lodge and could visualize Nicole that first night with golden moonlight in her hair.

"You look about as worn-out as I am. What happened?'' When Max opened his eyes and stared through him, Doug had a sinking sensation. ''I've seen that look before,'' Doug murmured. ''When you were mooning over Sandra.''

''I wasn't mooning.''

''From the way Nicole was glaring at you, I'd say you were your usual charming self and stepped on toes.''

''That's unkind. She thinks I'm a weasel.''

''You are.''

''Jeez.'' Max pressed his fingers to his eyes. ''She found out we're working for Bedford and won't speak to me now.''

Doug leaned his shoulder against a column, crossed his arms and grinned. Max looked almost as bad as he did, and he had an excuse by the name of Charlie. ''You're supposed to be an expert at keeping secrets. How did she get that out of you? No—don't answer that. I know you better than to think you'd ever use sex.'' Doug was joking, but when Max didn't answer and deliberately shifted his gaze away, he straightened from his lounging position.

''Don't ask,'' Max snapped defensively, ''and I won't have to tell you to shut your mouth.''

For a second Doug was speechless. ''You know a shrink would have a field day with your motives and actions.''

''Leave it be, Doug.''

''Okay, I will for now. But being the weasel you are, what did you end up telling her about Bedford?''

''Nothing. She wouldn't let me explain.''

''Well, you don't have to worry, then. I went to see Bedford yesterday and told him we were off the case.

That I didn't like his business practices and underhand tactics.''

''When did you step up to such high moral ground?''

''Screw you, Max.'' Doug smiled. ''Just because you messed up, don't take it out on me.''

''Sorry. What did Bedford say?'' Max was having trouble paying attention as he debated whether to tell his partner his scheme or wait until he'd made a couple of phone calls to see if what he had in mind was feasible.

''He didn't take kindly to being told no. So, he threw me off his ranch.''

Max's dive into the dark waters of self-pity was saved by curiosity. The fact that Doug had turned down a paying client was a shock. That he'd actually done the job himself was stunning.

''Aren't you even going to ask why I did it?''

''After I swallow my surprise.''

''I like Charlie. He's a rounder. Drinks too much, gambles too much, but he's a straight arrow. An upright kind of guy. He's honest—well, sort of—when it suits him, and he does love the ladies. The thing is, he's like a kid, Max, and I know that's no recommendation for a man his age, but somehow it fits Charlie.

''Hell, he nearly killed me, but I don't believe I've ever laughed so much or had so much fun. And I like this place.''

Max's gaze narrowed on his friend. ''You're not thinking of becoming a cowboy, are you?''

''No. I don't know. Sara would divorce me in a minute if I even dreamed of something so crazy. There's this little place Charlie showed me... Oh, never mind. But we work too hard, Max, take life too seriously."

"I won't disagree with you there."

Doug was amazed at Max's response. He'd expected ridicule, and it threw him off for a moment. "Helen shocked the hell out of me by showing up. I had to fill Charlie in on everything. Even about Bedford and our association—" he chuckled "—and our sudden disassociation. I also told him we'd do everything we could to help him and Nicky with Bedford. That's another problem. Bedford's been playing dirty. Using every means he can to screw Charlie and Nicky out of their land."

"Nicky told me some of it."

Doug perked up. "Ah. See, she likes you enough to tell you about their problems."

"That was before she found out we worked for Bedford."

"Oh. Well, Charlie got taken for a ride. He's in the hole for about thirty thousand dollars he doesn't have. I set the office to checking it out and found that the deal was backed by one of Bedford's blind corporations. Charlie took out a hefty mortgage on the ranch for some bogus deal. Of course the get-rich-quick scheme fell through, Charlie lost thirty grand, and Bedford's just waiting for Charlie to miss a payment, then the bank's going to foreclose and the land will be auctioned off. The bank's in Bedford's pocket, so he's going to start squeezing soon."

Max cursed. He didn't need more problems.

"By the way, Nicky doesn't know her father's in trouble. We thought it best to run it by you first, see if we could come up with a plan before you tell her."

"Kill the messenger, right?" Max took a stab at humor, but the diversion didn't help.

"You want to spit out what's been chewing on you, besides Nicky?"

"I think I've come up with a plan to get Gillman." He thought he heard a noise at the door and motioned for Doug to move farther down the porch.

"Oh, hell, Max. I thought we were through with that. John Gillman's beat the system and us. He's gotten away with murdering Sandra, and there's nothing you can do about it."

Max loved a challenge. "Are you so sure about that now that you've seen Nicole?" He smiled at the way Doug's puzzled expression changed as his meaning dawned on him. For once his partner was speechless. "Come on, man. It's simple. We resurrect Sandra through Nicole."

"You've lost your mind," Doug said, but there was doubt in his voice and he began to pace in front of Max. Suddenly he stopped and swung around to face him. He pushed at his glasses, then ran his fingers through his hair. "Have you got a plan mapped out?"

"Down to dotting the i's and crossing the t's. It'll work, Doug." His friend and partner wasn't above taking on a challenge, either. Max could feel Doug's growing excitement.

"He's a killer," Doug whispered, as if Gillman, thousands of miles away, might overhear him. "Nicky could end up like Sandra."

"No, she won't. Because I'll be with her every minute of every day and night that it takes to pull it off. And you'll be there, as well as a security force from the office. Nicky's Sandra's identical twin, right down to the birthmark. It's simple. We'll trap Gillman with Nicky, but he'll think she's Sandra.''

"You're going to bring Sandra back to life? That's a mighty big leap of the imagination there, pal. Maybe you better tell me everything—in detail."

They both jumped when the screen door was pushed open and Helen Applewhite stepped out. "Maybe you should tell me this plan, too." She smiled when they glanced guiltily at each other—like boys caught looking at a girlie magazine. "I have excellent hearing, and at my age eavesdropping has become a great source of entertainment."

"Where's Nicky?"

"The last I saw, she was coming out of the dining room with Charlie. She seemed pretty determined to get him alone for a talk, and he seemed equally determined to get away. I think she won, because as I passed the stairs, they were heading to her room. I imagine she has a lot of questions."

Doug groaned and shook his head. "Worse than that. I think she's going to put Charlie on the hot seat. He told me Nicky has this radar that tells her when he's in trouble. And he's in big trouble this time."

NICOLE SHUT her bedroom door firmly and turned to face her father. "Okay, Dad. What have you done and what's it going to cost?"

"Sugarplum, I'm crushed." He reached for the knob, but she shoved his hand away and planted herself directly in front of the door. "We have guests, darling, who are getting ready to leave. You know I have to give my farewell speech."

She shook her head. "Dad, please."

Charlie gave a heavy sigh and limped over to the

bed. He sat on the side and wrapped both hands around his cane. "You remember Ben Jessop who was here a month ago? The chemist with Agi-Chem Laboratories?"

Nicole nodded and felt the chill of dread. She hadn't liked Jessop much. "Go on."

"He told me about a new strain of range grass that he and a couple of his egghead agriculture-scientist buddies had developed. It was going to be great stuff. Great for cattle, even wildlife, and able to withstand some pretty cold temperatures. It was supposed to cut down, if not cut out, the cost of winter feed."

She'd picked up on the operative word—*was*. She swallowed her fear and gathered her courage enough to ask, "How much did you lose?"

"I was set up, Pumpkin. Doug found out that Bedford was behind the deal. He's going to help us."

The thought of Max and Doug sent a surge of rage through her. Now was not the time to tell her father that he'd more than likely been taken in again. "Please, Dad. If I don't know how much, I can't help you."

Charlie tapped the cane against his cast and stared at the floor. "Thirty thousand."

For a moment she thought she'd heard wrong, but when her father lifted his head and looked at her, she saw the truth in his eyes. Her knees felt suddenly weak, and she barely made it to the bed before she collapsed beside him. "Oh, Daddy," was all she could say.

"That ain't the worst of it. I took a mortgage out on the ranch to come up with the cash. Doug thinks Bedford's got Penkins at the bank in his hip pocket. They're going to wait till I miss the payment and foreclose, then Bedford can pick up the ranch and mountain at auction.''

"Thirty thousand dollars.'' The amount was astronomical, and it was all she could think about.

"Sounds like a lot, I know.''

"Sounds? It *is* a lot, Dad. More than we have.''

"I think we can put it together, though. There's Missy and Polo. You know how much Shannon Bartlet admires those horses.''

"Missy and Polo are mine, Dad.'' The fact that he was willing to sell her prize quarterhorses, ones she'd raised from foals and trained herself, was enough to make her take a good look at him.

He was pale and drawn and looked older than his years. She checked the urge to wrap her arms around him and tell him they'd figure it out together like they always had. But she doubted if he would hear her. As he continued to talk, she realized that, for the first time in his life, he was really afraid he was going to lose the ranch and maybe the mountain.

"The herd, Nick. If worse comes to worst, Ash will give us a good price for them.''

"It's not enough, Dad.'' He met her eyes again, and the desperation and shame she saw in his face almost broke her heart.

"Close?'' he asked, his voice raspy.

Nicole shook her head. "Maybe. Maybe half.''

Charlie perked up a little. "What if we filed a lawsuit against Bedford for setting me up and cheating me out of the ranch? It could stall him until we come up with the money. Better still, we could win.''

"Stall him *until* we come up with thirty thousand dollars? We can't get blood out of a turnip, Dad. As for a lawsuit, I don't think so. Lawsuits mean lawyers, and we don't have enough for a retainer." She didn't want to tell him that Bedford's attorneys would eat them alive in court.

He took a deep breath, patted Nicole's leg. "We'll think of something. We always do." He used the cane to stand, then looked at his daughter. "I love you, Button. Your mother loved you, too. And I'm sorry we didn't know about your sister. We would have taken her, too, if we had." He started toward the door and paused with his hand on the knob. "Our guests are getting ready to leave. You need to come say your goodbyes."

She stood up. It had all been said. Everything out in the open, and her father would, in all likelihood, try to ignore the fact that their lives were heading down a trail they never thought they'd have to follow. Losing the ranch would break his heart as much as hers. Maybe he was right. Maybe it was best to wait until all the guests were gone. Then they could sit down and try to figure what they were going to do to get out of this disaster.

"Right," she said. "The guests. We'd better go see them off." She followed his slow descent down the stairs and into the dining room.

The men were gathered around having a last drink together. Nicole shoved all her problems, including Max, to the back of her mind, plastered a smile on her face and joined them. In the commotion of saying goodbye and escorting the men out of the house, she had a second to wonder where Max and Doug were. Surely they would be leaving with the rest. Only after Hal, the last guest, passed by and gave her a quick kiss on the cheek, did she spot Max, Doug and Helen Applewhite on the porch. She and her father escorted the men to the two waiting Suburbans and watched as they were driven off by a couple of the cowhands. They gave a last wave when the vehicles were almost at the end of the long driveway.

Max met them at the top of the steps. "Nicky. Charlie. We'd like to talk to you. How about the living room again?"

Nicole had a quick flash of her and Max in bed together and could almost feel his mouth on hers. She forcefully shoved the picture away and followed her father, noticing that his steps had suddenly become lighter. If he thought Max and Doug were going to be their deliverance, he was in for a rude awakening. Mr. New York, better known to her now as the champion of all weasels and Bedford's lackey, was, she had a feeling, about to take them, metaphorically speaking, for a ride. Dammit, but she hated to let him win.

As she sat between her father and Helen on the sofa, she did a brief tally of her assets, wondering how much she could make from her two gold fillings and Roger's diamond engagement ring, which she'd refused to return. But even adding the horses, cattle and some antiques, it wasn't enough to cancel a thirty-thousand-dollar debt. Then the absurdity of her hocking her fillings got the better of her and she smiled.

Max thought it was a good sign and decided to plunge right in. "Nicky, you know now that the reason Doug and I are here is that we were working for Bedford. He wants the mountain and the ranch, and we were to help him get enough background and information on your family so he could mount his campaign.

"The thing is, we only took the case in the first place because we'd been working on Sandra's murder for over eighteen months. We were burned out, and the idea of fly-fishing in Montana, staying at a mountain lodge for a week, was too good to pass up. Can you imagine the shock we had when we saw you? We never had any idea that Sandra had a twin. Then there you were. I was sure you were Sandra, and I knew her better than anyone.''

Max left his seat in front of the fireplace and took the chair next to Doug and across from the others. ''What we couldn't figure out was how or why Sandra would change her name and hide out here. How did she get here? Why didn't she contact her mother? You threw us for a loop, and we were groping around for answers without tipping our hand as to who we were.''

Nicole was surprised how easily she accepted what he was telling her. ''What about Bedford?''

''Bedford's not the issue or the problem other than the dirty game he sucked your father into. I know how much Charlie's into the bank for, and we might be able to help you.''

''Why?'' Nicole asked. ''And who do I have to sleep with or kill?''

''Nick!'' Charlie barked, appalled.

''Money like that doesn't come without strings, Dad. You of all people should know that.'' She'd regretted her rude remark the minute the words were out of her mouth, but she wasn't going to apologize. At some point in his life her father was going to have to stop his games and good times and realize there could be disastrous consequences to being a wheeler-dealer.

''Your daughter's right, Charlie. There *are* strings, but the payoff isn't mine, it's Helen's.'' He decided to tell them up front how much money was involved to sweeten the pot and Nicky's sharp tongue. He knew her well enough to believe she'd do just about anything to keep the ranch and mountain. He was counting on it, in fact, and ready to put his conviction to the ultimate test. "Helen's willing to pay Nicky a hundred thousand dollars for a couple days' work."

The air was knocked out of Nicole's lungs, and before she could regain her breath, her father surprised everyone by speaking out.

"No," Charlie said. "Do you think I don't see where this is heading? I know the entire Sandra story. Helen told me. Any fool can see what you want Nick for."

"So call me a fool, Dad, but I'd like to know what you all seem to know that I don't. And should I remind you what's coming up in a couple of days?" The reminder of the bank note forced Charlie to sit back with a scowl.

"Helen tells me she hasn't told you about Sandra's murder," Max said. He didn't know how she was going to take what he was going to say about her twin, and wanted more than anything to sit next to her and make his revelations less painful.

"First of all, let me tell you about John Gillman, Sandra's husband. He's a highly trained ex-Navy SEAL, an expert with explosives. He's charming and good-looking. Has that rugged, outdoors, male-model type appearance. He's a con man with expensive tastes who preys on women. When he met Sandra, he charmed and seduced her. I imagine she found him totally different from most men in her social set."

Max noticed Helen's distress. "Do you really want to hear this again, Helen?" She bit her lip and nodded, and he continued, "John used sex and his charm to make Sandra fall in love with him—fall hard enough to defy her mother and elope with him. Then the real manipulation and control started. Slowly, meticulously, he began to drive a wedge between Sandra and Helen, but not so big that Helen would cut Sandra off from her money.

"John didn't work and never intended to. He figured Sandra was rich enough to keep him in style. But for all his charm and looks John has a dark side he has trouble controlling. He likes to dabble with drugs and pain. Believe it or not, those idiosyncrasies of his are expensive. At first Sandra kept trying to get him to go out and find a job. After all, she kept busy with her charity work. But work was against John's nature.

"I know from my investigation that he abused Sandra, not physically, but emotionally. He belittled her, undermined her self-confidence and self-esteem. He was unfaithful and flaunted his affairs. I don't know what goes on in the mind of that sort of man, but maybe he thought he could subdue her and control her forever while he drained her funds. But like a dog that's been kicked too much, she finally turned on him and threatened divorce.

"He **was** not about to lose his easy life or his gravy train. I'm certain that's the exact moment John started planning her death. From then to the day she was killed was five months. Everything changed abruptly. John changed. He got a job. He dropped all his women and gave up the recreational drugs. He agreed to go with her to a marriage counselor, and they were each seeing a therapist. Those were his ideas. He started treating Sandra differently and fooled her into believing he was truly sorry. During this period of miraculous changes he and Sandra took out hefty life-insurance policies and had their wills drawn up. John even tried to patch things up with Helen and win her over."

"I never trusted him." Helen couldn't keep quiet any longer. "But what was I to do? Sandra was happy again. She'd gained weight and looked so much better. She was talking about having a baby, and John would smile that charming smile of his." She shivered with loathing. "There had already been...strain between Sandra and me, and I couldn't take the chance of creating more. So I decided not to interfere when she told me John wanted to rekindle their love and take a second honeymoon. They were going to take Sandra's yacht, the *Looking Glass,* on a cruise down to the Florida Keys, then around the Caribbean. I didn't want her to go, and...and it was the last time I saw her alive."

"How did he kill her?" Nicole asked.

"They'd been anchored in the harbor off a small island for two days, fishing and doing the tourist thing—shopping and dining at the local establishments. On the third day, around sunset, while Sandra was cooking dinner, John rowed the dingy to shore to pick up some supplies at the local market. While he was gone, there was an explosion on the *Looking Glass.* The boat disintegrated in a ball of fire. Sandra's body was never recovered. Of course John was part of the search party.

"There was a local inquest. John played the devastated inconsolable husband like the pro he is. It was probably John's testimony, backed up by a couple who'd had dinner on the yacht with them, about Sandra's habit of leaving things cooking on the stove and forgetting about them that made Sandra's death be ruled accidental. There was no evidence to suggest otherwise.

"John flew home, and the first stop was the insurance company to file his claim. Helen's lawyers, through legal maneuvering, have managed to delay his collecting on Sandra's estate. But in a few months John's going to be a very rich man."

Nicole felt an instant loathing for this John Gillman. "What am I supposed to do for a hundred thousand dollars?"

"You resurrect Sandra from the dead."

Charlie struggled to get up, walked to the bookcase, pulled down a couple of books and retrieved a fat cigar from his hiding place. He turned to face the others and defiantly lit it. "It's crazy." He blew out a thick cloud of smoke. "You're asking my girl to put herself in the path of a murderer. I'd rather lose the ranch, the mountain and everything else I own. Not my daughter."

"That's very noble of you, Dad. Now put that nasty thing out or you'll be the one I'll be losing." She watched, amused as he puffed hard and fast until his entire head was almost obscured. "Dad, you know what Doc Shotwell said." Waiting until he'd crushed out the cigar, she said, "Now come back, sit down and let Max finish. He's much too good at lying and scheming for us to pass up hearing his plan."

Max and Doug traded grim looks. It was obvious she wasn't ready to forgive him, so he plunged on. "It's all beautifully simple. No extravagant lies. We let Gillman know that Sandra's alive and living on a privately owned island in the Caribbean. And the island is close enough that an injured woman clinging to a life ring could have been picked up and nursed back to health. It's a believable lie. By the way, a friend of ours owns that island, and he'll be more than willing to let us use it. But this mystery woman can't remember who she is, only that she doesn't want anyone to find her.''

Nicole shook her head. She couldn't believe he'd come up with such a lame story. "Amnesia? Really, Max. That's pathetic. He'd never fall for it. And even if he did, do you think a man who so meticulously planned Sandra's murder is going to confess the minute he sees me?''

"No." He tried to control the urge to join Charlie in the calming effects of smoking a cigar. "But it's going to scare the hell out of him. Then we're going to have to play with him a little. Run the best con game and flimflam on him. Nicky, I mean, Sandra, has been living on the island for over eighteen months. We make him believe that though you lost your memory, you're beginning to get little pieces back. That ought to unnerve him."

Max couldn't sit still any longer. He got up and began to pace. Everyone was looking at him as if he were a madman, even Doug and Helen, and they'd already heard part of his scheme. "The kicker, the thing that's going to drive John Gillman over the edge, is that Sandra is in love with another man—me, or rather, me as Dr. M. Adair Gibson.''

"The owner of the island?" Nicole asked.

"Yes. Adair is a wealthy scientist with two Nobel prizes for his research in cancer. He's also a recluse. Our story is that Adair picked Sandra up and took her to the island. You're in love with each other, and your idyllic existence would have gone on forever, but Sandra—that is, you—doesn't want children because, without knowing who she is, doesn't feel it's right. Adair, however, does want children, and so decides to quietly do some investigating. He learns that Sandra must be the woman presumed killed in the boat. He convinces her to call Helen.

"Helen and I can tell you all you need to know about Sandra, but only for the purpose of instilling those timely memories that are designed to undermine his confidence. Listen, Nicky, John Gillman is a jealous man. He's going to see his wife in love with another man, see him touching her, and it's going to be the catalyst that drives him over the edge."

"And who's going to be there, besides you, to protect me when that happens?" His plan leaked like a sieve, but she figured that was only in the telling. She was sure Max had all the leaks plugged in his mind.

"There are only about five or six permanent residents on the island, and they all work for Adair. We'll give them a paid vacation and replace them with the highly trained security staff from Warner and Hart. We'll totally take over the island.

"Look, there are a thousand details I'll go over with you, but I want you to know that before John arrives on the island we'll have cameras and microphones installed. The entire place, inside and out, will be under surveillance. We'll be watching and listening. There won't be a move or a word said that we won't hear or see. And there will always be someone close at hand. I swear you'll never be alone with him."

Max stopped his pacing and planted himself in front of Nicole. "There's only one hitch. We can't waste time. We need to do this fast, get the wheels rolling. John's about to inherit Sandra's entire estate. After that, for sure he's going to skip the country with the money."

Everyone was staring at her, and Nicole realized that Max was finished for the moment, and they were waiting for her to say something. She caught a glimpse of her father and knew he was being swayed by Max's sincerity.

She stood up. "I need some air and time to think it over."

Max gave her half an hour, then went in search, leaving Helen and Doug to reassure Charlie. He found her sitting on the porch steps, staring out at the pasture. He sat beside her. He wanted nothing more than to explain that what had happened between them had nothing to do with Sandra, his work or anything else. But he had a feeling it wasn't a subject to broach at the moment. Besides, he selfishly didn't want her mind on anything but Sandra and the decision to help them catch Gillman. "I never meant to hurt you, you know."

"No. I don't know, because I don't *know* you, New York. You came up here thinking I'm some dead woman, and you gave no sign that you thought I was anyone other than Nicole Dawson. It makes me think everything you said and did were lies. And they were, because you thought you were dealing with Sandra."

It was a hopeful sign that she'd used her nickname for him. "Not for very long. Listen, at first I was trying to figure out why a woman of Sandra's background would lie about who and what she was. I was so damn shocked and stunned to see Sandra—you—that I couldn't think straight. Then, after talking to you and getting some answers from Reed, I realized you weren't Sandra."

"Well, to be honest," Nicole said, "I'm not sure about this scheme of yours. I'm having trouble believing a man as careful as this Gillman will crack the minute he sees me."

"Maybe not the minute he sees you, but after we get through with him, he'll slip up and we'll have his confession on tape."

Nicole gazed at Max, wondering if it was her imagination or *had* she sensed a change in him, a hardness she hadn't seen before. "You really want this man, don't you?"

If she only knew how much. "Yes. The fact that he murdered your sister is one thing. But he's a cold-blooded killer, Nicky, and if he's done it once, what's to say somewhere down the line he won't do it again—find some gullible rich woman and kill her. I'd think you'd want to stop him, too."

Without answering, she stood and returned to the living room. Max followed her, and as the room fell silent, she looked from one to the other. She liked Helen and pitied her. The woman was a tortured soul. Doug's reasons, she figured, had more to do with the amount of time Warner and Hart had invested in the case. Then there was Max. She wasn't as sure of him as she had been. Granted, he hadn't exactly lied, but she had a bad feeling about how he'd handled everything. If only he'd told her after he'd realized she wasn't Sandra. And there was something strange about him when he talked about Sandra, something she couldn't put her finger on, that struck a nerve.

Lastly there was her father. Maybe the severity of what he'd done and what it was going to take to put it straight would knock some sense into him. She had a hundred thousand dollars' worth of reasons to go along, and none to turn it down. She just wished her acceptance could have been nobler.

"When do we leave for the Caribbean?"

CHAPTER TWELVE

PARADISE.

A good description, Nicole thought, for a place as close to heaven as one could be without dying.

She adjusted the gauzy skirt, tied sarong-style low on her hips, then looked askance at the tiny bikini top and all the exposed skin. She hated to admit it and refused to show it, but she was more than a little self-conscious.

Glancing around, she couldn't see anyone, and it appeared she was alone. But of course she wasn't, not really. There were cameras on her, catching every twitch, every move. Hell, she couldn't even scratch her belly button without at least three people seeing. As daunting as the prospect of being constantly spied on was, it couldn't stop her feeling of enchantment. The view was breathtaking. Emerald green grass melted into a widening expanse of sugar white beach that ended by blending into the clear sapphire blue of one of the island's horseshoe-shaped lagoons.

The sun wasn't fully up yet. The lush tropical ferns and palms that ringed the lagoon were like silent sentinels standing guard behind the white beach, moving only when the light breeze brought them to life, catching the fronds and setting them fluttering. Beneath were the brilliant reds, pinks and yellows of flowers that seemed to pop up everywhere. Nicole inhaled deeply of the moist morning air, heady with the fragrance of jasmine and other scents she couldn't identify.

She stood on the patio for long moments soaking it all in, but the sun and the beach beckoned like an eager lover. When she stepped off the cool thick carpet of grass onto the white sand, she was shocked. It was hotter than she'd anticipated, and the bottoms of her feet were tender. She hopped from one foot to the other, cursing as she made her way to the set of lounge chairs stationed a few feet from the water's edge.

Once she was settled on a lounge, she leaned back and stretched out, pushed her sunglasses to the top of her head, closed her eyes and let the morning sun seep into her bones and take the tension away. But her mind kept turning to events of the past four days.

She'd spent many hours at the ranch being drilled by Helen, Doug and Max about Sandra's life. She couldn't see the logic of knowing how Sandra talked, walked and acted, nor could she see the reason for knowing every detail of her sister's friends, places she liked to go, the foods she liked and disliked. After all, she was supposed to have amnesia and wouldn't remember any of it. But they persisted with the "forewarned is forearmed" bit.

When she'd complained, Max had been the first to remind her that she had a hundred thousand reasons for doing this work. Reluctantly she'd agreed, but didn't appreciate having it thrown in her face every time she balked. And meanwhile, Max and Doug had pulled staff from their New York, Los Angeles and Houston offices and set them in motion. She'd never heard so many orders and was amazed at the meticulous details. Even down to a Houston employee buying a complete tropical wardrobe and making sure all the items had been washed, so they wouldn't appear new before she personally delivered them to the island.

Yesterday had been a surprisingly emotional one. Doug had departed earlier that morning for the Houston office where he was to gather the staff that would accompany them to the Caribbean. Max had deliberately made himself scarce with the excuse that he had phone calls to make and details to take care of, so that she, Helen and Charlie could be alone.

She didn't realize how much she was going to miss Helen until it was time for her to leave. Even though she'd see her again in a couple of days, she couldn't help the empty feeling she had. She'd insisted on driving Helen to the airport herself, so they'd have some time alone. Over the days that had followed their first meeting, Helen hadn't so much as drilled her about Sandra as talked like a mother. It was that sweet unconditional love, the understanding over the emotional upheavals and trials a girl goes through just growing into womanhood, that got to Nicole and made her realize for the first time just how much she missed having a mother.

Now, even thinking about their parting at the airport brought tears to her eyes. The sun caught the tears like crystals and almost blinded her. Nicole sniffed, pulled her sunglasses off her head and slipped them on. She'd become so fond of Helen, so moved by her loss, she'd even offered to help get Gillman without the hundred-thousand-dollar payment. But Helen had insisted they stick to the deal, and Nicole had trembled with relief all the way back to the ranch. She couldn't imagine what had come over her to have made such a crazy offer. It wasn't as if she had any feelings for Sandra.

Agitated, and a little too cooked on her front, she flipped onto her stomach and tried to relax. But thoughts of the journey to this island kept flitting through her mind.

Doug had warned her before they'd left Bartlet, Montana, that Max wasn't a chatty traveling companion. He'd said she might find him a little amusing at times, but overall she shouldn't expect him to be entertaining on the flight. Doug had tried to talk Max into leasing a jet for the trip, she knew, so they could have a direct flight to the island, but Max had refused. He'd warned them all about drawing attention to themselves or making a showy appearance.

But she should have detected that Doug had been warning her about Max. As they hopped across the United States, with numerous airline changes, she'd come to realize Max was a traveling companion from hell. He'd totally drained her of every bit of sympathy, strength and patience.

By the time they arrived at the airport in Dallas, she'd made so many calls to Doug that a Warner and Hart employee met them as they were changing planes. After the employee had recovered from the shock of seeing her—Sandra's twin—he then fought to conceal his amusement upon seeing his boss's condition. He passed Nicole a package of pills, swearing they could calm a mad tiger. The description had just about fit Max's demeanor.

She could laugh about it now, she thought, lying relaxed in the sun without the sound of him moaning and bitching. By the time they reached Miami, Max was so mellow she'd practically had to drag him off the plane. Then with the assistance of two airline attendants, who were more than willing to do anything to get rid of him, they helped her get to the commuter airline that was to fly them to the island of St. Thomas.

She laughed out loud, recalling how she'd pushed Max into Doug's arms the minute they got off the plane, heaved a huge sigh of relief and stomped away. She glanced around the beach now, feeling foolish for her amused outburst. But there was no one around, no one she could *see* that is. She'd stomped off, all right, and was immediately brought back to earth when three men, the size of linebackers, formed a wedge around her.

They were supposed to have been inconspicuous. But the instant her bodyguards moved in on her, they'd drawn the attention of every eye in the airport. That and the fact that Doug was struggling and cursing with a noodle-limp partner who had suddenly been pitched into a fit of the giggles.

Everyone had tried to ignore the other as they'd made their way across the lobby to the waiting van, drawing amused stares every step of the way. Then they were driven to a dock, where they boarded a motor yacht. Thirty minutes later they docked on Dr. M. Adair Gibson's island paradise.

Her thoughts were disturbed by a steady slapping sound. She raised her head and blinked a couple of times, unsure if she was really seeing what was coming toward her or if it was her imagination. Doug was making his way across the sand. It was the sound of his flip-flops that had announced his arrival. As she took in the rest of him, she checked the urge to laugh.

He was dressed in a gaudy tropical-print shirt with a pair of long loose-fitting walking shorts in a garish plaid print. The ensemble was topped off by a white panama hat with a saucer-size red hibiscus stuck in the brim. He noticed her expression, made a dramatic stop, kicked off his thong sandals and pivoted like a high-fashion model on the runway for Chanel. His feet must have transmitted the message of the hot sand, because suddenly he was skipping toward the lounge beside her.

"You look..." She was at a loss for words.

Doug balanced the hat on one knee, pushed at his glasses, then fussed with his hair. "Like a native?"

Nicole sat up. "No. That's not what I had in mind."

"How about an absentminded bumbling assistant to a great scientist?"

"You forgot nerd."

Doug glanced at himself. "You think my staff over-did it a bit?"

"No, not really. You just shocked me. Has New York awakened in his den yet?"

"Are you kidding? He ran me out of the room with his snoring. Jeez, Nick, how many pills did you give him, anyway?"

"I lost count after four—and don't gasp, but at that point I wouldn't have cared if I'd killed him."

Doug laughed. "Well, he's alive, but out for a while longer, I believe."

"What am I supposed to do until then? We never talked much about what was to go on here."

"He has it all worked out," Doug said.

"Oh, I'm sure of that." Her sarcastic tone wasn't lost on Doug. "He just hasn't told me, and that's what worries me."

Doug laughed. "You shouldn't be. Max is the expert at planning con games."

"I take it you've done this sort of thing before?"

"My, yes. Didn't you notice the eagerness and excitement of everyone you met yesterday evening? We have a lot more leniency than any police force, and we can bend the law to meet our means and ends. We haven't lost a case where we've set up a con yet.''

"That's reassuring.''

"Max is a great flimflam man. He did say one thing before he passed out yesterday. You have to be thoroughly familiar with the island, know where and what everything is.''

"Fine. But I'd like to know what to expect and how I'm supposed to act when Gillman shows up. The only thing Max said was that he and I are to appear to be lovers.''

"In good time, Nick. Max will reveal all.''

Nicole was sure Doug knew more than he was letting on, but he seemed reluctant to steal Max's thunder. They sat quietly, enjoying the breeze and the heat of the sun—until she heard the sound of footsteps. Without even looking to see who it was, Doug called Max's name in greeting. She glanced over her shoulder, then wished she hadn't. Unlike Doug's fashion statement, Max had donned only a bathing suit, and though it was the boxer-shorts variety, to her he appeared naked.

Max grunted a greeting, squinted up at the sun, then screwed up his face as if the brightness was painful. He took a long sip from the mug of coffee he was carrying. "Mornin'.''

She thought it strange that she'd been as intimate with him as a woman could be and still hadn't taken the time to study him objectively. He had great legs, and from what her hands had told her an equally great butt. His chest and shoulders were broad, brown from the Montana sun and with just the right amount of dark chest hair without looking like he should be dragging his knuckles on the ground.

She watched him cross in front of her and Doug, then settle in the lounge at her side. She didn't miss the way his eyes ran over her from head to toe, examining her lemon yellow bikini and her bare flesh. His thoughts were the same as hers, she'd have bet her life on it. Seduction and shared passion were hard to forget. Some memories had a way of cropping up at the most unexpected moments. His gaze caught hers and held her eyes captive, his thoughts as visible as if he'd spoken them aloud. She fought the urge to shiver but couldn't control the way her cheeks flamed with heat and color.

He hadn't once talked about what had happened between them, and she'd been reluctant to bring it up. All she knew was that he'd ruined something special, and she was loath to relive the pain his deception had caused. Too, there was this strange feeling she experienced every time he talked about Sandra. At first she thought it was her imagination, but now she wasn't so sure.

Glancing at Doug for guidance, she received only a shrug, then ventured to ask, "How are you feeling?"

"Like I'm coming off a three-day bender. What the hell *were* those pills you forced down me?"

"You'll have to ask David."

"Oh, sure. David from the Houston office." He glared at Doug. "I hope you're picking up his expense to meet us in Dallas."

"Hey, it wasn't me he was delivering medication to."

Max rubbed at the stubble on his cheeks and chin, then tried to finger-comb his hair. "Man, that was the most grueling trip I've ever been on.'' He thought he needed to explain his bad behavior. ''I've flown to Europe, Hawaii, Singapore and Australia. It's not the long flight that gets to me. It's the changing planes, the rushing through airports, the food, the booze, the cheerful attendants and the goddamm takeoffs and landings.'' He waited until they'd stopped laughing and asked, ''How many times did we change planes?''

''Three, no four, by the time we boarded the flight in Miami.''

''Next time, Doug, I don't care what I say, or the cost, we hire a private jet. If I give you any guff, just remind me of this trip.'' He gave Nicole a sidelong glance. She was so sexy in that little yellow thing she was wearing that he valiantly forced himself to keep his eyes locked on her face. But, hell, he was a boob-and-leg man and a sucker for cleavage. His gaze kept drifting downward.

Doug watched the interchange and the effort they were both making to keep from looking at each other. Max, when he wanted to, could charm the pants off the most cynical and experienced women. He was a man used to getting what he wanted, when he wanted. There was something odd going on between him and Nicky. At first, after they'd come back from the lodge, he'd thought, from the hostility, that Max might have seduced her. But he must have been wrong. Max acted as if he was walking on eggshells around her. It was out of character, and Doug was curious as hell to find out what was going on.

Nicole captured the fluttering skirt from the wind and tucked the ends between her knees. She wasn't ready to reveal the rest of herself to Max's gaze. ''Tell me something, now that you've talked me into doing this and I'm here on the island with no means of escape.'' She gazed from one man to the other. ''You knew all about me before you ever showed up in Montana, didn't you? I mean, that story you two cooked up might have convinced my father, but it was a little much for me.''

Max placed his hand over his heart. ''I swear, Nicky, we came to Montana only because of Bedford. We had absolutely no idea about your existence. It was just meant to be. Fate, pure and simple.''

''Kismet,'' Doug put in.

''Karma.'' Max wasn't about to be outdone.

''Chance.''

''Luck,'' Max shot back.

''Godsend.''

''Destiny.'' Max grinned when Doug glared at him.

Determined to have the last word, Doug said, ''Nick's been curious about how to handle Gillman. I told her you'd fill her in on all the details.'' He stood up quickly, secured his hat on his head and strolled down to the water's edge.

''Is he wearing what I think, or am I having a hallucination?'' Max asked.

''He's gone native.''

Max finished his coffee, then secured the mug in the sand beside the lounge. ''The natives have better taste.''

''Why is it, I wonder, that no one wants to tell me what I'm supposed to do now that I'm here?'' Nicole said.

''Maybe because we know you're going to be put in an awkward position. It's not going to be a picnic.'' Max immediately regretted the reference to ''picnic'' even though it brought back some lovely memories.

"Listen, Nicky," he went on, "everyone here is a professional. They know their jobs in this sort of sting operation. Above all, they know their first priority is to keep you safe and unharmed. I won't lie to you. As vigilant as everyone's going to be, as closely as you're going to be watched and the fact that I'm going to be with you every minute...nevertheless, there's always room for human error. One wrong move. One slip and you could be in a dangerous situation."

"Now you tell me," she muttered.

"That's why I have to have your word, no matter what's happened between us, that you'll do what I say."

She took a moment to consider what he'd asked, then nodded. "Fill me in."

"First thing to remember in a con game or a sting operation is to stick as close to the truth as possible. Don't fabricate or you're going to be tripped up. You're going to call yourself Nicole with no last name because you can't remember. The good doctor, M. Adair Gibson—me. By the way, the M. stands for Marion, but you like Max better. I don't think that'll bother Gillman."

She agreed it would be far easier to answer to her own name. "What am I doing here? Why haven't you informed the authorities of my existence? Tell me about Dr. Gibson." Suddenly there seemed so much to know for the scam to work that she began to doubt if she could do it.

"Don't choke on me, sweetheart. The ball's rolling and picking up speed and can't be stopped now." Without thinking, he reached for her hand and held it tightly. "Nicky, most of the explanations are going to be coming from me. Remember, you have amnesia and you can always fall back on that. But one thing has to be convincing—the fact that you're in love with me. You have to be rock solid in your love and devotion to me. It's the key, the one thing that's going to tip Gillman over the edge."

"I don't see it."

"Think about it. Gillman believes he's done the perfect crime and is about to reap the rewards and get his hands on his wife's five-million-dollar estate." Nicky gasped and he nodded. "Yeah, a bundle. Think how he's going to feel when he's told his wife is alive. It's going to shake him up really good. But remember this, too. From all the background and research we've done one thing was clear—Gillman was always possessive and jealous of what was his, and Sandra was his."

"Don't you think he'll suspect a setup?"

"Of course he will. He'll be suspicious and dangerous. But when he sees us together, so obviously in love, sleeping together—"

"Wait! Did I miss something? You kind of ran those last few words together."

"We're supposed to be deeply in love—husband and wife, in our eyes. Don't you think he'd be suspicious if we didn't sleep together?"

"I guess." She was having trouble taking it all in. "So when he arrives, you move in with me? In the master bedroom?"

"No. I've already moved in."

She opened her mouth and closed it, then slowly tugged her hand out from under his. "I don't think so."

"Do you see what you just did? You don't want me to touch you. You're still pissed off at me, and as much as you try not to show it, you stiffen up a little when I'm close. Gillman's a smart man—he'll spot the reaction. In the next couple of days we're going to be close—day and night, twenty-four hours a day. You have to get use to my touching you and being affectionate, even loving. Furthermore, you're going to have to reciprocate the feelings and actions.''

"Did you have this all planned in Montana?"

"Sure."

"I see."

"It's the only way, sweetheart. Dammit, you just made a face at me."

"Think of something besides 'sweetheart,' darling. My ex-husband called me that all the time because, I'm sure, he forgot my name. I hate it.'' She couldn't sit still any longer. Yanking off the skirt, she got up and headed for the water.

Max watched, his breath hanging in his throat and his heart hammering like crazy. The bikini bottom was no more than a tiny triangle of material. Her backside was taut and her legs long and shapely, with strong thighs and rounded calves. Years on horseback had hardened and defined every muscle, without making them overly muscular. He sat staring, drinking in the sight and remembering the strength of those legs wrapped around him. The way she'd squeezed him and held him inside her.

Max shook his head. He figured a dip in the water would be therapeutic. It would cool his desire and clear his head. Though the thought that he might get close enough to feel her wet-slick skin against him made him hasten his steps.

Nicole slipped under the water, letting it inch over her head, savoring the feel. The rivers at home were all fed by melting snow high up in the mountain and always cold. She'd swum in the Pacific, too, and found it cold, dark and unappealing. But the Caribbean water was different, sliding over her body like warm silk. She came up for air, wiped the water from her eyes, then squealed when she came face-to-face with Max.

"Wonderful, isn't it?" she said.

Max glanced around, taking it all in. He'd been to the island before and never noticed until that moment just how beautiful it was. "Yes. But you know, I don't like it half as much as your mountain in Montana."

She treaded water in front of him, laughed and said, "Sure, you can say that now—you've never spent a winter there." Then she started swimming parallel to the shoreline, her strokes long and sure.

Max watched her body slice through the clear blue water and started after her. He had no idea how they ended up in a race. One moment he was simply trying to catch up with her, the next they were beating their bodies against the water, fighting to outdistance the other.

Nicole finally admitted defeat and stopped, her breathing labored. Max swam circles around her, no more tired out than if he'd taken a stroll on the beach. "That's how you keep in shape—you swim?" she asked. She could barely get the words out she was so tired, and she flipped onto her back to float and catch her breath.

"Yes. Hard swimming takes some discipline. The first thing is to make yourself breathe slowly, the next is to remember to let your thigh muscles do all the work. You were exerting most of your power from the knee down, and that can wear you out real fast. Plus, you're not used to the way salt water can weigh you down and sap your strength."

"You're being too kind. You're just stronger, better and more experienced than I am."

"Oh, hell, Nicky. Stop trying to rub my nose in what I did."

"I haven't the foggiest idea what you're talking about." She glanced around and realized how far out in the lagoon they were and started doing a backstroke toward the shallower water. Max followed her.

"Of course you do. Everything you say to me has a sarcastic undertone." He grabbed her arm and pulled her against him, so she could hold on to him while he treaded water. "If I remember correctly, I didn't exactly force myself on you. You were as willing and, yes, eager as I was. You're just mad at me for deceiving you. Okay, I'm profoundly sorry. But how the hell could I tell you I thought you were another woman when I wasn't sure myself? Then when I was sure—well, hell, shoot me—I just didn't want anything to mess up what was happening between us."

She clung to him, her arms wrapped around his neck, her mouth a few inches from his. He was having trouble concentrating. "Nicky, you have to get over your anger. Be mad at me when this is all over with. But right now, for your own good, let's call a truce."

"Fine. Now will you shut up and help me get where I can stand up? I honestly don't think I can swim another stroke."

"See where always trying to be the winner gets you?"

"Tired?"

"That, too, Montana. And sometimes dead."

"Sorry, I'm not as strong a swimmer as I thought. It's a little humiliating."

"Don't let go of me. Relax." He began kicking and

using his strong backstroke. Her body settled on top
of his as he carried her to shallow water. When he was
certain her feet could touch bottom, he stopped, pried
her arms from around his neck and started wading toward shore.

"Okay, New York. You win. I'll do whatever you
want, without the lip service and sarcasm."

He glanced over his shoulder but kept moving.
"Sure, and I believe in fairies. You better move—this
isn't a Montana river. There are things in this water
that just love little white toes."

She went very still, then turned in a complete circle,
searching the surface for a triangle fin. When she realized he was teasing, she didn't so much as jump at
him as dive, catching him around the waist and dunking him.

CHAPTER THIRTEEN

THE PLAYFULNESS and banter of the morning swim set the tone for the rest of the day. Nicole decided she'd allowed the instant attraction she'd felt for Max to overrule her judgment and good sense. It was a bad habit, a flaw, this expecting others to feel the same way about her as she felt about them. She berated herself for her foolishness.

So he hadn't told her he thought she was another woman. And when he realized she wasn't Sandra, why would he have told her in the first place? It was a convoluted excuse, but it worked for her. It was obvious Max was attracted to her, and they had been lovers, but that didn't necessarily mean he had stronger feelings for her. Her problem was that she cared more about him than she wanted to admit even to herself.

As she'd stood in the shallows earlier that morning watching him walk away, she'd made a promise to herself. Why she ever thought there could be anything serious between them, she had no idea. They were miles apart. As opposite as day and night. When all this was over and she returned to Montana, she wasn't going to regret whatever happened between them on the island. She wasn't going to beat her head against a wall the way she had with her ex-husband, trying to figure out what she'd done wrong.

"Are you listening to me, Nicky?"

Max was amused by her faraway expression. He'd been taking her on a tour of the island, the places she needed to be familiar with. She'd changed dramatically after their swim. She seemed more relaxed and open.

He'd been so used to the tough capable Nicky that the delicate beauty who stopped to ooh and aah over some wild profusion of exotic flowers made him laugh.

"It's paradise lost, Max. Only we've found it." They were at the rear of the compound and heading toward the other lagoon and the boat dock. She glanced over her shoulder at the way the green hills rolled toward a thickly forested volcanic mountain that ended in a sheer dropoff into the ocean. "How can Dr. Gibson bear to leave it?"

"He spends most of his time in England working on his cancer research." Max glanced around. "It is beautiful, but I still don't think it compares with your mountain, the river by the lodge or the warm spring by the cliffs."

By speeding up and walking ahead of him, she was able to hide how it thrilled her to hear him compare her home so favorably with this paradise. When she reached the steps leading to the wooden dock, she paused and let him catch up with her. "When will Helen call Gillman?"

The dock looked like a long bony finger bleached gray by the sun and left to stretch out across the water. The deepening colors, from dark turquoise to almost midnight dark, and the fact that the doctor's yacht was tied here, made her realize the lagoon was very deep.

"We figured you'd need at least three days to get

familiar with the island and your role.'' She was so busy taking everything in he took hold of her arm and led her around a coil of rope before she tripped over it. ''Helen's in Miami waiting for me to give her the word to start her part of the sting. She'll call Gillman, tell him the miraculous news that Sandra's alive. Then she'll sadly explain that Sandra has amnesia and doesn't remember who she is.

''Gillman's going to die by seconds and inches until he sees Sandra. I hope the sight of you doesn't give him a heart attack—that would be too damn easy.

''Helen knows she's not to tell Gillman much beyond the fact that Sandra's been found. It's believable that she'd be so excited her details would be sketchy and jumbled. But she'll make sure he knows the location and the name of the island. After the call her jet will fly her to St. Thomas, then one of our men will bring her to the island.''

''What if Gillman doesn't take the bait?'' They were at the end of the dock, and she gazed into the water. ''And if he does, how will you know when he's coming?''

''He'll have to come. How can he not? A couple of things are going to happen very quickly. Never forget, Nicky, that John Gillman is a cunning man. First off, because he's guilty, he's going to suspect everything and everyone—a setup, a trap. When he sees you, everything will fall apart. He'll realize if Sandra's alive it'll cost him her inheritance, and he'll have to pay back the life insurance. Furthermore she's a time bomb waiting to blow up in his face. He'll never know when she might remember and expose him.

''So he'll be ecstatic his wife has no memory of the explosion, no inkling that her carelessness didn't cause it. He'll be thinking of ways to get you away from the island, and somewhere down the line, say in a couple of days or months, another accident will happen.''

Nicole felt a chill. Since they'd arrived on the island, the mere mention of John Gillman gave her the oddest feeling. A sick kind of fluttering in the pit of her stomach. A sensation she couldn't exactly put a name to, other than maybe fear. But that was strange. She'd known all about Sandra's husband back in Montana and hadn't had this feeling, this premonition.

They headed down the dock, and with the hypnotic slapping of their rubber-soled sandals against the wood planks of the dock, Nicole fell into the darkness of her thoughts. She hadn't realized she'd been so lost in her own world or that they'd walked so far until she was startled by Max's tug on her arm to stop. She lifted her gaze to the long sleek lines of the yacht, the gleaming brass and dark wood, and the man pushing the mop as he scrubbed the deck. She recognized him as one the bodyguards who'd met them at the airport. "Is he really working or just keeping an eye on us?"

"Not me. You, Nicky. Even when I'm with you, you're still under their protection."

"That's a comforting thought." And it was. She was just beginning to realize how seriously everybody took his or her job and how really dangerous the situation was.

They came alongside the yacht and Max stopped. "Nicky, this is James Thames—we call him Big Jim. When Gillman gets here, Jim will always be near you. He's an expert in self-defense, weapons and explosives. And don't let his size fool you. Jim moves as quickly and quietly as a cat."

Nicky smiled as the big man made an effort to clean

his massive hand before he shook hers. "I don't think with Jim around I have anything to worry about." The man grinned, and she had a feeling his heart was as big as the rest of him.

As they moved on she asked, "Besides the four I've already met, how many of your people are here?"

"Including Doug, about eight. Three are on St. Thomas watching for Helen and Gillman. One will ferry Helen over as soon as she arrives, and the other two will wait and follow Gillman over." He began to count off the ones on the island. "The ones who attached themselves to you at the airport are Jim, LeRoy and Elvis, your bodyguards. Where you go they go. Paul and John are setting up the outside surveillance, cameras, things like that. And Karen, a woman of many talents, is going to be our cook on this operation, and she's quite good at it. But don't let her culinary talents fool you—her expertise is languages, electronics and handguns.

"Last, there's Andy Harris—you saw her earlier. She's the little elf with all that wild blond hair. Don't be fooled by her fragile looks, either. She's a sound and video expert and has set up all the surveillance on the island. She's also deadly with a knife. I'd like her to give you some lessons."

Nicole would have laughed if he hadn't been so serious. "Max, I've been expertly handling knives since I was twelve. I've always won first place for knife throwing at the county fair. I might teach her a thing or two."

The more he tried to set her at ease the more worried she became. She didn't want him to think she was some silly weak female like her twin sister and forced down her growing fear. "I've had a feeling all morning that we're being watched."

"We are. Indoors and out someone will be monitoring your movements. When Gillman gets here and the sting goes into operation, you'll not only be electronically watched, but there will always be someone near you."

She'd lost count of the number of times he'd reminded her that she'd be guarded, but every time he did, her fear increased. They were almost at the house when she stopped. "You think he's going to try and kill me, don't you?"

So far he'd glossed over the dangers because he wanted to make damn sure she'd come to the island. Now he debated telling her the truth. But he knew from experience that keeping the "bait" in the dark could make Nicole too comfortable with the security. She needed to be on guard all the time, or she could end up dead. "If he believes for one moment that he's walked into a sting operation, he'll go for Sandra first—you as Sandra. If you're dead, anything after that is hearsay and accusations."

"But the video would be proof."

"Not if he screams setup and the authorities stumble just long enough for him to leave the country for good. Nicky, remember Gillman was a Navy SEAL. He's had training in areas most people can't even imagine. He can disappear in a flash. But that won't matter, anyway, because you'll be dead."

"Oh. Thanks a lot." She sat down on one of the patio lounges and stared into the swimming pool's mirror-smooth water.

"Did you think it was going to be so easy? That all you had to do was play a little game, act like someone else and collect a hundred thousand dollars? Nothing in life comes that easy. You of all people should know that.''

''Well, New York, I just didn't think I was going to be this scared.''

''Scared? You? The woman who faces down bears and sends them running with her shouting.''

She grinned and shook her head. ''Reed filled you full of tall tales, did he? I wonder what he wanted from you?''

''To tell him about New York and offer him a place to stay when he kicked the Montana dust off his boots.''

''He wouldn't! You wouldn't!'' She watched his smile grow and his eyes sparkle, then she threw back her head and laughed.

Max scowled. He'd thought it was *his* joke. ''You want to tell me what's so funny?''

''If you'd ever met Reed's mother, Shannon, you'd know. She'd eat you alive if she even thought you encouraged Reed to leave home.''

Max was pleased he'd made her laugh and forget for a moment what she'd gotten herself into. The problem was, he was beginning to have doubts. Although he knew a lot about Gillman from his investigation, there was still too much he *didn't* know. The man remained an unknown element in the game. Max didn't know how Gillman would react when the woman he thought he'd killed stared him in the face, when she smiled, walked and talked.

By ten o'clock Nicole was bone-tired and so frustrated she was almost reduced to tears. Max's trained team had a way of talking over, around and, if they could, under her. When she questioned them, they either ignored her or looked at Max as if he controlled her life.

The only thing that kept her sane were the flashes she kept having from one of her favorite movies, *My Fair Lady*, and the trials of poor Eliza Doolittle. She, Nicole, had no less than five people acting like Henry Higgins. She'd been drilled and lectured. She'd been taught to talk, walk, even laugh softly and shyly like Sandra. Every time she contradicted someone, she was shot down. She tried to tell them that if Sandra had amnesia, she wouldn't remember how she'd acted in the past. That statement created an uproar that made her throw up her hands and escape to her room.

NICOLE SANK DEEPER into the tub of steamy bubbles and closed her eyes. The hot water relaxed her knotted muscles, and the gardenia-scented bubbles soothed her ragged nerves. Suddenly something Max had said made her sit up and self-consciously pull her knees to her chest and wrap her arms around them. He'd told her there were cameras everywhere. She glanced around. Surely they wouldn't—not in the bathroom!

From the other side of the bathroom door, she heard the distinctive sounds of someone moving around. "Max, is that you?"

When he said yes, she told him she needed to speak to him.

He tapped on the door. "Are you decent?"

She looked down, then tightened her arms around her knees and said, "I guess."

He stuck his head in and caught his breath at the sight of her. Her hair was slicked back and soft bubbles clung to her wet shoulders. For a second he had trouble finding his voice, then when he did it was hoarse with a greedy need to strip and join her. But he managed to crush down his desire. The night was going to be bad enough without his imagination going crazy. "What's the matter? Did you forget to get a towel?"

"No. Max, are there cameras in here?"

"The bathroom? Heavens no. Is that why you're sitting here with your body in a knot, trying to cover every inch of flesh?" And such tempting flesh it was. He felt like a sex-starved teenager with an urge to jump her bones. "There are no cameras in any bathrooms and none in our bedroom." He ducked out, closed the door and took a deep breath as it clicked shut, then headed out of the bedroom. The only solution to his problem was a cold shower, and he didn't have time to wait for Nicole to vacate their bathroom.

Nicole sighed, stretched out and relaxed once more. For one heart-stopping moment she wished more than anything that she was back in Montana. She was out of her element here. The closer to the day John Gillman was to arrive the more she wished herself elsewhere. She didn't know how long she stayed in the bath, but when she became aware that the water hadn't just cooled to tepid but was actually cold, she decided it was time to get out.

Max settled the big bath sheet more securely around his hips as he dug through one of the bureau drawers for something to wear to bed. He'd just pulled out a pair of silky blue pajamas and was debating whether to wear both the top and bottoms when the bathroom door was yanked open. Swinging around, he froze with his heart in his throat and a throb in his groin.

"Am I supposed to wear this to bed?" Nicole asked. "If I do, I'll be haunted by the need to find a busy street corner. For God's sake, New York, did someone pick this stuff out at Victoria's Secret?'' She glanced down at the slinky white satin gown that hung on her shoulders by threads; the neckline plunged so low her nipples were barely covered. To make matters worse, the gown hugged her hips and butt to the point that her goose bumps were visible, then flowed outward and pooled on the floor around her feet.

She stood in front of him with her arms spread wide, too disgusted to be self-conscious or observant enough to register the range of expressions that flitted across his face. When she spotted what he was holding, she kicked the satin hem out of her way and went for her goal like a trout after a fly.

She snatched the pajama top from his hand, spun around and went back into the bathroom in a blur of white satin, pink flesh and the scent of gardenias. Max swallowed hard, losing control over all the good intentions he might have harbored. He jammed one leg then the other into the pajamas, yanked them up, gave the drawstring a haphazard tug on his way across the room and dived for the bed.

By the time Nicole emerged again, he was propped against the headboard with the covers neatly folded at his waist and wearing a smoldering look that was meant to melt the willpower of even the most virginal female. He couldn't decide whether Nicole looked sexier in the negligee or the man's pajama top. God knows, her long legs added a definite enticement to the latter. He could feel his blood pressure rise.

Nicole deliberately kept her gaze on her side of the bed. She'd never been particularly modest, but right now she felt more than a little naked, and it didn't help that she knew his eyes followed her every move.

Without a word she flipped the sheet back, got in, adjusted the covers up to her chest, took a deep breath and closed her eyes. "Do you really think it's necessary to go this far to get used to you?"

"If this evening was a demonstration of your performance, we have a lot to work on." That got her attention and she turned to face him. "Every time I just casually put my arm around you or even moved close, you either stiffened up or inched away. The thing is, Montana, I don't think you're even aware of what you're doing. But it has to stop. It's something Gillman will spot immediately."

He slid down under the covers, then rolled to his side in order to be level with her, instead of hovering above her. "It's not like we haven't been in a bed together or I haven't touched you. Are you still angry with me for not coming clean about Sandra and the Bedford mess right from the start?"

"No, not really."

"That doesn't sound very promising." When she looked at him, her short hair still damp and a mass of wavy curls, he knew something was wrong. "What's the matter? Do you want to back out of this?"

"No. Honest. It's just… Dammit, Max. I'm sick and tired of everyone telling me how to act. And I don't care how good your Karen, Paul and Andy are at changing people's personalities—they're bullies. I'm not shy, quiet or reserved, not by any stretch of the imagination. Trying to act like that not only makes me want to puke, but it's so phony I don't think I can pull it off. And the way they want me to talk! It's a joke, Max. I'd have to lip-synch my part to get that Kentucky accent. It's so…so…" She screwed up her face, struggling for the right expression. Nothing really apt came to mind. "It's so Southern," she finally said.

She thumped her pillow in frustration. "And have you seen the way they want me to walk? Karen said I stomp and swing, that I need to glide. Glide! For God's sake, New York, if I was wearing roller skates, I'd glide. Feet don't glide. What's wrong with a little hip-swing, anyway?"

He agreed, there was nothing wrong with the way she walked. In fact he liked the long firm strides and the way her hips moved in rhythm to her steps. He and Doug had been so wrapped up in helping the crew install the rest of the video and audio equipment that he'd left almost everything else to others. If there was ever a revolt about to happen, it was now. Everyone's nerves were strung out from being rushed and the severity of the situation.

"You're much too stressed out over this," he surprised himself by saying.

"First of all," she went on as if he hadn't spoken, "I don't think it's going to matter." She stopped and stared at him. "What did you say?"

"You're stressed out. Relax. You'll do everything right when the time comes. I have faith in you, Montana."

She did relax but was wary of his compliments. "You're not just pulling my leg so you can get into my pants tonight, are you? Because, if you are, I'm here to tell you it's not going to happen."

"It never crossed my mind," he lied, and smiled.

"Sure. That's why your eyeballs fell out when I walked out of the bathroom in that satin getup, then you rushed to get in bed. And I didn't miss that look you gave me, either."

"Well, I can dream. Besides, I bought four dozen condoms at the airport in St. Louis."

She couldn't help laughing and realized she'd relaxed. "So it never crossed your mind, huh?"

As much as he wanted her and knew she could be convinced if he set his mind to it, he decided to give it a rest. He leaned over, picked up a folder off the floor, then made himself more comfortable. "It occurred to Doug and me today that you don't know what John Gillman looks like. Helen certainly didn't keep any pictures of him around, and we didn't think about it—till now. Here's a photograph." He handed her the folder.

It wasn't as if she didn't know what sort of man John Gillman was or what he'd done. But somehow she'd never considered herself personally involved. Granted, it had happened to her twin sister, but she had no more feelings for Sandra than she would have had for any stranger. Still, she couldn't explain the sudden sense of revulsion that filled her now and kept her from opening the folder and looking at the picture right away.

If she didn't look soon, Max was going to start asking questions. Biting a corner of her lip, she opened the folder and forced herself to look at the eight-by-ten glossy. Her response was instantaneous, like the shock of feeling something slimy crawling over her skin.

She was stunned by the ferocity of her reaction. John Gillman was gorgeous. A man with lots of dark hair, dark bedroom eyes, a granite jaw and sexy mouth. She figured the body was as perfect as the face. His character was the antithesis of his looks. On the outside he was beautiful, with the exceptional looks of a male model. On the inside he was revoltingly ugly, cruel and brutal. And, she felt certain, vicious when cornered. She usually reserved such a description for an animal, but somehow it seemed to fit Gillman.

Suddenly, knowing what she was dealing with lessened her apprehensions and strengthened her resolve. She was no longer the odd man out, the outsider who had to be led around and shown how to walk, talk and act. It took remembering who she was and where she was from to clear her head. She'd lived her life with the constant threat of lurking beasts. She'd never learned what compelled a wild animal to kill, not for survival but for the sheer pleasure of it. It happened often at home, and they'd lost livestock, even pets. She'd tracked and killed vicious animals before and was skillful enough to know the rules.

Max was right. Bait needed to be planted. Patience was essential for the long hours of waiting, watching and learning the personality and habits of the enemy. Then the teasing and baiting to bring the beast out in the open for the kill. At that point someone better be a damn good shot. One way or the other, death was a foregone conclusion. The victor was determined by who was the smartest, not necessarily the fastest or the strongest.

She had a thought, like a whispered voice at the back of her mind, and it was warning her to be careful.

"Well!" Max said. "What do you think of Gillman?"

"He's okay." She shivered.

Max was taken aback by her lackluster description. The women he worked with thought John Gillman's looks were better than ice cream. He took the photograph and folder from her hand, pitched it on the floor with the rest of the file, then gently grasped her shoulder and turned her toward him. "What's wrong? Why so pensive?"

Nicole tried to shake off the sudden overwhelming chill that was like being ducked in ice water so cold the quick flash of pain was bone-deep. The strangeness of it made it impossible to articulate. "Someone just walked over my grave, I guess. Sorry." She needed a distraction, managed a smile and shoved all the upsetting feelings away. Here she was, she thought, in bed with a man who'd made her feel like a woman for the first time in two years, and she was being silly and morbidly reflective.

"Did you really buy four dozen condoms? Or was that a joke?"

He was suspicious, leery, but answered both questions. "Yes. And no."

"We could diminish the number a little." She didn't wait for him to comment but reached over, wrapped her arms around his neck and kissed him.

Max gave himself up to the kiss completely. His lips took command, and his tongue plunged into her mouth. Savoring the greedy way she responded to him, he didn't wait for an invitation and got busy with his hands under the pajama top.

Nicole pushed her hand between them. She chuckled against his mouth, pulling just far enough away to whisper, "Why, New York, what have we here?"

"Something that comes up quite often. I've been meaning to talk to you about it. You're going to have to stop wearing that bikini." He was the one to smile now, his lips moving lightly against hers as she gasped when his fingers found her. He loved her boldness, the way her hand and mouth were so sure what would please him. He shuddered, then chuckled when she grasped him firmly. "That will get you in a whole lot of trouble."

"I love trouble. Wait." She tried to pull away, but he wouldn't let her budge an inch and tightened his hold. "Wait! Max, are you sure there're no cameras in here?"

He rolled her onto her back and pressed against her. "I'd kill them and they know it."

The moonlight from the window cast mysterious shadows across his face, and his eyes were dark, narrowed with the intensity of desire. "I'm going to make love to you. Long and slow—and so hot and wild our bones will melt together and all that'll be left is the essence of what we were."

His words were enough to take her breath away. The only answer she could give was a kiss of unbelievable sweetness. Desire burned away any lingering remnants of anxiety over Gillman as the kiss deepened. Nicole hugged him closer, her hands roaming his back and shoulders. Her fingers pressed into the small of his back, pulling him against her hips.

Lips still locked in a passionate kiss, they struggled, making soft groaning noises as they frantically worked at removing their scant clothing. Max ran his lips down the smooth creamy column of her neck, then pulled back a fraction to look at her.

The light of the moon enhanced her beauty and illuminated her skin, reminding him of the luster of pearls. He ran the fingertips of one hand along her shoulder, over her breast, across her stomach, then traced the graceful flare of her hip. His fingers lingered there for a moment, teasing, tantalizing. With butterfly lightness they skidded across her leg and up her inner thigh. There they found their goal in the warm wetness of her womanhood.

She watched the way his gaze devoured her. Light shivers of pleasure ran through her from his touch, and when his fingers found her, she gasped, every muscle in her body attuned to the erotic sensations shooting through her. She touched his face, drawing his attention back, then set her mouth against his and slowly and deeply kissed him.

Max wanted to devour her. Felt that old primitive need to bury himself so deeply in her he'd totally lose himself and forget every woman who'd come before. He wanted to ease the knot of his loneliness, feel it melt away in the heat of their passion.

She gave herself over to sensation, tugged at his shoulders so their bodies were stretched against each other, chest to chest, then she wrapped her legs around his waist and raised her hips in the ultimate invitation. She gave herself over to him, letting him control the rhythm. When his mouth suckled her breast, all thought disappeared, replaced with nothing but pure pleasure. Desire was like a coiled spring pulling tighter and tighter, pounding and throbbing through her, fighting for release. The heat of passion turned to sheer physical force as their bodies, glossy with sweat and anticipation, exploded in a firestorm of emotions.

MAX STRUGGLED to catch his breath as he pulled the covers up over them. She felt good, right somehow, in his arms. It amazed him, but he believed he'd found in her an oasis where he could drink his fill and never get enough. He turned on his side and braced himself on his arm so he could look down at her. She was staring at him, laughter twitching at the corners of her mouth.

"You want to tell me what you find so amusing?" he asked.

"How is it that we start out with great expectations of making love for hours only to have our good intentions shot down in one swoop?"

He smiled, then became serious. "But the night's not over, and this time I don't have to leave your bed." He settled beside her. "Just let me catch my breath."

Max was a man who took his promises seriously. When they lay tangled in each other's arms for the third time that night, their bodies slick with the heat of passion and drowning in their own world of contentment and fulfillment, Nicole was the first to move.

"Max..."

He made a humming sound for an answer, too exhausted to form the words in his mind, much less speak them out loud. As he struggled back from that dark velvety place Nicole had thrust him, he tried to prepare for the usual female postcoital talk.

"Would you make Karen and Andy back off? Tell them I don't need my eyebrows plucked. And while we're at it, they stole my boots and jeans. I want them back."

He should have remembered Nicky was different from any woman he'd ever met.

CHAPTER FOURTEEN

NICOLE FOUND it strange to wake up in the morning with a man beside her. Stranger still that she was wrapped in a tangle of arms and legs with the soft sounds of breathing in her ear and it hadn't bothered her. Her ex-husband didn't like to snuggle or sleep close. He said it made him hot.

She grinned. Obviously it made Max hot, too, but not in the same way as her ex. One of her legs was wedged between his, and she moved it slowly in a back-and-forth motion.

"That's the nicest way to wake a man up I can think of. But unless you're prepared to follow through, I'd advise you to stop." His voice was husky with passion.

"Are you up for it? After last night, that is."

He disengaged his arm from under her head and propped himself up on one elbow. "I'm always up—as you can feel—for anything. Want to take a stab at finding out?"

She ran her fingertips over the stubble on his jaw, then outlined the shape of his mouth. "Am I too wanton for you?"

"I like a woman with a healthy appetite." He grasped her hand and kissed her palm.

"I have that. Roger—" He pressed his fingers against her lips so she couldn't finish.

"I don't want to hear what your ex-husband said or did. He's a fool and probably blamed his own inadequacies and shortcomings on you."

"If you're not careful, Max, you're going to end up a nice guy in my book."

He was tracing a blue vein that ran from her neck down over her breast. "Why, thank you. Nothing would make me happier than for you to like me."

"Oh, I like you all right." She tried to keep from shivering at his touch.

"And trust me," he said as his fingertips circled her nipple.

"Don't push it, New York." They both jumped when someone rapped twice on the door.

"Max, are you awake yet? Max!" Doug called as softly as he could and still be heard.

Max gave Nicole's breast a long hungry look, then threw back the covers, swung off the bed and grabbed his pajama bottoms. He held them up in one hand as he opened the bedroom door a crack with the other. "This better be good, Doug."

"We've got troubles and they're all headed our way."

Max glanced at his wrist, then realized his watch was on the bedside table. "What time is it?"

Doug tried to wedge his face sideways so he could see Nicole. "About eight. You overslept. Ouch." He rubbed his nose where Max had tweaked it.

"What's wrong?"

"The weather's in for a change. Paul tells me there's a disturbance brewing, and we might get some rain and winds. He's going to keep an eye on it."

Max knew damn well Doug's urgency wasn't about the weather. "What's the bad news?"

"Helen just called. She was in Miami, staying close to her plane, waiting for us to give her the green light—"

"*Was* in Miami?" Max snapped. He didn't like the thought of a hitch in his carefully laid plans.

"She was at the airport, in the gift shop getting some magazines, when guess who walked up on her? Talk about bad luck and worse timing."

"Doug, don't tell me it was Gillman."

"It was Gillman."

While Max was cursing under his breath, Nicole joined him. She figured the pajama top was enough cover, but managed to stand just behind Max to block Doug's view.

She didn't care a fig about Gillman or their great sting operation. "Is Helen okay?"

"She's a smart old bird. Thinks fast on her feet." Doug pushed the door open enough to see Nicole, then adjusted his glasses and combed his fingers through his hair. "Good morning," he said. "Don't worry about Helen. She's fine."

"What about Gillman?" Max wanted to know.

"I think Helen must have missed her calling in life. She could have been a great actress." When Max moved as if to grab him, he talked fast. "She acted shocked and very nervous to see him. When he pressed her as to why she was waiting around the airport, she pretended to break down. That must have given Gillman a jolt to see his hard-hearted mother-in-law crying like a baby." He paused.

Max took another step toward him, with Nicole close behind. "Okay, okay," Doug said. "But don't rush me. In a state of ecstatic happiness and hysterical fear, Helen let it slip that Sandra was alive. When

Gillman almost freaked out, she let another tidbit of information slip out about Sandra having no memory. Then she gave him some sketchy details about how and where she was found. At first he didn't believe her, but after more tears she convinced him.

"Of course he was furious and wanted to know, as Sandra's husband, why he wasn't notified first. Helen covered that, also, by playing the protective parent and making it clear she hadn't planned to tell him anything, at least not until she'd seen and talked to her daughter. To back up her statement she gave him another shock and let him see how much she hated him, something, for Sandra's sake, she'd always kept hidden.

"Anyway, after her Oscar-winning performance, Gillman demanded to know where Sandra was. He had to drag the location of the island out of Helen." Doug held up his hands to ward off any further questions. "She's fine. Unnerved by the encounter, and I imagine she's mad as a wet hen. But the crux of the matter is, Gillman took the bait. He demanded a seat on her plane, and when she refused, he took off to hire one of his own."

Doug looked at his watch. "Helen will be arriving in St. Thomas in about an hour. And Gillman's plane isn't far behind, only he's landing on Virgin Gorda."

"Figures."

Nicole glanced sharply at Max. "What do you mean, figures?"

"The murderer has returned to the scene of the crime." Max tried to bank the anger that threatened to boil over. "The bastard's as clever and cautious as ever. Unlike St. Thomas, which is in the United States

Virgin Islands, Virgin Gorda is part of the British Virgin Islands. It's where Sandra's inquest was held."

He could see Nicole still didn't understand. "When he planned Sandra's murder, he made damn sure they weren't in U.S. waters and wouldn't have to face a U.S. court."

"Which side is *this* island on?" Nicole asked.

Doug laughed. "Barely, just barely, U.S. territory."

Max thought it amusing, too. "Can you imagine the shock he got when he found out Sandra was alive? But he's still cautious and conniving. I don't think he'll have time to check that little detail about where the doctor's island is. He'll just automatically assume, if another murder's necessary, he'll have the same British officials to pay off as before. In other words, he's sure he'll walk again."

"Over my dead body," Nicole said, her macabre humor catching both men off guard. Max stared at her in horror. "It was a joke."

"Max doesn't take jokes about Sandra well."

"Goodbye, Doug." Max gave him a friendly nudge, making his partner take a step back so he was in the hall. "Does the team know?" When Doug said they did, he started to shut the door, then paused. "How much time do we have before he arrives?"

"He won't want to talk to anyone or call attention to himself. He'll take his time finding a boat to rent and the directions and coordinates to the island. I'd say he'll be here around noon." Doug found himself staring at the ornately carved door that had been shut in his face.

"Max." Nicole knew why he was suddenly so quiet. "It's all right, New York. I'm as ready as I'll ever be, and you and the others will be there. It's better this way.''

"How's that?'' He shook off the bad vibes he was getting.

"You won't have to tell Karen and Andy they can't pluck my eyebrows. There won't be time for it. But I still want my boots and jeans back—immediately.''

Max wrapped his arm around her shoulders and gave her a shake. "Let's dress and get something to eat.''

She expected him to be moody and distant, knowing that his thoughts were a million miles away. Then when Gillman arrived, she would simply be the means to an end. Bait to trap a murderer. She felt suddenly cold. Max was single-mindedly determined to get Gillman. No, she thought, he was more like a man obsessed with getting justice. It troubled her to realize she hadn't recognized it before.

SHE FELT like a fifth wheel. Everyone was busy discussing their jobs, and she was all but ignored. Actually she felt as if she was just in their way. She strolled out to the patio and found Doug comfortably seated in a lawn chair going through a file. She knew the paperwork involved in operating a company was never ending and couldn't imagine the amount of work needed to keep an outfit like Warner and Hart running smoothly. As she dropped into a chair next to him, he looked up, and she recognized the quick nervous movements of adjusting his glasses and fiddling with his hair.

"Max's checking and double-checking the video and audio equipment,'' she said when he glanced over her shoulder searching for her shadow. "And I sent Big Jim to get something to eat."

Doug tried to close the file, but succeeded only in knocking it off his lap. As she helped him gather up the papers, he said, "You're not supposed to give Jim orders and he's not supposed to take them from you."

"Give it up, Doug. Gillman's not here and I'm with you." She glanced down at the photograph in her hand. "I haven't seen this one." It was a picture of Sandra on horseback. She shuffled through a few more photographs and realized they were all of Sandra. "I thought I'd seen everything in Sandra's file. Where did these come from?"

"Max's file." Doug watched her thumb through the stack. "Most of those were gathered from her friends and the organizations she did charity work for."

"This one's good." She handed him a color photograph of her sister in a very brief bikini, her long hair wet slicked back from her face. Nicole touched her own short curls. "It's amazing how much we look alike here, isn't it?" She sensed more than saw him relax, but she hadn't missed his rather guilty reactions. "I wish Sandra and I... Oh, never mind. How did Max get all these?"

"Part of the investigation." He shoved his glasses up, then gazed out over the swimming pool to the sea. In the process the file slid off his lap again and scattered between them like an oversize deck of cards.

Nicole got down on her knees, bumping heads with Doug as they silently worked at gathering the photographs and typewritten notes. He was lying, she was sure of it, but she couldn't understand why. Out of the blue and for no apparent reason she felt a sinking feeling. One by one she handed Doug the pictures, her sister's face swimming and blurring before her eyes.

Doug was watching her. She could almost sense him holding his breath as she held out the last picture. She couldn't take her eyes off it and was almost paralyzed by one thought. Slowly she lifted her head. Their gazes met and held as she whispered, "He was in love with her, wasn't he?"

"I don't—" He glanced up. "Ah, Max!" He didn't bother to hide his relief. Then he got up off his knees, shoved the file into Max's hands, gave him a look of apology and quickly exited the patio.

Nicole was on her feet, too, and handed Max the last of the pictures she'd gathered. "How long were you and Sandra in love with each other?" She wished she'd walked away, given herself some time to absorb what she knew deep down was the truth. Every fiber in her body screamed for her to leave. She didn't want to hear his answer.

Max set the stack of papers and photographs on the table and began straightening their edges. "Sandra and I were never in love, Montana."

Her ugly suspicions were shattered, and she wanted more than anything to give a huge sigh of relief. But the seeds of doubts and uncertainty had been planted. Her instincts told her to back off. If she pressed the issue further, she might learn more than she wanted to.

"I never met her," Max said.

Turn away, she told herself. *Laugh it off. Keep your mouth shut.* But she couldn't tear her gaze from his hands and the gentleness with which he handled Sandra's pictures. She thought back to their first meeting and the time they'd spent together in Montana. The attraction between them had been instantaneous. She accepted it for what it was—honest emotion. She was sure Max felt the same.

But now she questioned his motives and feelings. Still, she didn't have the heart to voice her questions. She tried to convince herself that she'd let her imagination run away with her good judgment. But she was too honest, even with herself, to play that foolish game. She'd never been one to opt for ambivalence because the truth was harder to take or might be hurtful.

Nicole took a shallow breath and asked, "You never met her. But you were still in love with her, weren't you?"

Max felt as if the floor was being pulled out from under him. Tell a lie or the truth, either one was going to hurt her if she didn't let him explain. He wondered if he *could* explain. "I think I was a little."

"A little? Love triangles and obsessive behavior aren't things I like to be mixed up in, especially when one of the participants of the triangle is dead. I can't compete with someone who's perfect in your eyes."

Max set the file on the table, turned to face Nicole even though he was at a loss as to how to explain his behavior. "I'm not asking you to compete, just be yourself."

Nicole gave the file a hard look. "But who am I to you, Max? Sandra or Nicole?" He didn't have time to give her an answer as they were both hailed by Helen Applewhite, flanked by a taller younger woman that Nicole knew to be another Warner and Hart employee.

They watched as Helen jogged up the patio steps, her short gray hair whipped by the wind that had suddenly kicked up. Her cheeks were flushed, and her face was radiant with excitement. She headed directly for Nicole and hugged her tightly, pleased more than she could say when the embrace was returned. When she broke away, she wouldn't let Nicole go and threaded her arm through hers and faced Max. "John can't be very far behind me, Max." She glanced at Nicole and gave her arm a squeeze. "Are you all right? You're not scared, are you?"

Helen's smile lit up her entire face, almost making her look twenty-five again. "I thought he was going to drop dead when he finally believed me that Sandra was alive. Then when I played like I'd slipped up and revealed that she was suffering from amnesia... Oh, Nicky, he's finally going to pay for taking my baby's life!"

Nicole couldn't have gotten a word in if she'd tried, so she only smiled and waited for Helen's excitement to run down. When she felt a drop of water on her bare shoulder, she glanced up in surprise. The formerly clear blue sky was quickly turning dark as rumbling clouds rolled in above them. They made a dash for the door, barely avoiding a thorough drenching.

Yearning for someone to talk to, Nicole stayed close to Helen. But Max and Doug had other ideas. As soon as the two women were comfortable in the airy living room, most of Max's staff joined him and Doug at the opposite end of the room. Helen grasped Nicole's hand and held it tightly, then turned to her.

"You look relaxed and rested, Nicky," she said. "But I get the feeling you're wound up tight as a drum. Something's bothering you."

Nicole knew Helen hadn't missed the new tension between her and Max. "Maybe I'm just a little scared about all this."

Helen smiled. "I don't think so. It would take more than John Gillman to scare you. Is it Max? Has he hurt you?"

Nicole had only been half listening. Her attention was on the group knotted together about fifteen feet away, talking in low voices. She realized she hadn't answered Helen's question and said, "Max? He doesn't mean anything to me."

Helen released her hand, patted her arm and gave Nicole a kiss on the cheek. "I learned from losing Sandra that it's not wise to waste time being foolish." Like Nicole, she'd kept her attention on the group and didn't appreciate being left out of the discussion. She let go of Nicole's arm and strolled across the room. When she tapped Max on the arm, he jumped. "Nicole, and I are part of this drama. Would you mind filling us in on what's happening?"

Max skirted around Helen and walked over to Nicole. The others followed. "Gillman's landed in Tortola and he's looking for a rental yacht. Tom and Ray are tailing him and will call us as soon as he leaves the island."

Nicole nodded, her heart in her throat. Max noticed her apprehension and sat beside her. "We would have liked a couple more days to get everything under control, but it looks like it's going to go down quicker than we planned. Nicky, are you okay with the change?"

She noticed that none of them offered to call it off. Her gaze shifted to Helen, and for a moment they stared at each other. "Sure. I'm as ready as I'll ever be."

Helen nodded, her excitement resurfacing. "Thank you, Nicole. I promise you won't regret it." She realized everyone was listening but didn't care. "I wish Sandra had been more like you."

"Really? Why?"

"Because you're strong. I see now that Harry and I spoiled Sandra and tried to protect her from anything unpleasant. Because of our money and position, we thought we could shelter her from the hardships and dangers of growing up. We were wrong. She was too trusting, gullible, easily manipulated, and in the end she didn't have the experience, wisdom or the strength to fight Gillman's charm and cunning."

A terrific clap of thunder broke the uneasy silence that had hung over Helen's words. Time was winding down and Nicole felt suddenly nervous. "I'd like to call my father."

"Sorry," Doug said, looking more distressed with each passing moment. "Andy just told me the phones are out. Seems we're getting quite a squall. When the storm passes, we'll be back in contact with Tom and Ray."

They waited in silence until Nicole thought she might scream. Glancing at her watch, she realized she'd been standing at the window watching it rain for more than an hour. The storm had moved on, leaving everything glistening wet and sheened with silver. The sun hadn't made an appearance, but she figured it wouldn't be long. She'd hoped John Gillman would be delayed until the storm was over and the sky had cleared.

It wasn't to be.

Jim and LeRoy alerted them from the docks that a yacht had just entered the harbor. Max said, "Okay, folks. This is it, but before everyone scatters, listen up. Our mark is here. Don't for a moment let your guard

down. John Gillman is a killer, a trained professional
and dangerous. Our objective is to get a confession,
but our number-one priority is to make sure Nicole
doesn't get hurt. If anything goes haywire, it's Nicole
you cover.'' There was a flurry of activity as Max's
staff scrambled to take their places and pass themselves off as servants and employees of Dr. M. Adair
Gibson.

Max joined her at the window. ''He'll be coming
from the docks. You can't see him from here.''

''Well, now I know what he looks like. I don't need
to see him coming.''

Max grasped her shoulders and turned her so she
was facing him, with no distractions. ''Nicky, listen.
Oh, hell, I seem to make a habit of hurting you and
I'm sorry.''

''Do you remember what I said in Montana?''

''You said a lot of things.'' He knew what she was
referring to, but figured if he didn't admit it, she
wouldn't go on. He was wrong.

''It was just sex. You can't hurt someone if they
don't care.''

He gazed deeply into her eyes, searching for a crack
in the wall she'd erected, but all he could see was her
strength and determination. ''Liar,'' he whispered.
''You care. You care more than you want me to see
or you want to face.''

He could feel the heightened sense of excitement in
the room. Gillman was getting closer. It meant he
wasn't going to have the time he needed to make her
understand—but he couldn't leave things the way they
were. Glancing toward the doorway, he said, ''This is
important to me and Doug, also to Helen and everyone
who has worked their butts off on the case for more

than eighteen months. At first it was my job to put a case together against Gillman. Then I got caught up in the investigation.''

"And Sandra? You got caught up in her?''

''Yes. I admit there was something about her that touched some chord, some need in me that I didn't even know was there.''

"You fell in love with a dead woman?''

He could hear voices from the patio. They didn't have much time left. "Yes, but not the way you think.''

"There can only be one way, Max.''

''That's not so.'' The voice coming nearer was deep, demanding and angry. As he dropped his hands from her shoulders, he slipped one arm around her and slowly turned her so she was facing the room. ''We're on.''

John Gillman burst into the living room with Jim and LeRoy behind him. Nicole was the first person he saw, and he stopped, stone still, and stared. The high color in his cheeks rapidly drained away.

After the effect his picture had had on her, she thought she'd be prepared for seeing him in person. She steeled herself against the revulsion, even fear. He was a stunningly handsome man. Her single thought, looking at him, was that his pictures didn't do him justice. Animated, he had a sleek-cat quality and radiated sexuality. No one could have blamed or found fault in her sister for falling for him.

''Sandra?'' John started toward her, his long powerful legs eating up the distance between them. Then he became aware of the man at her side and just as quickly dismissed him. ''Sandra! Baby, can it be true? You're alive?''

CHAPTER FIFTEEN

JOHN GILLMAN was a dangerous man. She'd heard that enough to believe it was true. He was a man who liked to prey on women, play with their minds and destroy their self-esteem. Her sister had suffered.

She could almost feel Sandra's pain, the desolation and the mind-numbing fear.

Nicole was suddenly light-headed, disoriented, yet strangely rock solidly planted where she stood. It was as if she were outside herself, seeing the room and everyone in it as a whole picture and feeling all their mixed emotions bombarding her at once. For a second her breath caught and hung in her throat. Then she told herself she was not her sister, not Sandra Applewhite Gillman. A sense of calm settled over her. Odd, she thought, that she suddenly felt stronger, even serene.

The light in the room seemed to dim, making John Gillman the focal point. There was a fluttering sensation in her stomach, and her heart was racing. It amazed her that after her initial reaction, she felt detached from any emotions concerning him at all. It was the feeling she had when tracking a rogue animal that had taken to senseless slaughter. She was in control.

Several points of interest flashed across her mind at once as Helen filled in the sudden silence. The older woman had managed to put a damper on her hatred and played the mother hen whose chick had just been delivered from the wolf's jaws. She was even gracious enough to endow John with a tight smile of triumph.

Nicole knew by the way Gillman's gaze scanned the room, assessing and calculating, that there was nothing he'd missed. As he moved closer to her, she could see his anger replaced first with doubt, then fear. She almost smiled, thinking that as ironic as it seemed, he was just as scared as she was. In the space of time before he spoke, she had an amazingly rational moment. She'd once had a sister, a twin, a person who was part of her. Because of this man's greed, her twin was dead, and she was never going to know her. If it killed her, Nicole was going to make him pay for his actions.

"Sandra. It can't be."

The curtain had risen and it was time to play her part. Nicole braced herself. "I'm sorry. I know who you are and who I'm supposed to be, but you must understand I don't remember you." The voice she heard was that of a stranger, and it took a moment to realize it was actually her speaking. She'd taken on that mint-julep, sultry-nights tone. The soft slow Southern voice of Sandra. The transformation must have been amusing. She sensed, more than saw, the crackle of electricity in the air as everyone in the room reacted.

John took a couple steps toward her.

She watched him and the way his eyes squinted to pinpoints, taking in every detail, studying her every feature. Still mesmerized by her appearance, he reached out to touch her cheek to assure himself that she wasn't a ghost but flesh and bone.

As hard as she tried not to, Nicole flinched. In doing

so, she instinctively moved closer to Max's protective embrace. There was a flare of fire in John's dark eyes. It was only a flash, a split second, so fast she could only stand stiffly and feel the surge of triumph. His rage meant he believed she was Sandra, and his fear of what she could do to him was complete.

Max's hand tightened on Nicky's shoulder. "This is Nicky."

Gillman was like a man struck dumb. Those same eyes that had devoured Nicole suddenly shifted to his face. As jovial as possible, Max held out his hand. "I'm Dr. Max Gibson."

Gillman nodded but ignored the outstretched hand. His attention returned to Nicole. He seemed to manage to rally his survival instincts and regain his composure. "Sandra had—has—a crescent-shaped mole behind her left ear. May I?"

The final blow of reality, Nicole thought. That last nail hammered home. There could be no doubts. He would think she was Sandra. He moved closer, almost hesitantly, as if he had to screw up the courage to look. She felt the power behind the urbane good looks, smelled the rain and salt water on his clothes. Suddenly she was no longer playing a role. She *was* Sandra, only a stronger Sandra. One who wouldn't stiffen or flinch away. But not so strong she forgot that Gillman was a snake watching his prey, and even Sandra had to playact to escape being eaten alive.

She glanced at Max for guidance, as Sandra would. Her hand trembled, as Sandra's would, as she swept the short curls back and twisted her head sideways. She heard the way Gillman's breath caught and knew he'd been praying she wouldn't have the birthmark. When she dropped her arm and gazed at him, his eyes were wide with disbelief. He staggered back, grabbed the arm of a chair and almost fell into it.

"How? I don't understand."

"Understand what, John?" Helen asked.

Max didn't trust Helen to hold her wrath at bay for long, and he stepped into the sudden simmering silence to keep her from losing her cool. "Come on, darling," he said, guiding Nicole toward the couch. "You've given John the shock of his life. He must have a million questions."

Gillman apparently had recovered from his shock and rage. "You're damn right I have." He glanced around as if wanting everyone to disappear so he could be alone with Sandra. No one moved. "What the hell is my wife doing living here on this island? Why wasn't I informed of her survival and whereabouts until now? What the hell is going on? Why doesn't she know me? I want an explanation. Now."

Max knew Gillman's survival instincts had kicked in big-time. He was scared and angry, and like any cornered animal he was going to lash out. They were in for the performance of their lives.

"Someone better start talking fast or I'm going to call the authorities, then take my wife and leave."

Nicole whimpered, as she knew Sandra would have when forced into a confrontation. She turned her head into Max's shoulder. "I begged you not to do this. He's going to take me away from you." Wedged between Max and Helen, she turned pleading eyes to the older woman, who tried to soothe her fears away. Then she glanced at John again. "Nothing is Maxie's fault." She felt the muscles in Max's arm tighten, his fingers digging into her upper arm, warning her not to

get cute. "You must believe that. I never want to leave
the island—or him."

"This is absurd," Gillman snarled. "Helen, do you
know how Sandra came to be here and why she's still
here?"

Max gave Nicole's arm another warning squeeze.
"It's not hard to understand." He twisted the knife of
jealousy deeper. "You heard her. Nicky doesn't want
to leave the island or me."

"Her name's Sandra. Sandra Gillman."

"That's the rub, Gillman. She's not Sandra Gillman
or Sandra Applewhite, not anymore." He watched as
John's eyes narrowed to slits, and for a moment he
rested his head in his hand. Then he seemed to gather
himself together and glanced up. Max continued, "I
found her drifting in the sea, holding on to a portion
of a boat. My crew and I fished her out and brought
her here."

"She didn't say anything? Tell you who she was?
For God's sake, man—" Gillman's voice rose in anger
"—didn't you take her to the mainland to a doctor?"

"I am a doctor, John." He deliberately used that
detached reserved way he'd seen the real Dr. Gibson
employ to drive his colleagues crazy. "Nicky—"

"Sandra," Gillman snapped back.

"—was very sick. She had cuts, burns, contusions
all over her body. There was severe trauma to the head
and neck area. Added to all that, she was seriously
dehydrated and hallucinating. She was hanging on to
life by a thread. It took months of care to get her back
to health, and I wasn't overly concerned when she
wouldn't talk. When she finally did speak, it was only
when I mentioned I was going to start making inquir-
ies about her identity. To put it in unprofessional

terms, she freaked. From then on every time I mentioned finding out who she was she nearly had a nervous breakdown. I stopped for her own recovery and peace of mind.''

''What about her family's peace of mind, Doc? Did you ever consider us?''

''No,'' Max said bluntly. ''I was worried about Nicky.''

''Sandra.'' John glanced at Helen. ''Don't you have anything to say about this?''

''No. My baby's alive and right now that's all I care about. When Dr. Gibson contacted me, he told me everything.''

''And you weren't going to tell me?'' John growled.

''Not right away. She's my daughter and I'll do—''

''—but my wife!'' John shouted back.

''Actually she's *my* wife,'' Max said, and was pleased to see that flare of fury in John's eyes quickly banked as he struggled to get control of himself.

''What do you mean, your wife? Sandra's married to me.''

''But *Nicky* is married to me.'' Max fought the urge to keep from smiling when he saw John's frustration.

Max was having fun.

Nicole wasn't. While she was being the sweet docile Sandra, she'd had more time to observe John. This was a supremely self-absorbed and selfish man. He wasn't going to take failure with a good-natured shrug. He was like a rumbling volcano just waiting to erupt.

She wondered if Max and his staff realized how strung out John was and decided it was time to put the focus back on her where it could be controlled. ''I was the one to finally decide that we needed to try and find out who I was, where I came from and if I had any family. Max and I want to have children, and there shouldn't be any question as to their legitimacy."

When John let loose a furious gasp and headed toward them, Max quickly rose to meet him. Nicole's breath escaped in a long hiss when John caught himself and stopped.

"I'm sorry." He held up his hands in surrender. "Really, I'm sorry." He turned to Nicole. "You're killing me, baby. To hear you say that, to talk about children when we planned to start a family—that's what the cruise was all about. A second honeymoon. A new beginning. I just can't stand to hear you— Surely you remember."

"I'm sorry, I wish I could. But I have no memory of you or anything that occurred before Max found me. Max is my life." She pressed her fingers to her temples and began to rub them. "I have a headache and need some fresh air."

Helen got quickly to her feet. "That's a good idea. Why don't I come with you and we'll leave the men alone to talk."

As soon as the door shut behind them and they'd moved out of view of the windows, Nicole leaned against the wall and closed her eyes. "I'm exhausted."

"Emotional turmoil will do that."

Nicole looked at Helen with new respect. She'd held up beautifully, through great strength of character and sheer determination. "Sandra was lucky, you know, to have a mother like you. She must have loved you dearly."

Helen ducked her head and blinked away the tears. When she lifted her head, it was to stare at the man they called Big Jim, who'd strolled out onto the patio and begun wiping down the patio furniture. He brought them two chairs and placed them under the canopy.

"Looks like another storm brewing," he said. He picked up a pool net and began cleaning leaves and debris from the surface of the water.

Nicole wanted to ask him how the staff thought it was going, but knew she wasn't supposed to talk to him. She shook her head at Helen in warning, seeing the same desire on her face to get another's opinion and approval. When the patio door opened, they turned. Her fingers tightened on the arm of the chair.

John glanced around, noting the pool man and another worker not too far away raking leaves from the grass. "Helen, I'd like to talk to Sandra." When his mother-in-law hesitated, he said, "Alone, Helen."

Reluctantly Helen started to leave, then paused. "Not too long. It's going to rain again and the wind's turning cooler."

Nicole loosened her grip on the chair and relaxed.

He waited until they were alone. "You've cut your hair." He lifted his hand to touch the soft blond curls.

"Max had to shave my head to stitch me up. I like it this way." She watched as Big Jim moved around so he was closer to her. As LeRoy raked leaves he also moved closer to the patio.

"This can't happen, Sandra." John grasped her hand in his. "I'm your legal husband. I love you. I was devastated when I thought you were dead." He picked up her hand and settled it on his thigh, then covered it with his own. "I wanted to die, too, that day. I think I did. Surely you must remember something about us. Anything. You can't have just cut it all out."

What was left of the afternoon light had been blocked by the rolling clouds. "No." She stared off into the distance, letting the silence stretch between them. When she thought he was on the verge of losing his temper, she said, "I'm sorry for your loss, but I'm just not Sandra. I'm Nicky."

Holding her hand, he began moving it up and down his thigh, and his voice dropped to a soft purr. "You don't remember anything at all?"

A gust of wind caught the leaves and debris Jim had piled beside the pool and sent them swirling in all directions, mostly back onto the water. The heat from John's body was apparent under her hand, as was the rock-solid muscle. She forced herself to keep a tranquil expression and gaze steadily into his eyes. His touch wasn't repugnant, just…bone-deep evil. Now was the time to bait the hook, but she hesitated. Once committed to traveling down the road Max and his staff had drilled into her, there would be no turning back. "Only little things," she said. "They don't mean much."

"What little things?"

There was a rumble of thunder and raindrops began to spatter lightly on the surface of the pool water. John was very still. She managed to slip her hand from under his. "I see bright flashes of light and feel a searing heat on my skin. Max says it could be the fire when the yacht exploded. And sometimes I hear a voice, but I can't make out what's being said."

"Are the memories the same all the time?"

"Yes. No. I started out seeing only the blinding lights. Lately, though…" The wind kicked up again, swirling, circling, picking at leaves on the trees, setting them fluttering. The thick ferns shook as if frightened of what was approaching.

"I see."

She hoped he did see. That was the plan. He was wondering if her memory would return in full. Nicole stared out over the pool to the darkening lagoon beyond. The storm was stealing the sunlight, and the water looked like it was capped with white lace. She turned and stared at John Gillman, barely managing to keep her expression as pleasant as Sandra would have.

"Ever since Max and I decided to find out who I was, we made a promise to each other that no matter what, we would always be together. I love Max with all my heart. I can't be your wife, John. You have to let me go."

He jerked as if stung by a wasp. "I can't do that, Sandra. But I'll tell you what. The doc and I discussed the possibility of my taking you back to the States to find a good psychiatrist who could help you."

"Max didn't agree to that, did he?"

"Oh, he's resisting, but he knows it's the only way. Besides, he really can't stop me, baby." John captured her hand from her lap and gave it a painful squeeze. "You are, after all, my wife. I'll do whatever is necessary to get you back."

She could sense the boiling cauldron of emotions just under the surface, needing only to have the flame lit and he would explode. Now was not the right time. "I can't leave here, John. It's my home."

He gave a snort of disbelief. "You can't be happy here. Not you who loves to keep busy with your charity work, your friends, shopping… Think of the parties, Sandra. Surely this desolate place is more like a prison. And what the hell kind of doctor is Gibson, anyway, that he hides out here with no patients—only locals and his servants?"

"I do cancer research," Max said.

Neither of them had heard him come out of the house, and both jumped. Max was leaning against the side of the house. John rose quickly to his feet and faced him. Max went on, "You're not taking Nicky anywhere, Gillman. Not unless she wants to leave." He couldn't risk getting into a staring match with John, couldn't chance the other man's seeing anything but an insignificant doctor who'd taken what was his. Deliberately he was the first to look away. John's victorious triumph was quickly squashed as Nicole got up and stumbled into Max's arms.

John stared from one to the other. "I don't think the authorities will agree to Sandra's staying here once they find out she's alive. You'll have to take her back to Virgin Gorda for a hearing and answer a lot of questions. I'll make my claim there. My wife needs medical care from a psychiatrist. The law is on my side." He swung around, intent on heading toward the dock and the yacht he'd rented.

Things had gotten out of hand, Nicole thought. Max wasn't supposed to butt in when they were talking. Dammit, it wasn't as if she and John were alone on the patio. Her bodyguards were within reach. There were cameras watching and listening. The plan was that she was to have more time to set the hook, to lead him on. She could have killed Max. Instead, she stomped on his foot to let him know she didn't appreciate his interference.

The wind played with her hair, tickling the back of her neck and sending a shiver up her spine. Or at least she persuaded herself that was the reason for the chill.

She'd already gone through so much and hadn't come all this way, accepted the money and endured being made into someone she wasn't, just to let John leave. She'd be dammed if she'd let that happen, and so she called his name, putting as much confusion into her voice as she could.

John stopped and she asked, "Was I a good cook?" She was ad-libbing, veering from the script, but she struck home nonetheless. Max covered his shock with a laugh, as if it was a private joke between them. But John didn't seem to find anything amusing in her question.

He slowly returned to the patio. Just as he ducked under the canopy, the black clouds opened up. Fat raindrops hit the ground and her bare legs and feet with such force they hurt. Nicole laughed and made a dash for the door. Max was right behind her, followed by John. Then Max yelled for Doug, and together they struggled to close the shutter doors to the patio.

As Nicole flicked the water from her shoulders, shook it out of her hair and wiped her feet on the area rug, John moved in close. Too close. She made herself concentrate on drying her feet.

"Why did you ask about cooking?"

"I don't like to cook. I'm hopeless around a stove. While I'm cooking, I have a habit of walking out of the kitchen and forgetting what I'm doing." She giggled. "I know it's silly, and it's something Max teases me about." She didn't know whether it was the question that caused the change in John or the giggle. She sensed that Helen had reacted with a jerk when she heard it. Whichever it was, John's reaction had been quickly disguised with a condescending smile.

"You used to do the same at home."

There was a roughness in his tone, and she could tell by the way his shapely mouth pulled in at the corners that he was controlling some violent emotion.

"Maybe I'm remembering the past."

"What?"

She decided she'd dangled the carrot in front of him enough for the time being, and now she backed off, relieved when Max's arm slipped around her shoulders. She rewarded him with a loving indulgent smile, the sort she might bestow on a pesky child. "See, darling? All those knocks on the head that scrambled my brains didn't leave me totally crazy. I've done it before. Do you think I might be remembering things?"

An earsplitting crack of thunder, loud enough to drown out Max's response, made them all look toward the ceiling and wait for silence to prevail. Max was the first to speak. "Doug tells me there's a small-craft warning out until after sunset, John. I don't know about you, but I'm lousy at night navigation. Maybe you should stay here for the night."

"I never planned to leave," John said. "Not without Sandra."

NICOLE CLIMBED into bed with a heartfelt sigh of relief. She rested her head against the soft pillow and closed her eyes. "What a night," she mumbled, too tired to raise her voice above a whisper.

"Did the hot bath help your headache?"

She turned her head. "Some. I didn't think I was going to be able to eat at the same table with him, though."

"He is single-minded, isn't he?"

"He never gives up. I wonder how many times and

ways I heard that I was his wife and needed a specialist, some expert medical care.''

"Enough to give me a headache, too." Max turned on his side and propped himself up on one elbow. "Where did the Kentucky drawl come from? I thought you couldn't and wouldn't do it."

She wiggled her toes and watched the covers move, trying to make up her mind whether to tell him. "It just came to me. Max, do you believe in ghosts? Or maybe not ghosts, but some kind of spiritual presence?"

"No. Maybe."

She chuckled. "Well, which is it?"

"I don't know. Why? Do you think Sandra's haunting us?"

"No, no. I can't explain it. But there's something. Like the accent thing. I couldn't get it right before, no matter how hard I tried. Then suddenly I'm talking like I was Kentucky-born-and-bred. Oh, hell, this is silly. I don't believe in ghosts, but maybe Sandra's...I don't know, watching over me."

Max nodded. "Like a guardian angel?"

She folded and creased the sheet neatly across her chest waiting for Max's scornful snicker, but it never came. She twisted on her side to face him. "Yes. Do you think that could be?"

"Just because you never met her or knew of her, she was your sister. Stranger things have happened between twins. I wouldn't rule anything out."

"I'm not scared of him, you know. It's sort of like he's no real threat to me. That I'm safe and he can't hurt me."

"That's a big mistake. Don't ever let your guard down around him."

"No, you don't understand. I *know* he can't hurt me. How do I know? I don't know, but I do."

"Dammit, Nicky, he's a dangerous animal!"

She agreed. "And I'm used to dealing with dangerous animals, the four-legged variety."

What Nicole was saying worried Max deeply. She seemed to believe she could handle Gillman single-handedly. "He's not a rogue bear you're tracking. He's not a crazed mountain lion or a cornered wolf. He's much more cunning and lethal."

"I'll be careful."

"Of course you will, because you won't be alone with him." He would have said more, reinforced his position, but the walkie-talkie on the bedside table buzzed. "Yeah, what's up?" he said, and turned up the volume so Nicole could hear.

Doug laughed. "You two should see him. He's sitting on the side of the bed staring at his feet. He's been like that for about thirty minutes. Just sitting and staring. You think he's trying to hatch a plan?"

"More than likely. Keep me informed." Max pressed the Off button and pitched the instrument between them.

"You have his bedroom bugged?"

Max laughed. "Yup. With hidden cameras, too. We know every move he makes, every expression."

"But not what he's thinking and planning?"

"What can he do with his every move monitored?"

Nicole thought back to the look he'd given her and Max when it was bedtime and obvious they were going to sleep in the same bed. He hadn't been able to mask the jealous rage but did manage to keep a hold on his temper, excused himself and went to the room they'd offered him. "He wasn't thrilled with our sleeping arrangements."

Max grinned. "That was the idea. It's got to be eating him up, thinking of us in bed together, imagining what we're doing together. He has all night to think, and he's going to start coming unglued. Mark my words, tomorrow we're going to see a dramatic change in Gillman." Max's mood became thoughtful. "I don't like it."

"What? That he's not punching holes in the wall?"

"No," he said, and touched her cheek. "I don't like it that we're not fulfilling his wildest fantasies."

She knocked his hand away. "Let's not get into that now."

"When, Nicky? After this is all over? I don't think so."

"Listen, New York, I've told you it's—" He placed his finger over her lips.

"Don't say it." He gave a short wayward curl a tug, and when she didn't move away or react, he said, "I want to tell you about Sandra."

Nicole shrugged indifferently. She told herself she didn't want to hear about a man in love with a dead woman. It was sick. But Max seemed determined to tell her, and in a sense she was his hostage.

"To set a trap for Gillman, I had to get into Sandra's head, think her thoughts and feel her pain and humiliation at his hands. I learned all that by talking and interviewing her family and friends, reading her letters and her diaries. It's an old investigator's trick if you want to snare the killer. I came to know your sister better than I knew myself. Sandra was everything I thought I wanted in a woman. She was sweet-natured, shy, loved children and animals. She had an inner softness, a goodness in her that reached out to people and those she loved.

"The more I researched and investigated her life, the deeper I sank into a fantasy world of my own making. Sure, I fell in love with her. She didn't talk back, didn't argue. And I was like a man possessed, in my need to get Gillman. She was too good a person, too sweet to be forced to endure what he put her through, and just because she was rich, he killed her. Long before that, he used and destroyed her gentleness and kindness. He took her from those who loved and cared for her, took her to a strange place and cold-bloodedly murdered her. No matter how you look at it, it wasn't right. He has to pay.

"My obsession wasn't being in love with Sandra. I got those emotions into perspective very quickly. It was to bring Gillman to justice for taking her life." Max ran his knuckles across Nicole's cheek. "I haven't mixed you up with Sandra. I know the difference, believe me. Except for looks, you are nothing like her."

Nicole realized she wanted more than anything to believe him, and in wanting to so desperately, she understood something else—she'd gone and fallen in love. But what would it leave her with? Nothing, she figured, but heartache. He was sophisticated, rich, with a demanding and thriving business and friends. They were so far apart he might as well have lived on the moon. Montana was not a place for Max Warner, and New York would destroy her. She closed her eyes and told him it would never work and why.

His only response was a laugh and a kiss. Desire

bloomed like a field of flowers in a spring shower. Afterward, as she lay spent, secure in his arms, she wondered how it would all end.

CHAPTER SIXTEEN

DAWN BROUGHT more than light. With it came an op-
pressive heat, an unnatural stillness and a sky that
looked as if it had been slashed and bruised. Ominous
dark clouds boiled and churned over the sea, moving
fast and spreading out as they devoured the sky. Even
the sun looked strange, as if it had been draped in red
gauze. Last night's storm had cut them off from all
communications except the ship-to-shore radio on the
yacht tied at the dock, and they were all waiting for
Jim to return with a weather report.

Nicole stood with her back to the usually cheery
sunroom and sipped her coffee, watching as the wind
came up. She was tired of the endless angry arguments
that had been going on for more than an hour. When
John shoved back his chair, cursed them all and
stormed out of the house, she didn't even bother turning around. He seemed more determined than ever to
take her back to the mainland. Over Max's dead body,
she thought.

She guessed Max was the reason she was so pensive. She desperately wanted to believe everything
he'd told her last night. Honesty was hard to judge; it
could get so damn tangled up with needs and denial.
She knew deep down she trusted him, and she had let
her own uncertainties and insecurities blind her. But
no matter how she felt about him, it wasn't going to

make any difference. When Gillman confessed, and if his earlier behavior was any indication he was close to the breaking point, what was left for her and Max but to go their separate ways?

Mentally exhausted, she leaned her head against the window, then jerked her head back in surprise. The glass was clammy, sweating from the stifling heat outside and the cooler interior. Her gaze was drawn to the abrupt change beyond the window. Shrubbery was being whipped and the palms were bending with the force of the wind, looking as if they were going to snap in two. Wet leaves and small branches were sent skidding and dancing across the grass, to be sucked up into the air and scattered in all directions.

A heavy lawn chair tumbled and banged across the patio, stopping only when it hit the wall of the house. Nicole jumped. She was turning around to tell the others about the change when the door flew open and slammed against the wall, shattering the glass. Jim struggled inside looking windbeaten and holding his left arm. Everyone started talking at once, demanding to know what was happening.

"That little tropical disturbance has turned into a full-fledged hurricane, and it's heading right this way."

While Doug and Paul struggled with what was left of the door and Andy raced to get a broom, Max led Jim over to a chair, but the big man waved him away. "I was tying down the yacht more securely and got knocked right off my feet. I landed on my shoulder."

The wind suddenly howled and everyone listened to the bumps and crashes against the house. Max glanced around. "Doug, take Paul and John and batten down all the outside shutters. Andy, Karen and LeRoy can

come with me. We need to get the table and chairs off
the patio. The wind's going to make anything that's
not tied down a flying missile.'' He turned to Helen.
''You stay here with Nicky.'' In the state of excitement and a real sense of emergency, no one gave John
Gillman a thought.

Nicole followed Max to the door. ''Helen and I can
bring in the furniture from the patio. You worry about
getting the windows and doors covered. Go on, don't
worry about us.''

The patio and pool were somewhat protected on
three sides. But the wind still managed to beat mer-
cilessly at their backs. She'd never been in a hurricane
before and didn't know what to do or what to expect.
With a chair between them and the wind playing tug-
of-war, she started laughing. Helen joined her—but
then abruptly stopped as she looked past Nicole's
shoulder.

It took a moment for Nicole to realize that Helen
had gone still. She glanced over her shoulder and
froze. John Gillman was jogging up the steps.

Helen looked around frantically for one of the men.
Nicole set the chair down and touched her arm in
warning, then said, ''John, thank heavens! Jim says a
hurricane is headed this way. Help us drag this stuff
into the house.''

There was something wrong with his eyes. They
were vacuous, unblinking, the pupils dilated into bottomless pits of darkness. She'd seen that steady dead-
eyed stare before in animals about to attack. ''John!''
she screamed as she tried to distract him. The wind
snatched her voice from between them and he leaned
closer. He reeked of whiskey. She recoiled, and when
she did, he grabbed her arm.

Helen couldn't hear what was happening. All she could think was that he had his hands on Nicole. She panicked, knocked his hands away and stepped between them. "Run!" she yelled. "Now!"

Nicole knew better than to run, but the horrible face John turned on Helen and the desperation in the older woman's voice sent an erroneous message to her feet. She suddenly found herself heading down the patio steps, running with one goal in mind—to find Max or one of his staff. But as she stepped on the grass and out of the shelter of the house, the full force of the wind caught her, stopping her dead in her tracks. Twisting sideways, she tried to use her body like a wedge, a knife, to cut through the wall of wind. As she turned, she caught a glimpse of Helen on the ground, John standing over her with the chair raised above her head.

She screamed his name, but her voice was sucked away as if she'd made no sound. Horrified at the tableau playing out before her, she kept screaming and started back to help Helen. What she couldn't understand was why Helen wasn't looking up, pleading with John, but staring at her. Though she couldn't hear what the older woman was saying, she could read her lips. *Run!* Helen was saying. *Run!*

Nicole turned around again and ran.

Bent double, against the wind, she ran.

But her feet didn't seem to be making much ground. The fierce wind kept pushing her back, making her stumble. She tried not to think about John Gillman, just kept moving as best she could, struggling to put one foot in front of the other.

Then, making her attempted escape worse, it started to rain. Solid sheets of water, it seemed, that pum-

meled her head and shoulders until she stumbled under
the intensity. Once she almost fell to her knees but
managed to catch herself and stagger off again. She
was soaked to the skin and shivering from cold and
terror. Raising her head, she faced the storm, straining
to see through the silver curtain and get her bearings.
She thought she saw the corner of the house and
started in that direction. But suddenly her arm was
caught in a viselike grip.

She turned her head and came face-to-face with
John Gillman. Her arm hurt and she wanted to jerk it
free, but she made herself stand perfectly still and give
him stare for stare. It didn't do any good. He smiled
and the water rolled over his face and poured off his
nose and lips.

Well, Nicole thought, she wasn't about to go quietly
into the night.

Surprise was her best defense. She shoved her
shoulder into his chest and at the same time yanked
and twisted her arm. Free, she managed two steps before she felt a blinding pain on her neck. A sensation
of numbness spread through her body like an icy chill,
then came a paralysis. It radiated outward to her arms
and down her legs. Her knees gave out from under her
and she crumpled, unable to stop or brace herself.

Soggy grass cushioned her fall. *Get up. Get up!* But
her leaden body barely obeyed her. She managed to
lift her head in time to see Max as he rounded the
corner of the house. She knew he hadn't seen John.
His attention was on her. Her mind screamed, trying
to warn him, but as she watched, John's fist caught
Max by surprise and he went down like a felled tree.
Then John was leaning over her, touching her neck
again. The pain was excruciating, every nerve ending

in her body was on fire, then just as abruptly she turned cold. Her vision blurred, images wavered and dimmed. The last thing she saw before darkness claimed her was John's beautiful maniacal smile.

MAX GROANED, rolled over and sat up. His jaw throbbed and he was dazed. He couldn't figure out what he was doing sitting on the wet ground in the rain, or where he was, for that matter. Then it all came back in a blind flash of pain, fear and rage. He struggled to his feet, and then weaved, dizzy from the movement. Once his head cleared a little, be began looking around. The wind shoved at his efforts to move, pulling at his hair, whipping at his clothes.

John had Nicky. The accusation stung, and the pain was so intense it felt like the sting of a million bees.

John had Nicky. Max knew he'd failed to keep her safe. Guilt ate at his gut. He was sick with dread.

John had Nicky. It was all Max could think about as he frantically looked around. Then hope surged through him. From the corner of his eye, he caught a movement and sprinted up the patio steps. But no, it wasn't Nicky. His heart plummeted as he fell to his knees at Helen's side. He wanted to know what had happened, everything, but was struck dumb by urgency and fear.

With great effort, Helen tried to get up, but she was hampered by the pain in her shoulder where she'd taken the brunt of the blow. When Max leaned over her to help her, she gazed into his ravaged face and cried, "He's got Nicky, Max! You have to stop him." She brushed away his helping hands. "Don't worry about me. I'm okay. Go. Go on. Now, Max, before he hurts her."

He didn't need encouragement and turned to leave. Doug and Jim caught him as he reached the corner of the house. They'd been battling to get the shutters secured over the front windows when they realized Max hadn't returned.

Max was like a wild man.

"John has Nicky!" he shouted, and kept moving, heading for the only place John could have taken her. The wind and rain were twin demons, pulling, tugging at his efforts to run. He knew Doug and Jim would follow him.

As he ran, heading for the lagoon and the dock, he kept telling himself that John might be a killer, but he wouldn't do anything to endanger himself. Surely he wasn't foolish enough to think he could take the boat out. Max prayed he was right. But that sick feeling that he'd misjudged John rushed back.

The wind almost knocked him off the steep steps leading to the dock. The rain made it difficult to see. Waves crashed against the wooden pylons and sent a sheet of water up in the air, making his footing precarious, but he kept moving, bending into the force of the wind. When he reached the end, he gazed through the gray rain at the empty space in disbelief and horror. He cupped his hands over his eyes and stared out at the lagoon.

Waves slammed around him, sending up sprays of water that stung his eyes until tears ran down his face. He watched as a yacht struggled, dipped, rolled and bucked its way out of the lagoon, heading for the open sea. He cupped his mouth and screamed Nicole's name.

Doug and Jim made it to his side. For a moment the three men stood like pillars of stone, watching the yacht being swallowed up by the wind, rain and the angry sea. With water pouring from his face, Max looked from Jim to Doug. "I'm going after her."

"Have you lost your mind?" Doug yelled over the howl of the wind. Then saw Max's face and had his answer. Doug grabbed Max's arm as if the act would hold him back. "They'll never make it, Max." Max brushed him off and headed toward their own boat. Jim and Doug ran alongside him, keeping him between them. "It's suicide."

As they came close to the huge yacht, LeRoy met them at the gangway. "I saw you running across the yard. I've already been on board." He leaned closer so they could all hear him. Max was impatient to get on board, but LeRoy planted himself directly in front of him. "The bastard sabotaged some wiring. She's dead in the water."

Max glared at LeRoy and ground out between clenched teeth, "Fix it."

"Come on, Max," Doug said. "We'll contact the Coast Guard. It's the only thing we can do for now. As soon as the storm passes we'll start our own search. Listen, man. Gillman was a Navy SEAL. He knows how to handle boats and how to survive."

"But *she* doesn't." Max wiped at the water streaming down his face and met Doug's gaze.

"We can't go after her, Max."

"I didn't ask you to. I can handle the boat myself." He looked at LeRoy, then Jim. "Can you fix her? Can either of you get her running?"

Doug grabbed Max by the shoulder. "You can't do it alone, Max. You know it and we know it. If you try, you'll kill yourself."

"I'm going after her." He turned his tortured eyes

on LeRoy. "Get out of my way or I'll knock you out."
LeRoy looked helplessly at Doug and Jim, shrugged,
then did as he was told and stepped aside.

Jim grabbed Max's shoulder, and when his hand
was knocked away, he held both hands up in surrender. "I'll get her running, but I'm coming with you."

Doug and LeRoy watched them board the wildly
rocking yacht. Doug ran his fingers through his wet
hair, then pulled his glasses off, ineffectively wiped
them with the soaked tail of his shirt, then put them
firmly back on. His shoulders lifted and fell in resig-
nation, he timed the rocking of the yacht, then jumped
aboard. He looked at a startled LeRoy. "Go tell the
others what's happened. Call the Coast Guard." He
grabbed the railing, leaned forward and yelled, "And
say a prayer for us. We're going to need it."

SHE AWAKENED to the pitch and roll of the floor under
her. But that didn't make any sense. A floor didn't
move. Then she remembered…and was loath to open
her eyes. She was bodily lifted up and just as abruptly
slammed down. All she could see was dark wood, wet
with water and the shine of brass, as she stared at the
moving floor. It all came back to her. She was on a
boat. With John.

She struggled to sit up by using a corner to wedge
her body against the violent motion, then pushed herself into an upright position. Taking quick stock, she
was relieved to see she wasn't hurt or tied up. Using
the corner, she spread her feet and pushed up. The
floor bucked and pitched under her feet, and she
grabbed hold of the brass railing and glanced around.
The yacht was smaller than the one she and Max had
used to get to the island. What was it Max had called

it? The helm or navigation station? It bothered her that she couldn't think straight.

Her gaze shifted around the glassed-in area. Suddenly she didn't care what it was called. Her attention was centered on John Gillman. He was standing with his feet spread wide and his hands on a round wooden wheel. Like her, he was soaking wet, his hair plastered to his head, his knit shirt like a second skin showing the bulge and strain on his muscles as he fought to hold on to the wheel.

It was as if she was awakening from an awful dream. She was holding herself upright, then everything tilted sideways and she was sent stumbling and skidding across the floor only to have her momentum stopped as she slammed into John's body. He shoved her away without a word or a look. As she lay still and tried to catch her breath, everything heaved sideways again, only in the opposite direction, and she was sent rolling back to her corner.

She grabbed for the brass railing with both hands and hung on, struggling to catch her breath again. Her fear almost choked her. She knew he had actually taken them out of the safety of the lagoon into the mouth of the storm—and they were about to be swallowed whole.

"John!" she screamed. "Are you crazy? Take us back." He couldn't hear her over the roar of the wind and the waves smashing against the boat. Hand over hand she began to pull her way toward him, only to be stopped as a low wooden storage door slammed open. It smacked her in the shins, and as she fought to close it, a couple of big neon-orange life preservers tumbled out. She grabbed one, her fingers just catching the straps as it slid by. She quickly put it on and secured it as tightly as she could.

Once again she began pulling herself across the slick heaving floor. Just as she was within reach of John, she turned her head and gazed in horror out the window. The sea around them was wild and angry, and the yacht rode it like a cork on a roller coaster. As she watched, the yacht was plunged into a valley of dark green water as if it was being sucked to the bottom of the world. Just when she thought they *were* being pulled to the bottom of the sea, they were suddenly riding out of the dark hole, only to have a wave crash over the bow.

She could hear the big engine whine and groan as the yacht shook and trembled under her feet. Slowly she dragged her gaze from what was happening outside and faced another danger. John's face was set in a grimace as he struggled to keep them afloat. "You fool," she screamed, "turn back! You're going to kill us!" Of course that was the idea, she realized, only he hadn't planned on joining her. "John. John!"

He tore his gaze from the front window and the water smashing into it and finally acknowledged she was there. There was real fear in his eyes, and her heart sank to her toes. He knew they weren't going to make it.

"You bitch, why the hell aren't you dead?" He growled like a wounded animal. "I had it all planned." Keeping one hand on the wheel, he grabbed her around the throat with his other.

His eyes glowed eerily in the green fluorescent lights from the instrument panel. His mouth curled into a cruel smile as he squeezed. Nicole fought to get free, slapping, scratching, but his hand only tightened.

When the yacht heaved and rolled sideways, she found herself free and struggling to breathe. He reached for her again, but she jerked away, and he was only able to catch hold of her life preserver. He shook her like a wet dog.

Wonderful, she thought fearing her teeth would come loose in her head from the shaking. *He admits he killed Sandra and there's no one around to hear.* No witnesses—just her, and now they were both about to die. The yacht pitched sideways again, and the force tore her from his grip. She stumbled and skidded across the floor, windmilling her arms to regain her balance until she grabbed hold of the vacant captain's stool to stop her slide into the wall.

He fought the wheel, cursing and ranting like a madman. She managed to catch a snatch of what he was saying. Instead of the fear she expected to feel, she was calm, warmed by her anger. He was bragging about how smart his plan had been. "How the hell did you survive?" he yelled, the deep rage rumbling like thunder.

The wood deck under her feet trembled and groaned. She thought she could hear a splintering sound below. She wasn't about to die letting him think he'd won. Hell, she wasn't a quitter and she wasn't going to die, not if she could help it. The only way to stay alive was to take her chances in the sea. Odds were she'd never make it in the water, but from the ripping and tearing sounds around and beneath her, it was her only option.

She had one chance.

One chance at survival. She had to get herself clear of the boat before John could get his hands on her. A sense of resolve filled her. She wasn't going to let him take her, too. Nicole smiled and raised her voice above the noise of the storm and the waves crashing against them. There was nothing to lose now.

"You didn't plan so good, did you, darling?" Even though she was yelling, he couldn't miss the sneer in her tone.

"Sandra." His lips said her name, but no sound came out. "You remember?"

She heard the last part and smiled. "I never forgot, John. Did you think I would or could forget what you did to me?" The yacht shuddered and rolled violently from one side to the other as another wave caught it. John didn't seem concerned with trying to set a course through the water that curled over the bow and crashed against the window.

Once she regained her footing, Nicole edged toward the doorway. She heard a strange popping sound. "You forgot how I hated cooking." She wasn't sure if she'd been right, but remembered Max telling her that John had been an explosives expert. Sandra had been cooking dinner when he'd rowed to shore, saying he had to pick up something they needed. That was when the boat had exploded. "All your carefully laid plans, and I simply walked away from what I was doing. Remember, I had a habit of doing that. I went out on deck to wait for you."

Now John was stalking her, as surefooted as a cat on the bucking deck. He'd left the wheel, didn't seem to notice that the yacht was breaking apart under their feet. All she needed to do was get to the deck, vault over the side and let the water take her away. Her fingers tightened on a buckle of her life preserver. She kept her back to the wall as she inched her way toward the doorway.

He was gaining ground, getting closer. As he moved carefully toward her, crazy with the rage of failure, his back was to the bow of the yacht. They rode the top of the wave for a moment as if suspended. She saw what was coming and grabbed hold of the railing as the bow began to dip. All she could see was the dark chasm of water. He was thrown backward, sent crashing into the instrument panel. She threw back her head and laughed. "If I'm going to die again, I'm taking you with me this time!"

She had no intention of dying. They were sliding down into the trough of the wave. The momentum, as hard as he tried to fight it and reach her, was holding John against the panel and window. She fought to keep her balance against gravity and the angle of the yacht by wedging her feet against the floor and leaning as far back as she could. All the while she kept moving, inching her way along.

The doorway was within reach when she stumbled and almost lost her precarious hold on a life preserver that was hung on a railing support, which had been ripped from the flooring. Scooping up the jacket, she hooked it over her elbow just as she felt the change in the yacht's descent. They were about to be sent upward.

Nicole made her move. She stepped into the open doorway, one hand on the doorknob and the other on the jamb. She hung there waiting, watching. Then she smiled. "It's your turn to be sent to hell, John."

The yacht tilted upward, and she was thrown backward through the doorway, managing to pull the door shut as she fell through. The knob was ripped from her hand, and she was pitched to the deck just as a huge wave broke over the bow of the boat. Her last sight of John before she was washed overboard was of him being slammed bodily into the door, his eyes wide with fear, his mouth open to scream as the glass shattered and broke.

Cold dark water washed over her head and pulled her under. Nicole hugged the extra life preserver against the one she had on, held her breath and started kicking as hard as she could. She was tumbled and rolled in the wave, then, just when she thought she couldn't hold her breath any longer, she was bobbing on the surface and gasping in air. Clutching the life preserver, she fought the churning water, trying to swim.

Soon she realized her efforts were only going to exhaust her. She forced herself to relax and ride the huge waves, imagining her body to be a human cork bobbing on the surface of the water. She didn't know how many times waves broke over her head and she was sucked under the surface. Or how many times she came up coughing, spitting, praying for air only to inhale rain. Whatever happened, she was on her own. It was up to her to stay alive.

After a while she realized she'd swallowed a lot of salt water. She stuck her finger down her throat and threw it all up. Then she relaxed and rolled and swayed, pitched and sank with the sea. There were times she thought she'd actually fallen asleep only to be awakened by coughing up water.

It was dark, and though the sea was somewhat warm, the rain was cold. She had no idea what time it was or how long she'd been in the water. She only knew she had to stay alive and rational.

Max would come, she assured herself. He wouldn't let her die. She held on to that thought for as long as she could, but when help didn't come and only darkness met her shouts, she began to cry. John had won, after all. The thought made her angry, and once more she made herself throw up and expel the salt water she'd swallowed.

She must have fallen asleep again. When she was unkindly awakened by a watery slap in the face, she opened her eyes, then wished she hadn't. The sky was growing lighter, and the sea had settled down to a nauseating roll, with waves only as big, she judged, as a car. She shook herself awake and looked around, twisting her body in a full circle when she was carried along on the crest of a wave. There was nothing, nothing but water and sky. No boats or land. But with the light came new terrors. Sharks.

She was a river person, never fond of the ocean because she couldn't see what was swimming around her or below her. Now her mind decided to play tricks, and snips and snatches of every documentary she'd ever seen on sharks crossed the screen of her mind. Bone-chilling fear was something new to Nicole, and she deeply resented it. She refused to look around any longer, afraid she'd see that distinctive triangular fin cutting through the waves.

Instead, she studied the life preserver she still clutched in her numb fingers. Something caught her eye, and one by one she forced her fingers loose and turned the jacket around. There were some boldly printed black letters. It took a moment to clear her mind enough to read the writing. She was weary and had to read it three times before the meaning sunk in. Her chin touched the top of the life preserver as she studied the words, then the black object on the shoulder of the jacket. Following the directions, she pulled a cord.

A red light began to blink rhythmically, and a moment later it started emitting a beeping sound. Pulling the life jacket she'd been holding closer, she rested her head on it. This time, instead of crying, she started laughing. Just when she'd been about to give in, there was hope, after all. Now it was up to Max. She thought of him, keeping him close, talking to him in her mind when she felt herself going to sleep.

CHAPTER SEVENTEEN

MAX STOOD on the deck of the yacht, his legs spread wide for balance, his bare feet clinging to the slick surface. Waves smashed against the bow of the boat, sending up fans of water that rained down on him. He didn't feel it. He didn't feel anything but desolation.

After a night of battling the sea and the wind, struggling to keep the yacht afloat and stay alive, they were all exhausted. Morning crept up on them. The sky was gray and still dotted with clouds, though they were light gray, instead of boiling black. He sighed and thanked heaven the wind had died. It had almost been the death of them last night. They'd weathered the hurricane.

Max wiped the spray of water from his face, his gaze on the horizon and the water around them. Nicole was alive. She had to be. He refused to think otherwise. Still, his pain was like nothing he'd ever felt before. It was the pain of guilt. If he hadn't been so damn obsessed with getting John Gillman, none of it would have happened.

He'd promised her he would take care of her, that she would be safe, and he'd failed. Crossing his arms over the thick life preserver, he shifted his weight with the motion of the ship and watched the waves roll by. He hadn't heard Doug's approach over the sound of the sea battering the bow, but felt the heavy hand on his shoulder.

"She's out there, Doug, waiting for us to find her."

"You're going to have to face the truth, Max. Our boat is twice as big, the engine more powerful than what Gillman rented. And we almost didn't make it."

Max shook his head as he continued to search the sea as far as he could see. "She's alive."

One of Doug's lenses was cracked, and the frame sat cockeyed on his face. His hair was wet, sticky with salt and stuck to his head like a cap. Still, he adjusted his glasses and tried to finger-comb his hair. "Jim's managed to get the Coast Guard, and they're going to mount an air-and-sea search as soon as they can." He tightened his grip on Max's shoulder. "That boat couldn't have made it through last night."

"Maybe. Maybe not. But what if they were close to an island? She could have managed. She could have saved herself."

Finally Max looked at Doug with eyes that were dark pools of fear and a face gaunt with strain. Doug swallowed, then bit his lip to keep from inflicting any more pain on his friend. He patted the stiffly held shoulder. "We won't give up."

Max jerked away, not from Doug's pity, but because he'd spotted something bright riding the ridge of a wave before it plunged down and out of sight. He moved to the side of the yacht and stared, waiting for it to resurface on the next wave. When it did, he spun around, pushed Doug out of his way and raised his arm to get Jim's attention on the navigation deck. He pointed to where he'd seen the object, then felt the big Rolls-Royce engines dig into the water as Jim changed direction.

Doug grabbed hold of the railing to keep from being knocked over, thankful for the millionth time that he had on a life preserver. "What'd you see?"

Max didn't hear him, didn't even know his friend was standing at his side as he kept watch for the object he'd seen. For ten minutes they circled the area, rolling and rocking with the waves. Finally it was Doug who spotted it again, and Jim steered the big yacht closer.

A destroyed boat bow, the wood crushed and ripped apart, scraped the side of the yacht as it swept by. Max closed his eyes. He knew in his heart it had to be from Gillman's boat. His hands tightened on the railing and his body bent forward as he swayed back and forth with the weight of loss and pain. He'd been so sure he wouldn't lose her. Now, faced with the truth, he was haunted by the agony of his loss, knowing she couldn't possibly have survived.

Jim's shout and the urgency in his voice roused Max from the dark pit of despair. Suddenly Doug was tugging him across the deck and up the steps to the fly deck. He stopped in the doorway, watching as Jim pointed to the radar screen. Hope surged through him. For a second he lifted his gaze toward heaven and said a quick prayer.

"I'm getting two blips on radar." Jim turned his back on his bosses, opened the throttle and changed the yacht's course. "It's an emergency homing device with a light that emits a signal. I may be wrong, but I think it's the kind used on life vests."

Max decided to stay on the navigation deck with Jim and Doug. He had a better view of the surrounding water. He was the first to see the red blinking light. Then he caught sight of something orange and knew Jim was right. His heart leaped into his throat. He shouted orders at Jim and Doug, then scrambled down the steps.

Doug was directly behind him and had to bodily tackle Max to keep his friend from diving over the side. "Don't be stupid." Max reared back as if to hit him, then caught himself and waited.

"Get the safety line." When Doug didn't move, Max forced his muscles to relax and said, "Please do it, and hurry." He endured the torture of waiting for Doug to return with the safety harness and rope. Waited longer for him to secure the rope to the loop in the harness. As soon as Doug had tested the knot, satisfied it wasn't going to come undone in the water, Max pushed himself over the side of the yacht. He came up fast out of the darkness. With strong steady strokes he battled the roller-coaster waves and began swimming toward the blinking red light.

Nicole heard Max calling her name. But she ignored it, telling herself it was just one more hallucination. She'd become accustomed to the lulling motion of the waves, comfortable with it, and longed to go back to sleep. Her limbs were like leaded weights, and she'd long since stopped trying to swim to stay awake and alert. If it wasn't for her life preserver, she would have simply sunk to the bottom of the sea.

Max's voice wouldn't go away. It was like a pesky fly that refused to let her go back to sleep, and it was getting closer. She struggled to open her eyes, then lifted her head. As the motion of the wave pulled her upward to the crest, she thought she saw a face cutting through the water. But then she rode the motion of the wave down and lost sight of it. She must be dreaming. Then she saw the face again and heard her name.

Max. Her lips were cracked and swollen and her

tongue was too big for her mouth, but she strained to call his name. Then she felt his hands on her shoulders, her face, heard his strong voice crack with emotion. She thought she saw tears in his eyes. "I knew...you'd come," she croaked.

"Hush. Hush, honey. You're safe." He couldn't believe it—she'd survived! He touched her face, her hair, reassuring himself she was real. Filled with wonder and relief, he let his eyes drink in the sight of her. He wanted to take her in his arms and hold her so she'd never get away or be scared again. But the bulky life preservers they were wearing kept them at arm's length. Suddenly Doug was in the water beside them, lending his help to get her to the yacht.

The sea didn't want to give her up, and it took all three men to pull her out of the water and on board. Then she was in Max's arms, and he carried her across the deck, through a door and into the beautiful stateroom. The air-conditioned interior made her shiver and shake, but before she could voice her discomfort Max was stripping off her life preserver and wrapping her in blankets. He placed her on the white leather couch, sat beside her, then pulled her into his lap.

She couldn't talk, just watched as Doug brought over a couple of bottles of fresh water and Max helped her drink. It tasted like heaven and she would have emptied it if Max had allowed her.

"Sip, don't chugalug it, Montana. You'll get sick."

She wanted to laugh, wanted to tell him how many times she'd been sick already. But she was too exhausted to talk. Her smile, when she tried, hurt, and she touched her mouth and winced.

Max captured her hand to keep her from exploring further. "Prolonged immersion in salt water ravages the skin, but it's nothing that won't heal with some attention and time. You'll be fine." He gave her a big sloppy grin when she glared back. She was going to be fine. "Of course, right now you look a lot like a white shriveled-up prune."

"Thanks." She closed her eyes for a moment, and when she opened them, she was clear in her thoughts and felt more alert. Her voice no longer sounded like a frog. It resembled a foghorn and made the men laugh.

"Let me do the talking," Max said, "and I'll see if I can answer all your questions before you ask. Jim's calling the island to let Helen and the others know we found you, then he's setting a course for Charlotte Amalie on St. Thomas. We'll get you to a doctor and make sure you're okay."

"John?" she asked, knowing she didn't need to say more.

Max shook his head. "We saw some wreckage. I'm not even sure if it was his boat. Was he wearing a life vest?" She shook her head, and after a thoughtful moment he said, "I wouldn't hold out much hope for his chances. The Coast Guard's going to make a thorough search. We'll just have to see what they turn up." He shifted her weight in his lap so he could hold her closer. "I'm sorry, Montana. I almost got you killed."

She should have said something to relieve the pain and guilt she saw in his face, but she was safe, warm and in his arms. She closed her eyes. Surely, whatever their problems were, they would be gone when she opened them again.

NICOLE AWOKE on the third day after her rescue with the same feeling of dread and hopelessness that had plagued her since she was taken from the yacht. She spent the first day in a clinic under a doctor's care, then she was transferred to a luxury hotel where everyone from the island was now staying.

Staring at the ceiling, she heaved a long soulful sigh and thought over the past two days of answering endless questions. The authorities wanted to know all about John and what had happened on the yacht before she was washed overboard. At first the island officials had trouble accepting her story, until Max, Doug and Helen gave their statements, filling in all the details of the setup to trap Gillman. Then she had to relate how John had confessed to killing Sandra. It was confusing at times, and when she found herself reduced to uncharacteristic tears, Max stepped in and called a halt to the proceedings.

She'd found out the Coast Guard, with the help of Doug and Jim, had conducted an extensive search for John. They found the remains of his yacht washed up on one of the many smaller islands in the chain—but no body.

Nicole turned her head and smiled. Helen seemed to have taken up residence in the chair next to her bed and refused to budge, no matter what. "Hi," she said.

"You're awake again?"

"I don't understand why I'm so damn tired."

Helen stood and stretched. She grasped Nicole's hand. "Shock, the doctor said." She turned when the door opened and waved Max in. "Max, tell her everything will be fine, that she's just suffering from shock."

Nicole fell silent and closed her eyes. When she opened them, they were filled with tears. "It's more than that. More like a guilty conscience."

"You have nothing to feel guilty about!" Helen said fiercely.

Max moved to stand on the other side of the bed. "You did what you had to do, Nicole, to stay alive."

"I killed a man, New York."

"A man who was trying to kill you."

"I know that, but..."

"You did what you had to do."

She ignored him. "Methodically. Deliberately. I planned it from the moment I realized where I was. It didn't matter that John was trying to kill me. When I knew for certain that the boat wasn't going to make land anywhere, and if it did, he was going to make sure I wasn't on it, I started mapping out my moves to force his hand. I pushed him until he lost control. Not only his temper but the boat. All I could think about was that he'd killed my sister and gotten away with it, but he wasn't going to do it a second time."

Helen rested her head on the edge of the bed and cried. Nicole squeezed her hand. "It's over now. You can let go of her."

Helen sat up, pulled a tissue from her skirt pocket and wiped her eyes. "I know she's at peace now. But you're not, are you?"

"No."

Standing, Helen motioned for Max to take her chair. "I'm sorry we got you mixed up in this, Nicky, but I'm not sorry John had to pay with his life. He got what he deserved. Poetic justice, even if it *was* staged. A greater power than us will be his final judge. Personally I hope he rots in hell."

Max waited until the woman had shut the door behind her. "I think Helen'll be okay now." He looked at Nicole. "Well, Montana, it's been a hell of a ride, hasn't it?"

"Yes." So this was it, she thought. He was going to write her off and walk out of her life. She'd done her job. Now it was all over.

He was rarely at a loss for words. But now he couldn't seem to find where to start or the right thing to say. There were a hundred things he wanted to tell her, but nothing came to mind. His conscience kept reminding him that he'd almost gotten her killed. The guilt was hard to swallow. "I've talked to Charlie every day. He's doing fine but misses you."

"I know. I've talked to him, too." She couldn't bring herself to ask, *Where do we go from here?* It stuck in her throat like a burr. Instead, she said, "I think it's time I got up, don't you?"

"Try out your land legs?" He couldn't take his eyes off her. She was so damn beautiful and fragile. "Only if you're feeling up to it." He got quickly to his feet. "I'll get Helen to help you."

He couldn't wait to leave her, she thought. He'd just walk away after all they'd shared, all they'd had together. Then she reminded herself of something she'd told him—it was only sex. Maybe he realized she was right. Well, it was great while it lasted, but obviously it was over. There was an awful pain in her chest, as if someone was squeezing her heart. She wasn't going to cry. She was strong and tough and not a crybaby.

When Helen opened the door, she found Nicole sobbing and rushed to her side. "What did he do?"

Nicole struggled to control her tears. "Why would you think Max has anything to do with it?"

"Only a woman deeply in love cries like that when a man walks out on her."

"He's nothing to me."

"Sure, and you're nothing to him. That's why he looked like someone had just ripped out his heart and stomped on it."

Nicole accepted a tissue from Helen and attempted to wipe away the tears, but they kept dripping like a leaky faucet. "I thought… Oh, never mind."

"You thought he might be in love with you, too?"

"No." Nicole sighed. "Yes."

"Now we're getting somewhere." Helen began to pace the small area beside the bed. "He does love you. Maybe he just doesn't know it yet. Like most men he needs a kick in the butt to make him think." Helen smiled. "My late husband used to tell me a little story. Do you want to hear it?"

She didn't wait for Nicole to answer. "Well, you see there were these two bulls standing on top of a mountain looking down at a herd of cows. The young bull says, 'Why don't we run down there and mount one?' The old bull says, 'Why don't we walk down and mount them all?'" Helen started to pace again.

"What do bulls have to do with me and Max?"

"Oh, nothing. Just that timing is important, and you can get more by taking things slowly than rushing." She smiled at Nicole. "Maybe Max needs to be forced down the mountain."

She had no idea what Helen was talking about, but the smile and the glint in the older woman's eyes made her uneasy. "I want to get up. I want my boots and jeans, and I want to go home."

"Of course you do. I think the authorities are through questioning you, but I'll find out. Then I'll call my pilot and have him fly you back to Montana today."

HOME. HER HAVEN, her comfort zone. Home. The mere word gave her a warm fuzzy feeling, a sense of oneness with what was familiar.

Home offered peace and shelter, and if her heart hadn't heeled completely, the love freely offered by her father and friends helped make her days bearable. But even her father had finally become sick of her long face, heavy sighs, seesawing moods and ill temper. He kicked her out of the house and told her to go stay on the mountain, and not come back until she could behave like a normally functioning adult. His words stung, but she knew he was right. She had to find some emotional middle ground to deal with what she'd done and the vivid memories.

Nights were the hardest. That was when she allowed herself to think of what had happened—and, of course, Max. He'd let her leave the island without a word—just a brotherly peck on the cheek and some inane comment about taking care of herself. By the time she reached Montana, she was furious with him and herself. Despite her vow, she'd been a fool once more.

Parking the Jeep under the overhang of tree limbs, she climbed out and headed down the trail to her private spot—the warm spring. It had been almost two weeks since she'd left St. Thomas, and no matter how much she worked at forgetting Max, he would pop into her head when she least expected it. The memories had the power to wipe her out and leave her an emotional wreck.

Her boot slipped on the pebble-strewn ledge, and she grabbed the side of the cliff and pressed her face against cool rock, then closed her eyes and waited until her heart stopped hammering against her ribs. She'd never been careless before, no matter how distracted.

Her anger made her careful as she edged along. But she was puzzled by something and stopped to inspect the ledge. She noticed the smattering of small rocks that had been pulled free from the cliff. The wind usually swept the ledge clean of any rubble. She moved on, watching where she stepped and keeping her mind on what she was doing.

More than anything she needed the serenity of her own little paradise. She jumped from the ledge to firm ground, then came to a halt, cocked her head and listened. For a moment she could have sworn she heard sounds of movement, but whatever it was it was gone now. She scrambled down the slope, rounded the outcropping of boulders wedged into the cliff, then stopped in shock.

"Did you think I was going to let you just walk out of my life?"

"Max!" She couldn't believe it. He was standing no more than a few feet away. She noticed the blanket spread beside the pool, the picnic basket, the bottle of wine and two glasses. But her gaze was only for him. "How? Why?"

"The how...well, I called your father a couple of days ago and told him I was coming, but didn't want you to know until I was here. He's good at keeping secrets."

She smiled. "And lying his head off."

"Yes. But so are JD, Penny and Reed. JD met me at the airport, Penny took care of me at the lodge and packed the picnic, then Reed led me to this place."

Nicole bit her lip to keep from smiling. "How did you know I'd come here? How did you know my father would kick me out of the house?" She wanted to touch him, to be held in his arms, but she was afraid to move, afraid that this was just a figment of her imagination.

"I didn't. All Charlie was supposed to do was send you to the mountain. It was JD and Penny who told me you'd head for your secret place." He studied her carefully as he talked, happy to see that she looked better than the last time he'd seen her. The strain and sadness were gone from her eyes, and there was color in her cheeks.

She couldn't stand it any longer and asked, "Why are you here, Max?"

"Why? I'd think it was obvious." She scowled at him and he grinned.

"I must be getting dense. The last time I saw you, you were sending me away without a backward glance. You let me leave thinking you didn't care."

"Never that, Montana. I let you leave because I cared too damn much." He wanted to take her in his arms, but knew Nicole was likely to be put off by any show of passion at the moment. She wanted an explanation. "I was responsible for what happened to you. I almost got you killed. Worst of all, Gillman's death was on your conscience. Things never should have happened like that, Nicky. I know what you must have felt, and knowing, I thought you needed some time alone to heal." He took a step forward. "Doug and Helen told me I was a fool to stay away any longer. Helen's not a woman easily dismissed."

Nicole grinned. "I know. Did she lend you her plane to get here?"

Max laughed. "Yes. Once I'd agreed to come, everything was taken out of my hands. Between Helen and Doug, I didn't have a chance." He could have told her the plans Helen had, but thought Helen would skin him alive if he let Nicky know she was about to become a very rich woman. Helen was making sure that Nicky inherited her sister's portion of the estate. He thought he'd hold off telling her that Doug, Helen and some of the others were on their way to Montana to make sure he didn't mess up again. He took another step closer to her. "I love you, Nicky."

She stared, unsure she'd heard correctly. "What did you say?"

Max rubbed a hand over his face, then back through his hair. She wasn't going to make it easy. "I love you."

"You love me? Why?"

"How the hell do I know why?" he snapped. "I just do." Then he realized she was teasing and relaxed. She had that sparkle in her eyes that made his pulse race. It was time he gave her a real shock. "I've gone into a new line of business and taken on a couple of partners. I'll have to do some relocating."

"What does that have to do with— What business? You already have a business in New York."

"I still have that, though on a limited interest." He stepped closer. "Want to know who my new partners are?"

"Yes." She couldn't understand why her heart was suddenly pounding as if it knew something her head had yet to know. Her hands were shaking, and she jammed them into the back pockets of her jeans. One thing she was sure of, Sandra was no longer in the equation. Nicole could see the change in his eyes, the way he looked at her and saw only her, Nicky. "You're not going to be happy until you tell me, are you?"

"No."

"Okay, I'm asking. Who are your new partners?"

"Dawson Outriggers. Charlie sold me an interest in the business, so I guess you and I are business partners."

This time it was Nicole who took a step forward. "I don't believe you. He wouldn't..." Then she thought about all the secret smiles and trips to the lawyer's office in town. "You'd never survive a winter here, New York."

"I'm tougher than I look."

"I won't live with you." Although she was calm on the outside, she was shaking on the inside. She was hot and cold at the same time. Then she took a deep breath, and before she could stop herself, the words popped out of her mouth. "You'll have to marry me." She couldn't believe what she'd said and went still.

They were only an arm's length apart. Max could see the way the corners of her lips twitched, but she refused to set her smile free. He couldn't stop his own. He'd never been so relieved in his life. "I could do that. But haven't you forgotten something?"

"Oh. You want to hear me say it, do you?"

"It would be nice."

To hell with it, she thought. She didn't want to play any more games. Instead of an immediate answer, she threw her arms around his neck, and as he laughingly swung her around, she wrapped her legs around his waist. "I love you, Max."

"Well, isn't this a touching scene?"

Max froze.

Nicole twisted in his arms, unable to believe the voice she'd heard. The fear that swept over her was all too real. So was the sight of John Gillman standing at the top of the ridge. He was carrying a rifle loosely in one arm, and she knew if they so much as moved he only had to raise the rifle and pull the trigger. Shock evaporated quickly to be replaced with a deep sense of relief. She squeezed Max's arm and whispered, "I didn't kill him, Max."

"I don't die so easily," Gillman said. "Though I must say your efforts were better than most. I never saw it coming."

Max tried to gauge the distance between the rocky waterfall and the time it would take Gillman to shoot them. His heart sank. They were pretty much in the open, with no quick route of escape.

Max studied Gillman, noting that he didn't look in top physical condition. His clothes were dirty and he had a good week's growth of beard. He imagined the man had to keep on the run. But it was John's eyes that drew his attention. They were wild, filled with hate and crazy with the madness that comes only with defeat.

Gillman was among the walking dead. He had nowhere to go. He had nothing. No money and no access to what he did have tucked away. He wondered how the man had come this far, but then John, if nothing else, had always been resourceful. He had nothing to lose now. Killing the two people responsible for bringing him down would only be a perk.

Max wondered if Gillman's physical and mental deterioration had slowed his reflexes. It was evident that if he and Nicky didn't do something, they were dead. If they were lucky, they might beat him and reach shelter before he could take aim and shoot. But he didn't want to bet Nicky's life on ifs and long shots. He had to distract him, keep him talking until he saw his chance to push Nicky to safety.

"How did you survive the wreck, Gillman?"

"Navy SEAL training. It's not something you forget."

Nicole saw the way John was looking at her, his eyes as savage as they'd been on the yacht. If there were any doubts before that he might not kill them, they disappeared with that realization.

John laughed, a maniacal sound that echoed off the cliff. "Man, who'd have thought that Sandra had a twin or that she'd be found and used against me? It's downright spooky."

"Or maybe poetic justice," Max said. He nudged Nicole with his elbow, then jerked his head in the direction of the waterfall, but just enough for only her to notice. "You're a master planner, John. Don't you see the beauty of it? You kill Sandra, and her twin ends up killing you? How did you know Nicole was her twin?"

"My good luck. The fishing boat that picked me up dropped me off at Charlotte Amalie. It's a small town and the place was abuzz with what had happened. I hid out and kept my ears open. Some of the local law likes to talk. Some of the men drink too much, and it's not hard to get the keys to offices where depositions are filed. I'm an old hand at breaking and entering, so it wasn't hard to find out everything I needed to know. Mind you, I had a few bad moments. One was when I realized I didn't have any money, and since I was officially dead, I couldn't access any of my accounts in the States. It took some fancy computer work to get to my foreign accounts. Even then I had to stay hidden."

Nicole realized he was enjoying himself, making sure they knew just how resourceful and intelligent he was. She figured that, since he was so sure of himself and bent on bragging, she ought to ask him all the questions about Sandra that she hadn't asked on the yacht. She was about to do just that when the pressure of Max's elbow against her ribs warned her. His touch also drew her attention to the movement behind Gillman.

Max could have sworn he saw Reed's young face through the shadows of the trees. He prayed not. If spooked, John wouldn't hesitate to kill a boy any more than he would at putting a bullet between Nicky's eyes. He suddenly felt her hand on his thigh, the tap of a finger.

She'd seen Reed and had the same thought as Max. She'd just cleared her conscience and didn't need another death to haunt her. Suddenly she saw more movement in two directions and managed a brief glimpse of the sheriff, Jeff Hall.

When the end came, Max realized, it was quick and effective. Before Gillman could react to the sounds behind and above him and turn around, the butt of a rifle swung wide and then it slammed into the side of his head. He dropped like a stone.

Max was as surprised as Gillman. He'd expected the attack to come from behind. He'd even seen the sheriff moving from tree to tree to get a better shooting position. Now he watched as the tall muscular man jumped with the agility of a monkey from the top of the cliff.

"Dammit, Ash," Jeff groused as he nudged the fallen man with his toe, then handed a pair of handcuffs to Reed Bartlet and watched as the kid knelt beside the body. "Frisk him carefully, son." He looked over at his best friend and Reed's father. "You could have waited for my signal."

Ash, senior, slipped off his Stetson, scrubbed at his sun-bleached hair with his free hand, taking his time, then replaced the hat and laughed. "I didn't like his looks or his tone much. Couldn't see any reason to wait." He turned his sharp gaze on Nicole. "You okay, hon?"

Nicole laughed and led Max to where they were standing. When she introduced them, she asked, "How did you know?"

Jeff was the one to answer while Ash eyed Max. "I got a call from Doug Hart. He explained that your office had just been informed that one of Gillman's foreign bank accounts was being activated, he knew something was wrong. I did some checking and found out about a stranger in Bartlet asking all kinds of questions about the Dawsons. I called Ash. When we arrived at the lodge, JD told us where you'd gone. Young Reed's the only one who knows about this place, so he was our guide."

Nicole, beaming, kissed all three. She was so relieved she hadn't killed Gillman. He was going to stand trial for Sandra's murder, and his punishment would be far worse than death. Gillman was not a man who could live in a cage. That thought made her smile widen even further.

Ash and Reed started dragging Gillman's limp body up to the ledge, and Jeff hung back. "I guess you two can go back to whatever you were doing." His eyebrows waggled suggestively. Then he stuck out his hand to Max. "Welcome to Montana. I know you're going to be happy here." He chuckled when he saw Max's stunned expression. "This is a big county with even bigger gossips.'' He turned to leave, then stopped. "Just one thing. You hurt Nicky and you'll have to answer to Charlie, me and Ash, then half the town. It won't be pretty."

Max figured his smile was as big as Montana. "I get the picture. But you don't have anything to worry about." He put his arm around Nicole's shoulders. They stood side by side, watching as the three men half-carried, half-dragged Gillman away.

"Where were we?" Max asked.

"I think you were about to go down on one knee."

"I don't think so. After all, you were the one who asked me." He saw the worry in her eyes and captured her face in his hands. "What now?"

"Max, this—" she swung her arms wide to encompass the mountain and ranch "—is not an easy life. Ranching and running the outriggers—is a tough way to make a living. The winters—" She never got any further, stopped by his mouth on hers. There were a thousand questions she wanted to ask, but as soon as his lips touched hers, the questions completely disappeared.

Max was the first to break away. "Don't you realize by now, Montana, that if we're together, if we love each other, there's not a thing in hell that can keep us apart? Haven't we already proved it? Just look what we've come through and think about where we're going."

Of course he was right.

She had a lifetime of love with Max to think about and plan for. His life was never going to be dull.

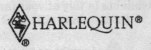

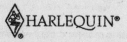

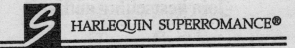

HARLEQUIN SUPERROMANCE®

WOMEN WHO *Dare*

*They take chances, make changes
and follow their hearts!*

WHERE THERE'S SMOKE... (#747)
by Laura Abbot

Jeri Monahan is a volunteer fire fighter in her Ozarks
hometown—and Dan Contini, former navy officer, is the
fire chief.

Jeri's a natural risk taker—and Dan's a protector, a man who
believes women shouldn't be exposed to physical danger.

Jeri's a woman who wants it all, including marriage—
and Dan's a divorced father embittered by his ex-wife's
unfaithfulness.

There are a lot of sparks between Jeri and Dan—and a lot of
problems, too. Can those sparks of attraction be fanned into a
steady fire?

Find out July 1997 wherever Harlequin books are sold.

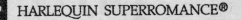

HARLEQUIN SUPERROMANCE®

When love needs a little nudge...

SWEET TIBBY MACK
by Roz Denny Fox

Tibby Mack is, at twenty-seven, the youngest resident in Yaqui Springs, a retirement community near California's Salton Sea. The folks there have become her family, her friends...her matchmakers. But what chance do they have of finding Tibby a husband when the youngest man in town is sixty-six?

Then Cole O'Donnell arrives. *Age:* 30. *Looks:* good (make that great). *And* he's inherited his grandfather's property in Yaqui Springs. He's the answer to their prayers. Not Tibby's, though.

But the matchmakers know that these two should be in love and that once in a while, love needs a nudge....

Watch for *Sweet Tibby Mack* (#746) by Roz Denny Fox

Available in July 1997 wherever Harlequin books are sold.

He changes diapers, mixes formula and
tells wonderful bedtime stories—he's

Mr. Mom

Three totally different stories of sexy, single
heroes each raising another man's child...
from three of your favorite authors:

MEMORIES OF THE PAST
by Carole Mortimer

THE MARRIAGE TICKET
by Sharon Brondos

TELL ME A STORY
by Dallas Schulze

Available this June wherever
Harlequin and Silhouette books are sold.

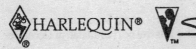

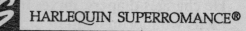

HARLEQUIN SUPERROMANCE®

Come West with us!

In Superromance's series of Western romances
you can visit a ranch—and fall in love with a cowboy!

In June 1997 watch for
The Truth About Cowboys

by award-winning author
Margot Early

Erin Mackenzie considers herself a candidate for the Dumped
by Cowboys Hall of Fame. One in particular—rodeo cowboy
Abe Cockburn, who's also the father of her baby daughter. And
then there's Erin's *own* father, rancher Kip Kay, who's never
acknowledged her.

Erin does a risky thing: she goes to Colorado to tell Abe about
his daughter. And to tell Kip about *his*. She goes to Colorado to
find the truth about cowboys—and about fathers.

Look for upcoming HOME ON THE RANCH titles wherever
Harlequin books are sold.

And look for Margot Early's next Superromance novel,
Who's Afraid of the Mistletoe?, available in December.